Praise for
THE IMITAT

'*The Imitator* gripped me to the end: I devoured it. Rebecca Starford has created an exceptional work of historical fiction, bringing 1940s England to life in formidable, compelling detail and thrusting the reader into a world of wartime spies, betrayal and surprising revelation. What a rare treat to find a novel that offers both white-knuckled suspense *and* evocative, beautiful prose. I loved it.'

HANNAH KENT, author of *Burial Rites*

'A poignantly rendered narrative map of one woman's journey from misfit to spy—and a thought-provoking examination of the gently human desires that lay the groundwork for pernicious extremism. Rebecca Starford has given us a rousing reminder of the power of our choices.'

JULIET GRAMES, *New York Times* bestselling author of *The Seven or Eight Deaths of Stella Fortuna*

'Rebecca Starford seems to be the inheritor of the cool, narrative elegance of Graham Greene and John le Carré. Her building of the tale to reach the critical moral apogee of this book seems effortless, and she has found a fascinating and unexpected World War II corner of espionage and intelligence to exploit for a plot that runs like milk and honey.'

TOM KENEALLY, author of *The Dickens Boy*

'Wholly compelling . . . Starford shows the complex ways in which patriotism develops into something murky.'

LOUISE SWINN, *The Saturday Paper*

'A fantastic debut . . . *The Imitator* is a riveting and powerful novel about identity and the choices we make. A highly recommended read.'

The Canberra Weekly

'I can't think of a single person who wouldn't love this novel. Both a gripping thriller and a deep character study, it will appeal to those who love espionage epics as well as lovers of literary classics. Starford's handling of her protagonist's internal divisions is assured and completely engrossing, the scene-setting rich in historical detail but never overdone. You'll tear through *The Imitator* in one weekend, I guarantee it.'

BRI LEE, author of *Eggshell Skull*

'Class and ideologies collide in Starford's consummate debut, a clever combination of homefront drama and espionage thriller . . . The author does an excellent job of recreating London before, during and after the war, and in Evelyn has created a complex heroine whose sense of duty gets her in way over her head. With suspense worthy of Hitchcock and a moral reckoning straight out of le Carré or Graham Greene, this is a winner.'

Publishers Weekly

'A beguiling and compelling tale with a finely attuned sense of time and place.'

THUY ON, *The Sydney Morning Herald* and *The Age*

'A fast-paced tale with plenty of plot twists, *The Imitator* lives up to expectations [and] adds to the canon of texts that counters the traditional depiction of wartime women as simply holding down the fort.'

ZOYA PATEL, *The Guardian*

'Wonderfully detailed with characters deftly and fully fleshed out, *The Imitator* is a satisfying, convincing and absorbing tale.'

The Herald Sun

'An elegant piece of writing, richly observed and engagingly told.'

The Weekend Australian

'Starford's control of the plotting is exceptional, her dialogue is precise, and her ability to evoke London at that time is superb. A highly recommended, cracking read.'

Good Reading

'Beautifully written . . . *The Imitator* explores the act of betrayal and the devastating effects that last well after the war is won.'

Books + Publishing

'A subtle yet moving story of personal and professional camouflage, of hidden selves fearing the light.'

Booklist

'A bold character study from a versatile and adept writer.'

Readings

'A solidly researched and compelling drama, full of page-turning intrigue, period detail and an engaging heroine who has to navigate conflicting loyalties both in her job and personal life.'

The Big Issue

'A well-crafted spy novel examines the perils of espionage's foundation in personal relationships . . . rich with historical details, right down to clothing styles and furnishings. The novel's depiction of Evelyn's career is exciting, but it also suggests the human cost: No matter how skilled her performances, to those above her in the social hierarchy, she's expendable.'

Kirkus Reviews

'Prepare to fall in awe with Evelyn Varley, the titular unexpected MI5 agent in this fast-paced thriller filled with more twists than a bag of pretzels. Set during World War II, memoirist Starford's fiction debut is a must-read for historical fiction buffs.'

E! Online

the visitor

REBECCA STARFORD is the publishing director of *Kill Your Darlings*. She is also the author of *The Imitator* and *Bad Behaviour*, which was recently adapted for a limited series by Matchbox Pictures and streamed in more than twenty countries. Rebecca currently lives in France with her wife and children.

the visitor

REBECCA STARFORD

ALLEN&UNWIN
SYDNEY • MELBOURNE • AUCKLAND • LONDON

First published in 2025

Allen & Unwin
Cammeraygal Country
83 Alexander Street
Crows Nest NSW 2065
Australia
Phone: (61 2) 8425 0100
Email: info@allenandunwin.com
Web: www.allenandunwin.com

Allen & Unwin acknowledges the Traditional Owners of the Country on which we live and work. We pay our respects to all Aboriginal and Torres Strait Islander Elders, past and present.

EU Authorised Representative: Easy Access System Europe, Mustamäe tee 50, 10621 Tallinn, Estonia, gpsr.requests@easproject.com

NATIONAL LIBRARY OF AUSTRALIA

A catalogue record for this book is available from the National Library of Australia

ISBN 978 1 76147 114 8

Set in 12.75/21 pt Minion Pro by Bookhouse, Sydney
Printed and bound in Australia by the Opus Group

10 9 8 7 6 5 4 3 2 1

MIX
Paper | Supporting responsible forestry
FSC® C001695
FSC www.fsc.org

The paper in this book is FSC® certified. FSC® promotes environmentally responsible, socially beneficial and economically viable management of the world's forests.

For Theo and Eira

My soul is like a house, small for you to enter, but I pray you to enlarge it. It is in ruins, but I ask you to remake it. It contains much that you will not be pleased to see: this I know and do not hide. But who is to rid it of these things? There is no one but you . . .

ST AUGUSTINE, *CONFESSIONS*

Prologue

THERE HAD BEEN no time to pack.

It was approaching dusk when Eliza climbed inside the car. The bats were going berserk in the fig tree across the street. Anita's place next door was dark; she must have gone out. Eliza felt a pang of guilt at not saying goodbye to her friend, but how could she explain what was happening? Anita would think she was mad. *We can write to her from Charleville, send a postcard*, Eliza reminded herself. Besides, in the coming days Anita would receive the letter and everything would make more sense.

Eliza clipped on her seatbelt. She watched her husband, Bruce, pop the bonnet to check the water and oil, then she twisted around, surveying the empty back seats. Eliza remembered all those holidays with Laura, the car crammed with sleeping bags, eskies, a box of books, her little body squashed against the passenger door, never complaining. She closed her eyes, fighting the pain that came from thinking about Laura so far away. It was for the best, of course, but it did not make it easier. Laura had already been hurt; Eliza knew that. And what about Tilly, her granddaughter, who she had last seen on that cold, grey day in London nearly three years ago. What would happen to her if they didn't make this right?

'Okay.' Bruce slammed the bonnet and joined Eliza inside the car. 'You set?'

She nodded. As he brought out the key, she reached over and put a hand to the back of his neck, stroking his white hair that still grew thick, almost to the collar.

'Have we got everything we need?' Bruce asked.

Eliza nodded again. She returned her hands to her lap. The low beat of panic had started at the base of her skull. They needed to leave.

'Anything else we can pick up on the way,' she murmured.

'The photograph?'

'In the boot. We'll dump it once we're out of Brisbane.'

'And Laura—are you sure you don't want to tell her?'

Eliza folded her arms, constraining all those feelings swelling in her chest, pushing them down.

'No,' she said. 'It's better to keep this from her.'

Bruce was peering up at the house. He had left on the security light, which flickered with a dodgy bulb. The bedroom windows at the front were black, motionless. The garden stood still. When he turned to Eliza he seemed to hesitate, and she took hold of his forearm, squeezing it. They had lived here for nearly fifty years. Despite everything, it was always going to hurt to leave.

'Any thoughts about where to stop tonight?' he asked, coaxing the engine to life and backing down the drive.

Eliza took one final look at the house and shivered, then pressed her head against the rest. She could feel sleep bearing down on her, an exhaustion that she had been holding at bay for months. It would be so blissful to give in to it.

'I don't mind,' she finally said. 'As long as it's as far away as possible.'

Bruce turned on the radio. Country Hour was playing. 'A World of Our Own'. Eliza faced the front, the faded harmony of The Seekers settling over her like a trance. The Pajero trailed the quiet street, the indicator flashing orange as the car turned, and then disappeared down the hill.

ENGLAND

1.

LAURA PULLED UP outside the Oxford Castle & Prison on New Road and let the engine idle. Through the passenger window St George's Tower loomed at the end of the cobbled walkway, platinum light cast bright against the grey coral ragstone. The line of barred windows in the hall adjacent to it glowed like a row of teeth. Laura brought out her phone and sent Tilly a text, then leaned back and closed her eyes.

She felt a little tipsy, though she had only drunk a small glass of wine at Blackwell's across town earlier that afternoon. It had been her last event for the year, Christmas now less than a fortnight away. Still, there had been a good crowd at the bookshop, including a few colleagues from the university, and even a couple of current students, which had pleased Laura. And the new novel, a re-imagining of the early life of Mary Ann Cotton, had received good coverage. A large feature in *The Guardian*, a profile in *Radio Times*, a capsule in *The New Statesman*. It was selling well, too—better than Laura expected, in any case, though Anthea had been confident. 'It's the podcast effect,' her agent had purred down the phone. 'Everyone is desperate to discover real-life crime stories.'

Laura's phone pinged, Tilly was on her way, and a moment later her daughter stood by the car, cheeks red against her otherwise pale skin, breath a fog. Outside, a light rain had begun to fall. The twin sycamore trees on top of the castle mount bowed.

'How was it?' Laura asked once Tilly had climbed inside and pulled the front passenger door shut. In Tilly's lap was a paper plate and a piece of chocolate gateau with thick ganache. Her puffer jacket whished loudly as she searched for her seatbelt.

'JoBeth invited loads of kids,' she said. 'Even *Katie* was there . . . But, yeah, it was good. JoBeth's parents booked out the crypt, and had tables set up with food and drinks. Charli XCX through the speakers.'

Laura flicked on the indicator and began the drive down New Road. Though only six o'clock, it was pitch black, and the inky streets through Oxford were quiet and mostly deserted. After all these years, she was still not accustomed to the callousness of a British winter.

'Did you take that ghost tour?'

'Yeah.' Tilly slumped a little lower in the seat. 'It wasn't too scary. I mean, I only jumped a few times.'

Laura smiled. She imagined it had been more often than that. Tilly had always been afraid of the dark. Some nights she still slept with a night-light.

'You would have liked the guide though, Mum,' Tilly continued. 'She was dressed up like a chambermaid from the 1800s. You know, all in black, a bonnet and everything. Ms Morgana McGoul, she called herself.'

'I certainly would have liked that. Did JoBeth have fun?'

Tilly glanced at her, then away. She was turning over a piece of chewing gum in her mouth.

'I guess. She was cutting the cake when I left.' Tilly swiped some dark hair from her brow. 'She hadn't opened my present.'

Laura reached over and ran a finger down Tilly's smooth cheek. Lately, Tilly didn't like these gestures, but tonight she leaned into it, closing her eyes for a moment, and Laura felt the stir of unrest. Not so long ago, she had been able to scoop Tilly up and explain away any worry, or accident, or mistake. Laura had been the answer, usually to problems with friends at school. Tilly would turn fourteen in April, cracking her young life wide open, and soon that crevasse between adolescence and adulthood would become dangerous to bridge.

'Hey, shall we do a movie when we're home?' Laura suggested, returning her hand to the steering wheel, giving it a squeeze. 'Something light?'

'Not *The Castle* again, Mum. *Please.*'

'You can choose.'

'Okay.' Tilly leaned forward to turn up the heater dial, pressing her fingertips to the dash. 'That could be good.' But Laura could tell she was still thinking about JoBeth and the party in the crypt.

The drive to Swinbrook took around thirty-five minutes. Via Jericho and then north, before joining up to the A40 and heading out through the West Oxfordshire countryside. A smooth, familiar route for Laura. For the past three years she had taught in the Master's program at Ewert House in Summertown. Creative writing students, mostly mature-age, diligently chipping away at novel-length manuscripts. It wasn't especially glamorous work, and the pay was appalling, but Laura took pleasure from the discussions about character, voice, and how to integrate Big Themes into narrative. She took a technical, clear-headed approach to writing; she was logical, and chose to focus more on the craft than the art. She enjoyed talking to the students too, the camaraderie, even if it was somewhat confected. During the week it could be lonely working in her studio while Tilly was at school in Burford, and Andrew spent long hours at Mount House in Witney where he hot-desked at a council co-work space with graphic designers and media consultants.

As Laura was thinking all this, Tilly chatted easily at her side. In January, the family were to spend a week in Paris, and Tilly was reeling off all the places she wanted to visit: Père-Lachaise, the Catacombs, Moulin Rouge. Laura only half listened. The heat of the car, infused with a sickly sweetness from the gateau, suddenly reminded her of home. Not Swinbrook but Brisbane, which Laura hadn't thought of as home for many years. It was a strange, melancholy feeling that set her teeth on edge. 'Don't forget Dad wants to visit that Museum of Resistance,' she muttered.

As Laura took the overpass, coasting above a gloomy Travelodge, she thought about all the times Andrew had suggested a trip back to Australia: 'Snorkelling on the reef? Tack on Sydney. Climb Uluru.'

'You're not allowed to climb it,' Laura said.

'Well, *look* at it, then.' He didn't push it, though. Andrew wasn't intrepid; Europe offered him more than he needed outside of drizzling Oxfordshire. And recently there had been a more urgent impediment to such a trip—money.

Arriving in Swinbrook, Laura took the bridge and passed the Swann Inn, whose front windows glowed a warm lilac in the dark, a hint of smoke coming from the chimney. Two minutes later, she had pulled up the gravel drive. By now, the rain was falling hard, the wind thumping at the car.

They lived in a converted Georgian stone cottage. Out the back were three acres of untamed wilderness running all the way down to the Windrush, which after this downpour would probably breach its banks. Although they had lived here for nearly a decade, Laura's parents had still never seen the house. She had been coaxing them to visit for years, but it had just never happened. Laura often wondered what they would make of it—the smart fridge, the jacuzzi, Alexa. Eliza and Bruce weren't exactly ostentatious. Her father still wore sandals with socks.

The front door opened and Laura made out Andrew's bold outline, his big woollen jumper, a glass of wine in hand. Behind him, the comfortable house and its promise of refuge beckoned.

'Rain, rain.' Tilly sighed, drawing a square in the mist against the window. When she turned, Laura was surprised to find some new dimensionality to her daughter's face, as though they were only now meeting each other for the first time. They had never looked much alike—Tilly, more like Andrew with her dark hair and heavy-set brow, had not inherited Laura's spray of freckles, or the fine line of scars across her knees and shins from a childhood outdoors, exposed to all that grit and grime. No calloused palms, no dry skin at the elbow. Instead she bore the complexion of an easy life spent inside, unblemished as fresh milk. Again Laura felt that pang for home, or a version of it from her past.

She turned off the engine. 'Come on,' Laura said. 'Let's make a dash for it.'

A fire roared in the hearth. Andrew took their wet coats to hang from the rack in the boot room, then steered Laura and Tilly towards the lounge. The house smelled of caramelised onions; Andrew had made pizzas, now cooking in the wood-burning oven next to the stove.

'So, the party?' he asked, accepting the collapsing gateau from Tilly's outstretched hand. 'Spooky?'

Tilly flopped down on the L-shaped couch, kicking off her sneakers. 'A bit.'

She smiled at her father, and Andrew ruffled her hair.

He raised an eyebrow at Laura. 'And what about you, my good wife? Have you sung for your supper this evening?'

Laura sat beside Tilly, savouring the warmth from the fire. 'If you call supper cheap chardonnay and half-a-dozen Jacob's crackers.'

Andrew leaned down to kiss Laura's cheek. 'I'll take that as a no.'

She watched him move about the kitchen, humming quietly under his breath, his thinning hair standing on end. Andrew usually came to Laura's local book events, but this time he had spent the afternoon working from home. Spread across the dining table were blueprints covered in scribbles and half-finished mugs of coffee. Laura wondered how the Zoom meeting went with the Gordon brothers; Andrew gave no indication. She would ask later, once Tilly was in bed, in case it was more bad news.

Wind squalled at the windows, and a few stray branches from the climbing hydrangea slapped against the glass. Rain battered the roof. Andrew returned from the kitchen with a glass of syrah for Laura, a soda water for Tilly, and a small platter of antipasto. The pizzas would be ready shortly, he announced. They snacked together for a few minutes, Andrew flicking through Channel 4.

'Something funny,' Tilly said through a mouthful of tapenade.

In the end they settled on old episodes of *Black Books*. After dinner, Laura brought out her laptop, and wrote a quick note to Anthea, a sign-off for the year, with thanks. She felt exhausted, though this was not uncommon after events where she had to be convivial with so many people. Putting aside the computer, she settled against the cushions, contented, and the flat screen on the other side of the room had soon narrowed to a small sphere of gilded light, while the canned laughter receded, as if banished to the bottom of a deep well.

Laura's eyes snapped open at a loud bang. She sat up.

'Mum,' Tilly said, raising a lazy hand. 'Was that the door?'

She and Andrew both had their eyes fixed on the television, clearly not intending to move from the couch.

Laura sighed. 'I guess I'll go investigate.'

The noise sounded as though it had come from the front of the house, and Laura lurched off in that direction, blinking and unsteady on her feet. Her mouth tasted of ripe tannins from the wine. Though it wasn't far to travel, the hallway felt like an underground tunnel, with paintings and photo frames and side tables a blur as she guided herself towards the fan light above the solid oak door.

Eventually Laura reached the front, and when she drew back the door she was startled by the frigid air waiting to greet her on the porch. Two young male officers blinked nervously at her. Behind them sat a police car, its front beams trained on the pines lining the drive.

'Mrs Townsend?' said one of the young men. There were pimples on his chin. 'Mrs Laura Townsend?' He gripped the radio attached to his lapel as though it were the only thing weighing him to the spot. His fingers looked sore and chilblained, the nails bitten down.

'Yes,' Laura replied. 'That's me.'

The officers glanced at one another. The clear-skinned one removed his hat. His hair was very wispy and blond, like a duckling. 'May we come inside?'

The officers had come to inform Laura that her parents, Eliza and Bruce, were dead. Their bodies had been found yesterday, somewhere in the Outback. Since Laura was their only registered next of kin, the authorities in Australia had contacted the British Consulate, who in turn contacted the local constabulary. Thames Valley had received the call an hour ago.

'I'm afraid we have no further details,' the blond officer told her. 'We're simply here as a community liaison. The bearer of this bad news.'

They had gathered in the lounge room. Laura sitting beside Andrew on the couch, the policemen standing before the fireplace, more in ungainliness than formality. Tilly wasn't there—Laura supposed Andrew had told her to go to her room, but she may well have been lingering in the hallway. Laura stared at the policemen's chunky shoes, and the faint steam rising from the backs of their trousers. She hadn't been able to speak since they arrived; she could barely hear what they were saying now. It was as though a shutter had fallen, or a curtain on a stage. It had come down noiselessly and painlessly, but it was a collapse nonetheless. This must be what shock feels like, she thought dimly, for she wasn't scared, or tearful, or particularly sad. She felt immune. It was a curious, almost empowering sensation, like she could have taken off for a half-marathon in the bucketing rain and returned unscathed.

'They're *dead*,' she heard Andrew say through her blocked ears. 'Are you sure?'

'Yes, sir,' said the blond one. 'We're very sorry.'

'Mm, yes, very sorry,' his colleague affirmed. Neither of them looked at Laura.

'How did they die?' Andrew asked.

A stricken look passed over the officers' faces. 'We don't know.'

'But someone killed them, you're saying? Oh my god. They were murdered?'

'I'm afraid I can't answer that either, sir. The investigation is ongoing.'

Laura put her face in her hands and squeezed her eyes shut. Her fingers felt cool against her hot skin. An image of her parents, standing on the other side of a sun-drenched room, took shape in her mind. How could they be dead? She thought about the last time she had spoken to them. It had been in August, when Laura suggested a visit to Australia. The conversation had not panned out as she'd hoped it would. That memory would stay with her forever, she realised. That the last time Laura had spoken to her mother, Eliza had hung up the phone on her.

Eventually she sat up. She wanted a cup of tea. Laura knew this wasn't an appropriate response, but she didn't know quite what else to do. She looked to the blond officer, who had a waxy complexion and dark circles beneath his eyes, and thought about asking him to flick on the kettle.

He was checking his phone. 'We're expecting a call from the consulate in Australia.'

'They have been liaising with detectives in, er, Queens Land,' said the other. 'They'll provide you with more information on the scene, as well as any updates in the investigation.'

Laura gave him a weak smile. They had probably never done a death knock before, or very few. She wondered how long they had each been in the force. Six months, a year. Boys, really, only a handful of years older than Tilly. The blond one's uniform was a poor fit for his angular frame, his hat too wide and with the habit of slipping over his eyes. His gaze kept darting about the lounge room, and every now and then he squinted at the bright lights in the kitchen, pursing his lips as though he needed to speak but had forgotten his lines.

'Ah,' he suddenly cried, waving his vibrating phone with pantomime relief. 'At last.'

He spoke for a minute or two with his back to Laura. Beside her, she sensed Andrew, and his warm hand on her knee, twisting on the couch every now and then and taking deep breaths.

'All right,' said the blond officer, pivoting to Laura. 'Would you mind . . . ?'

'Oh. Yes?'

Laura took the phone and proceeded to talk to an Australian woman in Sydney who wanted to confirm her identity. Date of birth, maiden name, passport number—which had Andrew off scrabbling through the bureau in the den. The whole thing was ordinary; the woman didn't even offer any condolences. Laura preferred it that way. It distracted her from the feeling that her conscious self, the intellectual, thinking part, had left her body and was floating off somewhere near the ceiling. There was a lot of clacking and tapping at the end of the line, and a weird, whistling delay between Laura's replies and the woman's next question. She had the kind of blunt voice that sounded exasperated but probably wasn't, and she breathed loudly into the receiver. Laura imagined her name was Pat. Eventually she was told that the detective leading the investigation in Brisbane was on the other line and Laura could now speak to him directly.

'Well, I . . .'

Pat patched her through. While the phone rang on the new call, Laura watched the young officers and Andrew, who had now migrated to the kitchen. They spoke together in a quiet, amiable way, and Andrew wiped his nose with his woollen sleeve.

The detective, a man named Sandretti, answered. Unexpectedly he had a lisp, an endearing characteristic that must have served him well when dealing with bereaved relatives, softening the brute nature of their conversation. He explained to Laura that he was currently in Charleville in central Queensland, more than seven hundred kilometres west of Brisbane. It was the largest town before the desert plains began on the road to the Northern Territory. He had been flown in from the city to assist the local police.

'Your mum and dad were found in a place called Hell Hole Gorge National Park. It's desert country, the Outback. Do you know it?' Sandretti asked.

Laura stared at the orange flames of the fire. Blood shrieked through her temples. 'No,' she breathed. 'I've never heard of it.'

'Your parents never mentioned it?'

'Not that I can recall.'

'Travellers, though, were they? Keen on the Outback.'

An image of her father swatting a mosquito popped into Laura's head, the smear of bright red blood across his thigh like a flourish of Japanese calligraphy. 'Not particularly,' she said.

'Mm.' Sandretti sounded disappointed. 'Well, it's more than two hundred and fifty kays north-west of my position here in Charleville. So, yeah, a massive drive from their place in Paddington. Accessible if you've a decent vehicle, but still remote.'

Laura's eyes strayed to the coffee table in front of the couch. On top of Elsie de Wolfe's *The House in Good Taste* was a postcard from her father. Bruce sent them to Tilly now and then from overseas locations, never addressing Laura or Andrew as though it were a private communique, which recently had begun to sting Laura with the slimmest thorn of jealousy. This one showed off the colourful tiles of Escadaria Selarón in Rio de Janeiro, and in his spidery scrawl on the back Bruce had written: *Counted 215 steps to the top, well worth the effort to climb.* Laura took a deep, shuddering breath, then smacked a hand over her mouth to staunch the wail she felt pitching up her throat.

'Mrs Townsend? You still there?'

Laura straightened. She gave her head a brisk shake. 'Yes, I'm here. But tell me, please. Do you have any suspects?'

'Suspects?' Sandretti sounded surprised. 'Oh no, Mrs Townsend. I'm sorry, I should have made that clearer from the start. Fatalities like these always trigger an investigation. But after my initial inquiries, I'm not treating your parents' deaths as suspicious. In fact I'm finishing up in Charleville this morning and flying back to Brisbane to write up the case from there.'

'I see.' Laura wasn't sure whether to be relieved by that or not. 'So what do you think happened?'

Sandretti made a noise down the phone, and Laura pictured him leaning back in his chair, rearranging his feet on the desk, perhaps taking a fortifying swig of coffee.

'Well, here's what we know. Eliza and Bruce left Brisbane in a hurry,' he said. 'Drove through the night and into the next morning. Brought along very few supplies, and no satellite phone, which you really need in these parts for safe travel. They spent the next night in Charleville, at the Hotel Corones, then went on to the gorge the following day. They were alone out there—there is no evidence of any other campers during their stay. Some

Germans found the bodies when they arrived at the site yesterday. Your dad was in the tent, but your mum . . .' Sandretti paused.

'Yes?'

'Well, she was found below an escarpment a few hundred metres away. It appears she had a fall into the shallows below. It's quite a way down, you see. Early indications are that she drowned in the water.'

The edges of Laura's vision dimmed for a moment. The room and everything in it began to slowly rotate. 'She drowned?' she whispered. 'All that way inland?'

'Mm,' said Sandretti. 'Not something you hear all that often out here. We've had the forensic team out to examine the scene, but there's nothing to suggest foul play.'

'And Dad—what happened to him?'

'We think your father passed away first. A heart attack, most likely.'

'Oh, Dad. How . . . *awful*.' Laura let out a slow, shaky exhale. 'And Mum after that?'

'Yes, probably soon afterwards. We found a camera on the escarpment belonging to your mother. It seems she took the last photo at around seven o'clock that same evening. We can't be sure what caused her to fall. It might have been something sudden too, like her heart or a stroke. Perhaps brought on if your father had an episode in the tent. Or it could have been the exposure.

Cracked forty-five degrees on Thursday and they'd been at the site all day. Sun that intense can be lethal . . .'

Laura pictured heat coruscating off the ancient red rock, a soundless desert backdrop.

'But what were they doing out there? They were so far from home.'

'It's a curly one, that's for sure,' Sandretti conceded.

'A *curly one*?' Laura gripped the phone, belligerence rising. 'Is that the official police line?'

Laura heard Sandretti cough. He was probably running a hand through his hair. Short and grey, she imagined. When he spoke again, his voice was quieter, further smoothed out by the lisp, which did half the work of placating her.

'I appreciate you're not getting many answers right now, Mrs Townsend, and that's really difficult. I hope in the next day or two that I'll know more, and we can better understand what brought them out here. When I'm back in Brisbane I'll investigate further. This will be useful in building a fuller picture of your parents' movements, and their states of mind before they left. By the way, was their GP still Margaret Leong at the Red Hill clinic?'

Laura clenched her fist, nails digging into the soft flesh of her palm.

'I'm sorry, I've no idea.'

'No worries. We'll get that confirmed elsewhere.' There was another noise down the line, the sound of a car door slamming. Sandretti must have been on the move. 'For now, you just need to know that cases of unusual or unexplained deaths such as these are always referred to the coroner. So, once we've submitted our report, the coroner will review the evidence and make a determination as to whether there will be an inquest.' He paused. 'You're in the UK, aren't you?'

'Yes,' Laura murmured, her eyes drifting back to the dark window. The rain had stopped. The house was very quiet.

'I'm sorry this has happened so far from home. But I'll keep you updated on the coroner's report and any other developments that may arise in the meantime,' Sandretti said. 'We'll speak again, perhaps in person at Roma Street.'

'I'm sorry?'

Someone else was talking in the background, Sandretti's voice for a moment became muffled as he replied. Then, clearer, on returning to Laura. 'Well, I just assumed, that's all. That you'll make the trip back. To Brisbane. To collect your parents effects, and organise other matters.'

Stones crunched underfoot, the caw of a lonely bird. Laura could almost feel that throbbing sun.

'Oh, yes,' she murmured again. 'I suppose I will.'

A few hours passed. Andrew had walked the police officers out to their car in the drive, then went to check on Tilly. The house remained still, only the occasional crackle sounding from the last logs in the fireplace. It was nearly two a.m. Laura's skin felt clammy. The back of her neck itched. She sat at the kitchen island, tracing a fingertip around her mug of cold tea. Andrew leaned against the bench near the Aga.

'How did you go?' Laura asked.

'It was a lot for her to take in. She's upset.'

'Oh.' Laura's voice caught. 'Yes, she would be. Poor thing.' She thought about going to Tilly, to lie down next to her on the bed and breathe in the smell of her hair, but she was frozen to the stool.

Andrew blew out his cheeks. 'I can't fucking believe this. Jesus Christ. What a night.'

I'm an orphan, Laura thought vaguely. It was an antiquated term, like spinster or chattels, belonging to a Victorian novel.

'None of this feels real,' she murmured.

They gazed at one another, bleary-eyed. Something about how they were positioned in the kitchen, the icy tiles underfoot, that drunk feeling now laced with the queasiness of an approaching hangover, reminded Laura of what she always considered their first date, at the house party in Shoreditch. Where, as their friends danced away to Pulp in the courtyard, she had holed up inside with Andrew, sharing a durrie and a glass of cava, and he told her about his business. Buying up old, dilapidated cottages in the north and renovating them, and then selling them on for a small profit. He had already completed five projects that year with a team of labourers from Estonia. The following year, he was aiming for ten. And though he had been trying to impress Laura with those figures, it had been his description of the feeling he had when the before-and-after photos were placed side by side, the exaltation, that had unlocked something deep inside her—'It's like a rebirth, a complete and utter transformation,' he told her. She had kissed him, desperate for some of this power to rub off on her. Andrew hadn't known it, but that night he had laid a new pathway in Laura's mind—one that was always facing forward, never circling back on the past.

'I have to go to Brisbane,' she announced, pushing away her mug of tea. 'As soon as possible. I have to sort it all out.'

Andrew scratched at some stubble on his chin. The fretful, quizzical expression he'd assumed after the police broke the news had not left his face. 'Okay, I can see that. But let's just take a few beats. Get our minds around it.'

Laura shook her head. Her legs ached from the cold. She wanted to feel warmth again, real heat. She didn't look like someone who would take pleasure in the unyielding humidity—she was too neat, too buttoned-up. But she had missed desperately the muggy air, the fullness of it, like she could reach out and scoop up some of that moisture in her hand.

'Around what? There is no one else to do this, Andrew. My parents were only children. I have no aunts or uncles or cousins. Neither did they, as far as I know. There is no other family. I have to sort it. All of it. The police, the probate. The house.'

'The house?'

'Yes. It will need to be sold, I suppose. Their things, all their things . . .' Laura broke off and placed a hand against her breast, feeling for her heart. There it was, still intact.

Andrew took a step towards her. He looked paler, thinner, under the harsh kitchen lights. 'You can't do all that by yourself, darling. It's too much.'

He reached for Laura, and she drew his hand towards her, kissing his wedding band. It was like being touched for the first time in years; she shuddered from it. He wrapped his other arm around her shoulder and pressed his lips against her hair, and with her face against his jumper Laura inhaled the comforting smell of old smoke and ash. Suddenly, she reared back. 'How did it go? Today, with the Gordons?'

'What?'

'The interview? The new contract?'

Andrew withdrew his arm, blinking frantically. 'What about it?'

'Did they like the plans?'

'Oh, right. Well, no. It was a complete balls-up, to be honest, just like every other pitch lately, but that's hardly important right now.'

He tried to smile, but Laura could see it. Andrew's career had finally disintegrated. It had taken some time, nearly three years. First it had been the aftershock of Brexit, then Covid-19 put a stop to most jobs on his firm's books. Last year his partner left, and Andrew started applying for council projects, winning a few here and there, but then austerity hit and the work dried up almost overnight. Before this, Laura and Andrew had been comfortable; lately they had accrued serious debt, including a second mortgage on the house. Interest rates were punishing. Only last week, Andrew had suggested selling up and downsizing. They simply couldn't afford to live there anymore. The job with the Gordon brothers, a substantial project to redevelop an old dairy, had been the last chance to keep their heads above water.

Laura eased herself off the stool and went to the kettle, flicking on the switch. She stared out the window, which overlooked the stone courtyard and raised vegetable plots. In the distance was the bold imprint of the oak, the desolate rope of the old swing twisting in the wind.

'What if we all went,' she said quietly. 'The three of us. To Brisbane. You could work on the house. You know, spruce it up before the sale. The garden will probably need work. Fences. Pavers. A project. Start the building portfolio again, get back on your feet?'

'Laura,' Andrew said.

'We could live cheaply in Australia, you know. Cheaper than here, anyway. Send Tilly to the local high school, no fees, while you work on the house.'

Andrew stared back at her, fidgeting with the hem of his jumper. He shook his head.

'Darling, you've had an incredible shock. We all have. There's a lot to process. So we shouldn't be talking about any of this right now. It feels a bit . . .' He searched around for the word. 'Unseemly. I mean, bloody hell. Your parents have just *died*.'

He didn't sound like he meant it. Laura could see he was trying to conceal the fledgling excitement, though the flint in his eyes betrayed him. In the back of her mind, Laura agreed with Andrew: this was a freakish way of responding to the news. It was distasteful, mercenary. Perhaps if this had all happened in the harsh light of day she would have been terrified of cosmic retribution. But there was no escaping it: with the sale of her parents' house, they could pay off the mortgages back in England and have change left over. A lot of change. Debts wiped out. New, safe investments made. Andrew could take his time looking for another job, finding work he really wanted, or perhaps start a new business of his own.

'I know it's icky,' Laura said in a clear voice. 'But let's be practical. I need to get over there to sort out everything, and you need work. This could be an opportunity. To make something good out of these awful circumstances. To get ourselves back on our feet. The grief stuff . . .' She gripped the bench, setting her stance to brace for another tremor of horrible bewilderment. 'Well, that can come later.'

'And you can do that—compartmentalise all that emotion?'

Laura shrugged. For months she had been siphoning off feelings about her mother and father. It had started about a year ago, the estrangement, where her parents dropped out of Laura's life almost completely. There were no more WhatsApps or Zoom calls, no personal updates or news, no birthday messages or Christmas cards. Nothing except those blasted postcards. It was like they stopped knowing each other. For a while Laura assumed it had something to do with her staying on in England after all these years, her parents finally snapping at her for depriving them of seeing their granddaughter grow up. But Eliza and Bruce never said as much. In fact they had never said anything to indicate anger or bitterness. They had simply checked out.

It wore away at Laura, this bizarre indifference. It simply made no sense. 'Maybe they're just busy,' Andrew had said, trying to comfort. But on and on it went, the pain running deeper and deeper in Laura. Eventually she had enough, and one morning she phoned up the Brisbane house and asked her mother if they could visit over Christmas. A respite from another British winter. A final gesture to break the logjam. They couldn't afford to make the trip, but Laura had come to realise that this is what it would take for a reunion; that her parents were not prepared to trek to the UK again. But Eliza had said, 'No,' in a stern, flat voice. 'I'm sorry, but that is not going to work for us.' Stunned, Laura had asked, 'Is something the matter, Mum? We never hear from you these days.' But instead of replying, her mother had hung up. And that had been that.

Laura stared across the kitchen at Andrew. Couldn't she just absorb this new blow about her parents, however much it dwarfed all the others? Because for some time she had set herself rigid alongside this unspooling knowledge: that they would never meet again. That it was over.

'Tilly won't be happy,' said Andrew.

He was right on that, too. No teenager wants to be uprooted. But Tilly would benefit from some disruption, some adventure. And she had always loved Laura's bedtime stories about Brisbane, those tales of straw spun so many times you could almost see the threads of gold. About catching frogs by the stormwater drain at Norman Buchan Park, swimming in the river at Corinda minutes before a bull shark nipped a boater's finger off, the diamond adder curled up in the manhole in her bedroom, sugar gliders warring on the roof. The endless stretch of ocean to the east of the city, and flat barren scrubland to the west. As a little girl, she'd even kept a map of Australia pinned to her bedroom wall with coloured tacks marking each place she longed to visit.

'Tilly will be fine,' Laura said. 'Children are adaptable.'

'She's not a child anymore.'

Laura felt herself hardening. He didn't understand. Andrew had never lived abroad; he had never really left home, and the comfort of the familiar. Swinbrook was fifty miles from where he grew up; he still visited his parents on Sundays, while his brother stayed with Andrew and Laura every Easter break with his wife, Aseefa. Andrew's family had a pleasant, uncomplicated affection for each other, and Andrew had a pleasant, uncomplicated relationship with his childhood home. He had never had to start again. He had never felt the urge to leave, which meant he had never felt any resistance to return, no matter the circumstances.

'It'll be good for her to have a break from Burford and those awful girls,' said Laura, once again seeking out the oak tree in the dark. 'Feel the sun on her face, swim in the ocean. Besides, it won't be forever. We could go for a year. She can do it. We all can.'

Laura's reflection in the rain-spattered glass refracted, morphing like breaking sheets of ice. *I will never hear their voices again*, she reminded herself. *We will never have another moment shared.* Laura set her jaw against the persisting numbness coming over her brain like a film.

Andrew watched her, his arms crossed. He was trembling a little, from the cold, and from the shock of it all. None of this was easy to him. He seemed to be working out what to say next.

'But won't it be strange,' he finally asked, 'living in their house?'

Laura closed her eyes. There was a pulse, as steady as a drumbeat, at the base of her skull. She pictured herself at Central Avenue, planted on the coir welcome mat, knees locked. It had been years since she had been inside the house in Paddington. Perhaps she was a little afraid. Not of the house itself but of how it would make her feel during the months they would need to live in it. After so long away, it didn't feel like it belonged to her anymore. *But I'll have to take back some ownership, some control*, she told herself. *If this arrangement is to succeed, I must swell into something I've never been before: proprietary. I'll have to do this*, she figured, turning back to Andrew and giving him a wan smile, *if I'm to later relinquish it.*

They agreed to sleep on it. And in the morning, if on balance it still appeared to be a good idea, they would talk to Tilly and begin the preparations.

They went to bed in their clothes, both too exhausted to change. Andrew put an arm around Laura's waist and promptly fell asleep, his soft snores whistling through his nose. Laura stared at the ceiling, at the dark edges where it met the cornice. Until now, she and Andrew had been lucky. Both had lost friends to cancer, and Andrew's cousin had committed suicide when he was a boy, but they had reached their forties without having to seriously contemplate the mortality of their closest family. It seemed miraculous to have been spared such pain until now.

Laura rolled carefully on to her side. Hanging on the wall near her dresser was a painting. Andrew had bought it for her birthday a few years ago from an art dealer in Hackney. 'In case you're ever missing your wilful, lavish land,' he'd said. It was a large desert landscape, blue and grey sky marbled with dense cloud. A small, washed-out mountain range receded in the distance, while thick oils in the foreground had rendered a clump of impenetrable spinifex; clay and blood clotting the base of the shrub.

What had drawn her parents out there? Laura still hadn't allowed herself to really pick at that question, or to go near to imagining their last hours by that dry, rocky outcrop. She sensed an impatience in her bloodstream, anxious and writhing. Sandretti said the inquest would shed more light on why they had got in their old Pajero and driven in an almost straight line to Hell Hole Gorge. Why they had fled the house like that in the middle of the night. As impossible as it seemed, she would need to wait for those answers.

Laura closed her eyes. She didn't think she would sleep, but it wasn't long before she felt herself pulled down towards silky unconsciousness. Right before she surrendered, she thought back to the night she left Brisbane for London. Nearly twenty-five years ago. She had dwelled on this moment so often, each time the memory adjusting slightly, another layer of sediment settling, that she had started not to trust it. How her mother had come down to the street from the house, while her father remained on the deck, a mere shadow. The atmosphere had been strained, the air full of unsaid things. It was as if a triangular current had formed between them, like the beginnings of an electrical storm, creating a curious combination of fury and pain that made the house glower in the moonlight.

'He's bad at goodbyes,' Eliza explained, bent over to speak to Laura through the taxi's rolled-down window. 'He doesn't think you'll come home.' Her mother had smiled, reaching out to trace a finger down Laura's cheek. 'But I know you'll be back.'

Maybe that is where the real cleft began. Because even though the memory of that night kept changing, Laura had remained certain that something had grown between herself and her parents, some fraught and dangerous feeling that had never been explained away. Laura always put it down to her youth. She had only just graduated from university when the taxi rolled away down the street. She had been so young. She had never travelled, or been in love. But she had wanted more from life than she imagined Brisbane could deliver. She hadn't understood all the nuances of betrayal back then, or how easily her parents could uproot her sense of belonging. *You'll be back*. Laura had always remembered Eliza's smile as hopeful, but now she realised there had been something worried in her expression, something tense. Laura had not realised her mother's words might have been a warning.

BRISBANE

2.

DAZED WITH JETLAG, Tilly had gone to bed early the first night in Australia only to toss and turn inside her sleeping bag for hours. She hadn't slept on the plane either, and as she untangled her legs from the clingy polyester it occurred to her that this was probably the longest she had ever been awake in her life. She rolled over, grasping for her phone. The display told her it was only a little after midnight, but when she peered up at the louvre window the sky looked deceptively light, like the atmosphere was made of paler, almost metallic matter. Maybe it was, on the other side of the world.

Tilly scrolled through her pictures until her eyes hurt, then opened her laptop and stared at the wallpaper image of JoBeth, her arm slung over Tilly's shoulder. The girls stood out the front of the Tower of London on last year's field trip. Tilly wished she could talk to JoBeth about the smelly man on the plane and the Bose headphones she bought duty-free in Singapore. She chewed at her bottom lip, pulling away a piece of dry skin. The image of her mother's face as she gazed up at the house was still lodged in Tilly's brain. She had looked so . . . *It was weird*, Tilly thought. There had been such trepidation in her expression, but she could have sworn she saw excitement in Laura's green eyes. What the fuck was there to be excited about? They were living in her dead grandparents' house.

Tilly slammed her MacBook shut and shoved her hands behind her head. She glanced around the empty room, her eyes straying over the white walls where stick-figure shadows pitched up and down the panelling. It gave her the creeps, all this emptiness. It didn't feel like a house anyone had ever lived in, especially not her mother. Their home back in Swinbrook was full of things. Books, old magazines, shabby rugs, paintings and tapestries crowding the walls, a blazing fireplace, the noisy Gaggia, while all those wintery elements—wind, rain, hail, even snow—hammered away at the roof and threatened the doors.

Tilly traced a line down the panel, feeling the dust like old resin gather under her fingertip. She had only met Eliza and Bruce a few times in person, the last of which had been when she turned eleven. She and Laura had taken the train to London for the day, and joined her grandparents at the Natural History

Museum in South Kensington. Afterwards, they had all gone for afternoon tea at Fortnum & Mason in St James's. Tilly couldn't remember much else about the excursion, except that her grandmother called her *Matilda*, which no one ever did, and it gave Eliza a faintly aristocratic bearing.

Back in England, Tilly's other grandparents, Muriel and Ted, had more determined views on Eliza and Bruce, despite never having met them, bristling at their very mention as if a cold wind had blasted through the Cheltenham bungalow. Muriel, who had a purple rinse in her thinning hair, called them *oddballs*. Of course, that had all changed. During their last visit, on Christmas afternoon, Muriel spoke about them with a kind of reverence, one pudgy hand pressed against her bosom, as if she had lost someone too. '*Dear* Eliza and Bruce,' she sighed. 'What a thing to happen. Mind you, we all know how dangerous the Outback is. What were they thinking, driving out there like that?'

'Lots of people travel to the Australian desert,' Tilly replied. 'Most of them come back alive.'

'Not if you believe the news, pet,' said Muriel. 'And now Laura is taking you both there.'

'We're not going to the actual desert, Nana. Brisbane has about four million people in it.'

'I've done my research,' Muriel continued. 'I've read posts on Facebook. Oh, it looks a ghastly place, it really does. Everything closes early, and it's terribly racist, full of crocodiles and venomous spiders and evangelical Christians.'

'And don't forget all that horrible sunshine,' Andrew had laughed, stirring his cup of milky tea.

Her grandparents' antagonism made Tilly defensive, like some part of her had been slighted, which in a small way she decided it had. What did they know about Australia? They had never been. In fact, Muriel and Ted had never travelled further than the Costa del Sol on a package holiday. Sometimes, amid these conversations, Tilly liked to picture Eliza sitting across from Muriel, one corduroy leg crossed over the other and smoking a cigarette, giving Tilly a sly wink before she tapped a worm of ash on her grandparents' shag carpet.

Tilly had cried when Andrew came into her bedroom and told her Eliza and Bruce had died. Less than a month ago, but it felt like longer, like years; shock had the habit of stretching time like elastic. Tilly already knew, of course. She had been listening from her doorway when the police arrived at the house. After they had delivered the bad news, her father had himself cried for a few minutes, strange snivelling sounds, while her mother had exhibited nothing more than brisk calm, like something inside her, the emotional part, had also expired. Tilly supposed part of you must die when your parents do—how could it not? She guessed that had been where her own tears came from as her father told her, patting her leg beneath the duvet, not quite knowing where to look as her shoulders heaved up and down. The truth was she had been crying for Laura—for that part of her that Tilly had now lost too.

For this reason, Tilly had expected to find her mother altered the next morning—red-eyed and withdrawn. However Laura looked as she always did: dressed in jeans and a neat blazer, dark-blonde hair tied back, make-up sparse. She stood at the bench, working the coffee machine and humming under her breath. Tilly watched her move to the fridge for the milk, then the pantry for sugar, a sick feeling growing in the pit of her stomach. She knew she should say something about Eliza and Bruce, but wasn't sure what. She could only stare at the photo clipped to the fridge. Of newborn Tilly, a cigar-shaped bundle with a squashed-looking face, held awkwardly in her grandmother's arms. Eliza looked remarkably like Laura, her shoulders sloped, slender-looking hands. They had different hair, of course—Eliza's was thick and wiry, like a Scotch-Brite scourer—but they wore the same loose-fitting blouse, the same high-waisted trousers. And their expressions were similar as they gazed back at the camera: faintly amused by something going on inside their own heads.

'Dad and I have decided that we're going to Brisbane,' said her mother finally, leaning against the kitchen bench and drinking from a large mug. For a second, Tilly had thought she meant just the two of them, and went to protest that she wasn't staying with Muriel and Ted in Cheltenham. But no. Overnight her parents had decided to move to Australia for the year, and Tilly was coming with them.

'No fucking way.'

Laura had looked up. Her face was very pale, though her eyes were clear. She set her head at an odd angle, folding her arms. If Tilly hadn't known better, she'd have said her mother was about to laugh.

'But you always wanted to visit, darling. Remember those stories you made me tell? You couldn't get enough of them.'

'I was just a little kid.'

'Over and over, every night of the week.'

'It's different now.'

Tilly felt herself flush hot with the indignation of being misunderstood. Why didn't her mother know that it wasn't the stories that she had loved but the proximity of Laura during their telling? The warm press of her, the casual hand smoothing back Tilly's hair, the flutter of Laura's heart through her shirt. Being together like that, the place of her mother's childhood took on a mythical dimension, one entirely dreamed up in her imagination. Its power, its allure, was in not being real. But as Laura began moving about the kitchen once more, Tilly had realised that there would be no further negotiation. They were leaving. Done, dusted. Tilly hardly had time to register the enormity of this change sweeping over her before Andrew announced he had booked the flights, and three weeks later they were on a train to Heathrow.

'This is important for your mum,' Andrew told her as they boarded the plane, his voice low, in warning. 'Try to remember that.'

And it's important to you too, Tilly now thought angrily, sitting up in bed and kicking away the sleeping bag. She wasn't stupid—she had heard her father on the phone, seen his browser history on the family laptop. He was going to renovate her grandparents' house, and then he and Laura would make a small fortune on the sale. She had listened to them talking about it late at night, Andrew reeling off prices in Paddington. Quaint-sounding, but again—unreal. Another of her mother's stories. Apparently there was some kind of property boom in Australia, a nation obsessed with houses.

Tilly ran her hands down her bare legs. They felt spiky, irritated; she had started shaving a few months ago. Maybe she would ask Laura if she could get laser. In the fiendish Brisbane summer, she wouldn't be able to hide much of herself beneath clothes.

Tilly lay down once more. From the roof came a scuttling sound, then awful, high-pitch shrieking. This went on and on until an enormous bump made the ceiling shudder. Tilly clenched her eyes shut. It must be the possums. Laura had warned that the heat sent them ballistic. Sometimes they killed each other during these fights, a consequence that only became apparent when the walls began to stink of a rotting carcass.

'They don't put that in the tourist brochures,' Andrew had quipped.

Joke's on him, Tilly smirked. Dad will have his work cut out with the house, dead possums or not. Tilly had recognised this the moment the taxi dropped them off at the bottom of the drive.

It had been a sweltering afternoon, the air ripe with frangipani starting to turn. The house stood tall over them. It was a typical timber Queenslander—'an Ashgrovian, to be precise,' said her father—fronted with a gable roof to the right and sitting on a half-acre block. The faun-coloured paint was chipped and worn in places, the pink frosted glass cracked in the left-hand corner, but the square-shaped deck, which was raised around twelve-feet high on stilts, did have an uninterrupted view over the street. The front garden was wild with blue flax and chalky cocos palms, while the banister at the foot of the stairwell was rotten. *Ideal for a project*, Tilly imagined the real estate strapline. When she had turned to her father, she saw he was practically rubbing his hands together.

Her mother, meanwhile, behaved as though she was on some kind of assignment. When the paralegal arrived soon after with the front door keys and other paperwork, Laura had accompanied the young woman around the house, acting all gracious and polite at her questions and comments, while Andrew inspected the backyard. Tilly went from room to room on her own. She was not impressed. It was a small house compared to Swinbrook, around twenty-five metres in length from the front door to the sunroom at the back, and with an old, worn feel to it. The air had a thick, cloying quality despite the open windows.

The living and dining room was open plan and sparsely furnished. A small, two-seater couch with a circular table next to it. A piano that looked like it hadn't been played in years beneath an ancient air-conditioning unit. Some undistinguished paintings hanging from the wall. A Formica table for meals, and four chairs with cracked leather cushions, a drinks cabinet. A hand-crafted draughts board and matching stand, half-a-dozen pieces still in position from an interrupted game.

The bedrooms each opened directly from the living room. The small room in the middle of the bedrooms, which Tilly heard the paralegal say had been Eliza's study, still bore the seal of the police tape across the door. Tilly watched her mother pause before it, a hand raised as if to turn the handle. *Don't*, she wanted to say, though she wasn't sure why. It wasn't like a crime had been committed in there. In any case, Laura had soon moved on to the kitchen at the back of the house.

Tilly rolled on to her side. She heard a sound from the main bedroom; a murmur, then a mug being shifted. Her parents were sleeping in there. Of all the rooms, she had felt most weird looking around in there. For a start, it was still full of her grandparents' things. A large, ratty futon had been positioned in the centre, matching drawers on each side piled high with dog-eared library books, a dresser cluttered with old bottles and brushes and stray pieces of jewellery. The room had smelt of sandalwood and spice, an aroma Tilly immediately associated with her grandparents. But it wasn't comforting or familiar. It just made her skin crawl.

A draught worked its way over her shoulders, and Tilly pulled the sheet up to her chin. How could her mother stand it, sleeping in her parents' bed? She had asked as much as the three of them ate fish and chips for dinner, and Laura simply shrugged and said, 'Well, it's not like they died in there, is it?' Maybe not, but there had been a weird atmosphere in that room, something alive to a new presence, Tilly was sure of it. As she stood on the threshold of the room, which overlooked the lush front garden, she had made out through the large motes of dust the matching oval outlines against the paint. Maybe that's where the Melanesian masks Bruce had found in a local antiques shop used to hang, Tilly now thought, remembering a postcard from years ago. Spirit faces, he'd called them. Made of hardwood, stained with vegetable dyes. Cowrie shells for eyes. Commemorating the dead.

Another day passed, then another, full of work in the backyard. The lawn was tamed, flowerbeds and hedges pruned, the dry, prickly grass watered each night, leaving a pleasant smell of dew drifting through the house. On the third morning Tilly stood on the creaking front deck and watched Andrew trudge up the hill to the Given Terrace bus stop. Laura had sent him off to collect the Pajero from the police depot in Ipswich—apparently her mother had no problem driving around in her parents' old car, either. Tilly checked her watch: it was only just after eight o'clock and the day already sweltered. A trickle of sweat ran down her torso and dripped against the boards. Her bare feet left dark prints. Her mother had promised a trip to the local swimming pool in the afternoon, but first they had to clean.

Tilly went inside. Laura was in the bathroom, scrubbing at rust around the plughole of the claw-foot bath. Tilly began work on the kitchen cupboards. It was grimy stuff; like stepping inside an exhibit at the Imperial War Museum, one of those 1940s ration kitchens. There wasn't much left over that constituted food—a packet of starch, vinegary bottles of pickled onions, cocoa, Chinese tea that had never been opened—and most of it was out of date. On the top shelf were a few calico bags, and ancient bottles of port and sherry for cooking. Tilly started going through the items one by one, thinking she might salvage a few, but she soon found herself tossing everything in the bin. Weevils had got into the starch and the bag of self-raising flour she found stashed behind an empty soy sauce bottle. From the top of the fridge she cleared away a stack of old leaflets and brochures, among them a Bunnings catalogue and a faded 'Yes 23' flyer.

After a while, Tilly stopped her work to wander down to the tiled sunroom next to the annex at the back of the house. She remembered Laura saying her parents had built it after Laura was born, extending the house by about five metres from the kitchen. It was a pleasant, almost subterranean space, made cool by the terracotta tiles, with three windows positioned level with the slanted backyard. Outside, the welters of shrubs and weeds still clogged the back fence. A lonely poinciana stood in the middle of the yard, stooped as though it too were bereaved.

'Til!' Laura was calling her. 'Can you check under the sink for any spray? Quick, please.'

'What? Why?'

Tilly bounded up the steps. Her mother had crouched on the floor near the study door. At her feet was a swarm of around a dozen enormous black insects, travelling like a dark glove from beneath the door and moving in the direction of the opposite wall.

'What the hell are they?'

'Cockroaches,' Laura said. 'There must be a nest in the study. You'll soon get used to them. Cockies are everywhere in Brisbane, especially in summer.'

'I'll never get used to that.'

'The spray, Tilly?'

'There isn't any.'

'There must be food in there. Mum always left things lying around. I'll need to get inside to clean it.'

Laura edged towards the door, tugging at the blue-and-white checked police tape. It came loose and fluttered to the floor.

'Mum, is this a good idea?'

Laura raised her eyebrows as she placed a hand on the knob. 'Sandretti said it was okay. We can't avoid it forever.'

'Sure, but . . .'

Laura turned the knob and gave the door a firm shove. The room, unlike the rest of the house, was dark. Black-out curtains hung at large windows set above a built-in desk. Tilly followed her mother inside, her T-shirt pulled up to cover her nose—the air was stale and slightly rank. Two enormous bookshelves stood off to the left. It was cold in there, too; Tilly's bare arms prickled with goosebumps. She watched Laura cross the room and draw back the curtains.

The light struck Tilly like a slap. She raised her free hand to shield her eyes against it, and when her vision cleared, she took in a sharp breath of surprise. Covering the white walls were maps, magazine cut-outs and photographs of desert landscapes. Waterholes, gorges, billabongs. Stony tablelands and rusty-red vertical cliffs. Mulga, bendee and yellow and white and purple wattles growing across the plateaus. River red gums, coolabah and gidgee lining dry creek channels. Several Post-it notes had been attached to the pictures, with scribbles in Eliza's hand. Pinned on a corkboard near the desk were a couple of charcoal sketches. A dark outline with two hollow eyes.

Tilly stood near the doorway, her heart beating noisily. It was like stumbling across a murder chart from one of those ITV shows her dad liked. The pictures provoked a rare sensation in Tilly: both narcotic and transfixing, the energy swirling around her dark at the edges, blurry. Eventually remembering Laura was nearby, Tilly turned to watch her mother peer closer at one map that had been graffitied with a bunch of thick arrows. Laura's chest rose and dropped. Her brow was greasy with perspiration.

'Mum, what the hell is all this stuff?'

'I've no idea.' Laura pulled out her phone from her back pocket and started taking snaps. Her hand shook. Tilly looked around some more. On a table near a small wardrobe was a pair of scummy wine glasses, and a plate bearing what must have once been a sandwich.

'It's kind of freaky, considering . . .' she breathed.

'What is?'

'Well.' Tilly tapped on a photo of a dusty red campground. 'It looks like the same place where they . . . You know.'

Laura turned back to the desk, her shoulders hunched. Tilly couldn't see her face.

'Maybe,' she muttered.

Tilly found herself examining the bookshelves. There must have been close to two hundred books, and she soon realised they had been placed in strict alphabetical order.

'Grandma was a big reader, then?'

'Not when I was a kid. I was always the bookworm of the family.' Laura joined Tilly by the shelves, her eyes running up and down the spines. 'All Australian authors. That's weird. I don't remember these ever being in the house.'

'They look old,' Tilly remarked. 'Is that why the room was taped over? Like, to protect them or something?'

Laura didn't answer. She was frowning as she reached for a book, prising it free. It was a sturdy hardback.

'Let's get rid of them,' she said. 'I'll use those spare boxes in your room. We'll store them under the house.'

Tilly took the book from Laura. 'Are you sure? I mean, some of them could be valuable.' She sniffed the yellowed pages and made a face. 'They smell valuable.'

'They probably are,' Laura mumbled as she began to pull paperbacks from the top shelf and build a tower by the door. 'The first editions I'll donate to the university. We can't take them home with us. Better to do a clean sweep today.'

It was odd seeing her mother dispose of the books like that. In England, Laura had a library with thick carpet and fat armchairs and a gas fireplace. The room was full of beautiful editions she had collected over the years—none of them smelly.

Laura paused to look at a book at the top of the pile. It was in very poor condition, the mouldy cover coming away from the spine. Tilly couldn't make out the title, but the author was John Lang.

'How strange.' Laura reached for the hardback. 'You know, Mum borrowed this for me when I was about ten or eleven. I'd had appendicitis, and I was stuck in bed for a week. This was all before Netflix, of course. But these stories . . .' She shook her head. 'I couldn't stand them. I begged Mum to take them away, take them literally out of the room.'

Tilly glanced at Laura, intrigued by this odd admission.

'What were they about?'

Laura turned the hardback over in her hands, seeming to weigh it up. The dust jacket had almost torn in two.

'Ghosts,' she said. 'It's an old book, from colonial times. About dispossession, murder. In one story, a freed convict gets rich and buys up surrounding land. Fisher, I think his name was. Then one day his neighbour tells the locals that Fisher has gone home to England.'

'Lucky him,' Tilly muttered.

'A year passes,' Laura continued, pretending to have not heard, 'and this same neighbour tells everyone he's received a letter from Fisher, asking him to sell off all his holdings and send the money to London. Soon after, those same locals are walking home one night and they see the ghost of Fisher sitting on a rail on the side of the road. The neighbour had killed him.'

Tilly found herself smiling.

'But why didn't you like that story? It sounds right up your alley.'

Laura stared back at her.

'Because it scared me.'

'Scared you? How?

'It's hard to explain.' Her mother, whose face had been flushed only a moment ago, had gone white. 'It was a feeling sort of beyond that terror of what the stories were about, because really they are quite silly melodramas that don't stand the test of time. I'm not sure . . .' She cleared her throat. 'I think until that moment I had not realised how frightening the past could be.'

Tilly watched Laura rub her hands together, as though she were trying to wipe away an invisible stain. She had never heard her mother talk like this. She didn't like it.

'Maybe you were just too young for that kind of story? Like when I watched *Poltergeist* at JoBeth's and had all those nightmares?'

'No, it wasn't that.' Laura chewed on the edge of a ragged fingernail. 'Anyway, after that, Mum found me other things to read. More in her wheelhouse. *The Hobbit*, *War of the Worlds*. That kind of thing.'

'Grandma was a scientist, wasn't she?'

'Mm. She worked at the campus at St Lucia in the medical research department. Tropical diseases.'

'Kind of the opposite to you, then?'

Laura smiled tightly, but did not reply. Tilly hoisted a box into her arms. She had read a couple of her mother's historical novels. There were five in total, all centred around real-life criminal cases, the first being set in Edwardian Glasgow about a woman in an asylum and the young, guileless doctor treating her madness. Tilly found it grim and depressing. For a contented person, she thought it peculiar that her mother only wrote about death and madness, though other people seemed to like these stories. Laura had enjoyed some success. Her latest book, about Britain's first female serial killer, was in development with a producer from the BBC. *But she's never written about Australia*, Tilly mused. Curious.

On her way out, she glanced over her shoulder towards Laura, but her mother was again hunched over in the corner, intently studying a faded paperback. Tilly felt her knees lock, another wobble of sadness stirring inside her. Laura suddenly looked very small and far away on the other side of the room, and when Tilly tried to imagine her mother as a child afraid of a book, all she could picture was that four-wheel drive belonging to her grandparents driving into a deep black hole, only a pin-prick of light in the centre indicating a destination.

She walked out the front door and down the stairs. The storage area beneath the house was fenced off, with a padlock on a swing gate, though today this hung open. Adjusting the box in her arms, Tilly stepped inside. It smelt damp and sweet though not uninviting, and it was much cooler down here, like being in the mouth of a cave. There were cobwebs strung between the slats and boards above her, but it was all pretty neat and tidy, with a workbench on one wall. Where the concrete ended there was a step, and then a dusty, inclined surface, covered in rocks and clumps of earth, extending into the darkness.

As Tilly dropped the books on the workbench, she caught sight of a piece of blue tarpaulin further under the house, where space grew tight. She crab-crawled over to it, cinching a corner between her fingers and drawing the material back to reveal a typewriter. It was one of those black, bulky things she'd seen on *Mad Men*, with a few keys missing. Tilly dragged the typewriter towards her, brushing away the grey dust. The floorboards creaked above her, threads of a voice drifting through the gaps. The sound of the toilet flushing, a running tap. Tilly lifted the typewriter—it was lighter than she expected—and moved it to the workbench. She ran a fingertip over the cool keys before pressing down on the letter 'T'. It made a loud *thwack* in the dark.

'Cool,' Tilly breathed.

She started to think about how she might replace those missing keys, and how good it would look on the desk in her room, set against the stark white walls. *I might even write something on it for Mum,* she thought, though Tilly had never had much interest in storytelling. She preferred the visual. Paintings, photos. They were more buoyant, less loaded.

Emerging from the storage area, Tilly walked to the edge of the driveway and peered down the street. Heat shimmered from the bitumen road. From her back pocket, she brought out a bent cigarette she had smuggled into her luggage, as well as a lighter, and wandered over to the bricked-up partition in the middle of the street, which somehow managed to contain a line of enormous figs. Ducking beneath one of the low-hanging branches, Tilly sat on a boulder in a patch of shade. She had a few puffs, coughing behind her hand, and finger-ashed the rest of the cigarette on the road. Then she put her chin in her hands, admiring a sleek cat basking in the sun in the yard next door.

The cat returned Tilly's impervious stare. It was a handsome thing, slate-coloured, maybe a Russian blue. After a while, Tilly noticed him batting at a toy by his front paws. She stood up, hoping he might play with her, but as she came nearer she realised it wasn't a toy but a scrawny dead bird. The cat was pushing it from one paw to the other, every now and then managing to throw it up in the air, the bird's tiny head flopping about on a snapped neck. When Tilly took another step closer, the cat went still, fur bristling, and let out a low, feral growl.

'Okay, okay,' Tilly muttered, backing away. 'I'm encroaching. I get it.'

The cat's sharp eyes were trained on Tilly as she crossed the street. Ill at ease, she skipped up the front steps two at a time.

3.

THE HUMID AIR struck Laura immediately, the smell of jasmine and fresh lawn clippings floating through the open window. Lying there beneath the lazy fan, she listened to the postman's scooter, followed by the clap of the box and the rev of the engine. She had no idea what time it was, though she guessed it was still early, the warm indent from the other side of the bed tipping her towards the centre of the mattress. But when Laura reached for Andrew, her hand only brushed at thrown-back sheets.

Opening one eye, she saw she was alone. Brilliant light streamed into the bedroom. The damp hair at Laura's brow cooled. She had in those first few moments of waking forgotten where she was, and Laura longed to slide back into that absent-minded space. But then the memory of yesterday returned, and that sickening lurch in her guts as she laid eyes on the walls and desk and shelves in the study. Why had her parents become so interested in the Outback? Laura couldn't recall them ever travelling out there. They were urban people who, during her childhood, had barely managed a summer holiday to nearby Minjerribah. In more recent years, they had opted to visit big cities: Istanbul, Berlin, Seoul. Sandretti seemed to think they left the house suddenly, but all this paraphernalia indicated intent, premeditation. With a sigh, Laura kicked off the sheet. She had been back in Brisbane for nearly a week and still none of it made any sense.

She found Andrew down the side of the house, hunched over a fixie in the dappled sunshine. A podcast played from his phone on the ground beside him.

'Hello, love,' he said, wrenching on the bracket over the blackened chain. 'Look what I found sprouting rust.'

Laura admired her old bike. A Mercier. She used to ride it everywhere—to school, the tennis club, the river; no mean feat up the steep hills of Paddington and neighbouring Bardon. She had loved that bike, saving up enough pocket money to buy it second-hand from the local op shop on Ellena Street, along with a pair of denim dungarees and leather cowboy boots. She would often stay out riding all of Sunday, only rabid hunger forcing her home at dusk.

'It's not in bad nick, actually.' Andrew stood up and faced Laura. 'What do you think? Dare to take on the hills again?'

She smiled. 'I'm not sure the legs would cope these days!'

'Oh, they'd cope,' said Andrew, giving her a dewy kiss.

A few minutes later, he brought out croissants and jam to the trestle table in the backyard, along with a halved grapefruit and a canister of brown sugar. Tilly was still asleep. As they sat in the shade of the jacaranda, he spoke about the schedule for the house. On Wednesday, two builders would visit to quote on the job. He still needed to find the right painters, though that could come later. An arborist would have to look at the poinciana. Andrew was worried the roots might have spread to next door.

'But I adore that tree,' said Laura. 'We won't have to get rid of it, will we?'

Andrew shook his head. 'I'll talk to the neighbours.' He patted her knee and sat back, wrapping his hands behind his neck. He stared at his notes for a moment. 'But yeah, good news is I reckon we can keep the costs to under four hundred, all told.'

'Four hundred,' Laura repeated. 'Four hundred thousand pounds?'

'No!' Andrew exclaimed. '*Dollars*! Which means we'll clear, what, a million? Mil and a half?'

Crossing her legs, Laura matched his smile, though it didn't quite reach her eyes. *Careful,* she almost warned him. *Don't get ahead of yourself.*

'I need to get ready,' she murmured. 'I'm due to meet Sandretti at ten.'

Andrew nodded, brushing some crumbs from his lap.

'You going to be okay?' he asked.

Laura stared at the tabletop. She felt so tired, it was like she hadn't slept at all last night. But she had been looking forward to this meeting with the detective with something close to feverishness. She needed to ask him about what she had found in her mother's study.

'Hey,' said Andrew, reaching for the coffee. 'Don't forget to check about the release forms. The funeral directors have been calling me non-stop since I asked for the quote.'

Her parents were still lying in the mortuary in Coopers Plains. Sandretti had said she could arrange a viewing, but so far she hadn't made a visit. She told herself she would once she had spoken to the police, but she knew she was avoiding it. The cold, clinical reality of it. Their unliving bodies. Their unbeating hearts.

'The police won't release them until after the inquest,' she reminded Andrew. 'But I should find out the date this morning. We'll be able to plan a little more after that. Tell the funeral directors to cool it.'

'You sure you don't want me to come with you? Moral support?'

Laura shook her head again.

'I'll be fine. This is all formality. Dates, forms, signatures.' She had the boxes lined up in her mind, one beside the other. Tick, tick, tick. She didn't need Andrew distracting her while she travelled this neat conveyer belt of emotions. Nonetheless she leaned across the table and gave him a quick kiss, for reassurance. 'Anyway, you've loads to do here. I'll take the bike. Give her a whirl. See how the old legs fare.'

The sun was high in the azure sky, the hottest part of the day already upon her. After taking the steep hill off Central Avenue, Laura coasted down Given Terrace towards Caxton Street. She was eager to see how Paddington had changed. Every second shop was now a cafe with wooden crates for seats or a designer gift shop; there were yoga centres and bars, and ramen and gnocchi restaurants, while a line of men and women in exercise apparel walked sleek dogs along the shady side of the road. She knew it must have evolved; more than two decades had passed since she left and nothing remained frozen in time for that long. There had been hints of it on the trip from the airport, with the tunnel and the inner-city bypass that wound and dipped like a girandole, but she had never imagined the roads would grow quite so wide, blistering beneath the great depths of the brown river, traversing the kinks and bends of the ancient terrain; they may as well have been on a Bangkok motorway or lost in a maze of Los Angeles concrete. Buildings had grown grander, meaner, the double-glazing capturing the monstrous sprawl, and construction edged right up to the outskirts of the airport. *Brisbane isn't quaint anymore*, thought Laura, inhaling the musky humid air. It had grown wild, reckless. It had realised its own potential.

Roma Street, the headquarters for Queensland Police, was an enormous building on a traffic-heavy thoroughfare on the fringe of the CBD. Sandretti met Laura in the foyer, shaking her hand. He was accompanied by a tall, unsmiling female sergeant in uniform. Laura was sweaty after the ride, and the sergeant fetched her a bottle of water. Sandretti looked younger than Laura had expected him to be, with soft hazel eyes. His hair, as she had predicted, was grey.

'Shall we head upstairs?' he said.

They took Laura up a few floors in the lift to their department, steering her towards a compact room with a table and two chairs which they entered via the reception area. The sergeant flicked on a light, and after removing her cap she remained near the door, as though guarding it, while Laura and Sandretti sat on either side of the table. The room smelled of disinfectant.

'Thank you for coming in, Mrs Townsend,' Sandretti began. 'I appreciate a meeting like this must be incredibly difficult, so I don't want to take up too much more of your time. You must have a lot to arrange.'

Laura's eyes flickered from Sandretti to the sergeant, who had edged towards a pot plant in the corner, her strong-looking arms crossed.

'It's no trouble,' she said hesitantly. 'It's good to finally meet face to face. Obviously I'm eager for news on the inquest so I can begin to make funeral plans.'

Sandretti glanced at his sergeant, sniffed. Then he reached down to his briefcase and produced a document comprising a few sheets of stapled print-outs, which he pushed across the table to Laura.

'Plan away. Those are the coronial release forms.' He gave a listless smile. 'The good news is you won't have to go through an inquest. Your folks can now be laid to rest.'

Laura stared back at him.

'No inquest? I don't understand.'

'There's no need for one. I appreciate there was some initial ambiguity when your parents' bodies were first discovered, but you'll see in the reports that the coroner has made clear determinations of the causes of death for both Eliza and Bruce.'

Sandretti proceeded to explain that the post-mortems had revealed her father had indeed died of a heart attack. It seemed Bruce had been living with serious coronary artery disease that had gone undiagnosed. His death was estimated to have occurred in the late afternoon or early evening on 12 December, the day her parents arrived at Hell Hole Gorge and set up camp.

Eliza's death had been recorded as a drowning sometime later that same evening. It had been determined that, in an agitated state after Bruce died, she had walked out to the escarpment, where she became disorientated and tripped or slipped down the rockface into the shallow water below. She had abrasions on her knees and elbows, and a large incision on her forehead, which the coroner resolved had been incurred during the fall.

'A tragic accident,' Sandretti allowed, his expression contrite. 'An awful twist of fate.'

Laura gazed down at the coronial report, and the formal watermark of the Queensland Government in blue at the top of the cover sheet. She felt the valves of her heart open and shut like the whirr and ping of a pinball machine.

'But why didn't my mother go for help?' she asked quietly. 'The car was right there.'

'With no witness, we can only speculate,' said Sandretti. 'But without a sat phone she couldn't have done much for Bruce anyway. He most likely died instantly and—'

'But that doesn't add up, either,' Laura interrupted, pressing her knees together beneath the table, pinching at the skin. 'They weren't reckless. This Hell Hole Gorge—it's unfamiliar to them. They weren't outdoorsy by nature. For a trip like this, they would have been organised. And they certainly wouldn't have just taken off like that and not told anyone. It's completely out of character.'

'Yes,' Sandretti agreed. 'It seems that it was.' He paused, examining his hands clasped together before him. Laura noticed he had very large fingernails. 'But people change. Your parents weren't young anymore, and older folks don't always think and behave as we expect them to.'

'Mum and Dad were only in their early seventies.'

'Sure,' said Sandretti. 'But my inquires revealed your mother had actually had a few falls. The most recent, just a couple of days before she died.' He paused again, watching Laura carefully. 'Were you aware of that?'

Laura felt herself flush.

'No, I wasn't,' she admitted. She sat back, taking in the smooth line of Sandretti's jaw and the small mole just beneath his ear. 'What about my mother's study? Didn't that strike you as suspicious?'

'Not particularly,' said Sandretti. 'The shrine your mum had created in there further indicates an obsessive quality to their interest in the Outback, but it doesn't indicate malevolence. *Anything* could have prompted that curiosity. We just don't know.'

'So we've still no idea why they stopped at Hell Hole Gorge?'

Sandretti shook his head.

'As part of my investigation, I also interviewed your parents' GP, Dr Margaret Leong, at the Red Hill Clinic,' he said. 'She indicated that your parents had become more reclusive in recent months, and that she had transitioned them to the home-visit program. With all this evidence, it's safe to say they were in a state of decline before their deaths.'

Laura felt cold all of a sudden. She clutched her half-empty water bottle, the plastic crumpling under her grasp.

'So you're saying that my parents had become old and frail, and that's why they died? I'm sorry, but that doesn't sound plausible to me.'

Behind her, Laura heard the sergeant rearrange her stance, the creak of her leather gun holster amplified in the bright room. Sandretti regarded Laura with a level expression.

'What I'm saying is that I don't believe your parents were thinking clearly when they left the house. They weren't adequately equipped for the trip, which you yourself have said is out of character. I could have easily described their passing as death by misadventure. They got into strife out there and had no way of saving themselves. It happens more often than you might think.'

'And it's not relevant that they had all those maps and pictures pinned to the wall?'

Sandretti leaned forward, threading his fingers together on top of the table.

'I'm not sure that reveals anything beyond a desire to drive out there. I found no coercion, no third-party involvement. The thing is, Mrs Townsend, unless there is real cause for suspicion, I'm compelled to accept the coronial findings on these deaths and move on. I do understand that can be incredibly difficult for family members. Especially if there has been a rift.'

'A rift?'

'Well.' Sandretti cleared his throat. 'I understand you haven't been home to Australia for many years until now. That recently you hadn't been in touch with your folks. That can mean, in tragedies such as these, that things were left unresolved. Emotionally. And for some family members that can further complicate the grieving.'

Laura tried to assimilate this new humiliation. Meanwhile a light went off on Sandretti's phone, and it began to vibrate. The detective was needed elsewhere. Another case, another family. He pushed out his chair and stood up.

'Right now, Sergeant Lattouf will escort you to the evidence locker where she'll sign over your parents' effects that were found at the scene and used in our preliminary investigation. It isn't much. Some clothes, wallets with a bit of cash, house keys. Your mother also had a camera on her person, and we developed the film, so you'll find a copy of the prints in that package.'

Laura gazed back at him, dazed. Everything was happening too fast.

'You don't need them anymore?' she heard herself say.

'No. The investigation has now been closed. Thank you for your time. And once again, on behalf of Queensland Police, we're very sorry for your loss.'

Sandretti held out his hand, which Laura shook automatically. His skin was soft. She caught a hint of his aftershave. He held the door open for her as she walked out.

Laura unchained her bike and wheeled it away from the station and down towards the river. In the shade of the Kurilpa Bridge, she sent Andrew a text: *No inquest* with a sad face. A moment later he replied: *Why not???* Laura wrote: *Coroner determined causes of death. Natural & accidental. No mystery.* Andrew tried to call her then, but Laura let it ring out. Returning her phone to the front pocket of her backpack, she pressed at the hard outline of the binder folder containing the coronial report, and a separate sleeve guarding the photographs from her mother's camera. A humid breeze slapped against the bridge's iron meshing.

Laura climbed on her bike and pedalled across the river, following the smooth path up towards the gallery, GOMA, and across the courtyard to the cafe attached to the library. It was starting to get busy for lunch, and Laura ordered a pot of tea. She wasn't hungry; in fact, her stomach churned with what felt very close to rage. That Sandretti, and the coroner, and the whole of the bloody Queensland Police department had closed the investigation. That because her parents were in their seventies their deaths could just be signed away with a flick of the pen. Laura sunk further into her chair. She hadn't realised how much she had been holding out for an inquest. A process where all the questions that had been eating away at her since the police arrived on her Swinbrook doorstep could be aired. Because no matter how she looked at it, this was an equation that still didn't add up. It wasn't grief, or guilt. Laura watched a few pigeons scrabble over a breadcrust. The sun dipped behind a single cloud, a moment of relief against the relentless heat. She stirred through her tea one sachet of sugar, then another. The sun returned, pinging obnoxiously off the concrete. When Laura finally drank, she tasted nothing.

She found Andrew hunched over the barbecue on the patio, black smoke billowing from the grill, Tilly at his side. Hours had passed since she'd walked out of the Roma Street Police Station; down on Southbank, she had managed to frit away the whole afternoon. There was almost no heat or moisture in the approaching dusk. The fluffy alyssums in the far corner had sprung up, and lining the far fence was a garden bed of magenta-pink dahlias.

The smell of charred steaks filled Laura's nostrils as she took a seat at the trestle table and poured herself a large glass of rosé. A crisp-looking green salad, crusty bread, butter, a range of fresh condiments. Everything was garish and over-saturated, like watching an old technicolour film.

Andrew said something to Tilly, making her laugh as she flipped the steak over with a spatula. When she looked up, she fixed her gaze on Laura.

'Dad's bought a whole cow,' she remarked.

'It's not a *whole* cow.' Andrew gave Laura a strong hug and kissed her cheek before taking a seat beside her. 'Just everything but the horns.'

'Cows don't have horns.'

Laura studied the lines of shadow by the fence. The jacaranda at her back wavered slightly in the breeze, the house creaking like a sigh. She reached for her glass, her hand shaking. She swallowed down a mouthful, the wine burning a line to her stomach.

'Mum, are you all right? Dad said you had a meeting with the police.'

Tilly had come up beside her. Dabbing at her eyes, Laura was surprised to find her sleeve came away damp. She saw Tilly glance across the table to her father, a fleeting expression of confusion on her face. Laura braced herself for a joke, but instead Tilly bent down and wrapped her arms around Laura's shoulders. Tilly stayed like that, clinging to her, black hair tickling at Laura's nose, her breath ragged at her ear. She smelt of sunscreen and grass clippings.

'It's okay,' Laura heard her say, once, then twice, as you might to an unsettled baby. 'It's okay.'

She tried to make some reply but it came out in a whimper. Eventually she wiped her nose on her shirt and sat back.

'Your grandparents,' she stammered. 'They can be buried now.'

Tilly nodded, her smile like encouragement. Behind her, grey plumes of smoke billowed from the barbecue.

'That's good, isn't it, Mum?' she said. 'We can say a proper goodbye.'

Laura blinked back at Tilly, searching for her own reflection in her daughter's grey eyes.

Later, when shadows stretched longer across the garden and dinner had been eaten, they returned to the house. Laura helped Andrew with the washing up while Tilly watched an episode of *Married at First Sight*.

'Today sounded rough with the police,' he said, replacing a dry plate on the crockery shelf. 'I should have been there with you.'

Laura scrubbed at a bowl in the sink, gave it a rinse, and passed it over to him.

'It wouldn't have changed the outcome.' She stared at her hands, pickling in the hot, soapy water, and her shoulders sagged. 'I know I should be relieved. It makes things simpler, but I just feel so . . .'

The tears were right there. How easy it would be to just let them out. Release the valve. Decompress. The din of the television echoed about the house, the shriek of women dressing up in wedding frocks.

'You can't blame yourself, Laura,' Andrew said gently. 'None of this is your fault.'

'But why did they go out there, Andrew? No one can give me a straight answer to a simple question. It wasn't a retiree road trip, for god's sake. They took off like they were being chased.'

Andrew looked back at her evenly, folding his arms over his chest.

'Is that what Sandretti thinks?'

'No, it's what *I* think. All that stuff in the study . . . Something wasn't right in this house.'

'Well, yes.' Andrew sighed. 'There's no arguing against that.'

Laura turned her face towards the last threads of sun between the trees. Andrew's incurious and uncomplicated view of the world had always charmed her. He had no guile. But she needed more from him now. She needed him to better understand her questions about what had been going through her parents' heads. That she was starting to wonder if this hadn't been more deliberate? A message for her, a coded demand, to *come home*? Eliza and Bruce had never liked attention or fuss; theirs had been a quiet existence, and Laura had always considered it dignified, something to emulate. But this, she thought, taking a deep breath and holding it; *this* is all utterly monstrous, and despite the heat in the kitchen she shivered.

The house grew dark, the street quiet. When Tilly had gone to bed and Andrew sat browsing the internet in the living room, Laura retreated to the study with her laptop. She spent some time reading over a scrappy first chapter of a new project about Ruth Ellis, then closed the file with an unsatisfied sigh. Laura stared at the laptop screen, then clicked on her mail tab and scanned the latest email from her agent, Anthea. She had sent a few review clippings, another festival invite, and details on the results of the Waterstones Christmas campaign. *All tracking nicely*, she wrote. *Bravo!*

After a while, Laura found herself looking down at her backpack on the floor. She dragged it over to the desk, pulling out the folder marked 'Photos—Copy' and a slim envelope. She peered inside. The envelope contained a receipt for petrol from a 7-Eleven in Mitchell, and another from the Adavale Pub and General Store for three bottles of water, a loaf of bread and a meat pie with sauce. A piece of paper unfolded to reveal an invoice from the Hotel Corones, where her parents had paid for Room No. 1 in cash. Laura raised the paper to her nose, inhaling, in the hope of catching some familiar scent. But it only smelt a little stale, and she folded it away again.

Next Laura cleared a space, placed the folder in the centre of the desk and proceeded to take out one photograph after another.

Within a few minutes she had made a collage of landscapes—her father driving, hands gripping the steering wheel, his longish hair swept across his brow; a china doll in a lace dress, Eliza's ghostly outline transposed over the glass encasing it; desolate red plains beyond Charleville; a couple more of her father, walking ahead, his legs thin and pale against a brown boulder, his knapsack hanging loose and low on his hunched back. There was one photograph of the cairn near where the Pajero had been found at Powell Creek campground, and a selfie of her mother, an enormous wilga shrub in the background. Then around half-a-dozen snaps of the rocks around the unbroken brown water, a couple glimpsing an elegant wader in the shallows. The last picture had been of what looked like a burning sun, a pink thumb caught on the edge of the lens, though perhaps it had only been overexposed.

Laura stood above it all, feeling a little sick, aware that she had strayed someplace she shouldn't have, someplace dangerous and illicit. She had never been to the Outback. She had not been further west than Toowoomba. It wasn't for a lack of interest, though perhaps it did reveal something about her creative arrangement. Urban, familiar, organised. She thought back to the book she found in her mother's study, those peculiar ghost stories, and how when she was younger and had begged for its removal Eliza had stared at her incredulously and said, 'They're not real.' But the distinction between reality and fantasy had meant nothing to Laura back then: like some papier-mâché gateway, the books were destined to funnel the ghosts of the bush directly into the Paddington house.

Laura looked at the overexposed photograph again and felt a stirring of heat at the back of her mind. Eliza had scooped up the book under one arm, but Laura would never forget that look on her face as she closed the bedroom door. Was it possible that she had been afraid too. But of what? Laura glanced at her computer, at the glowing blank screen. Something was slowly unfolding in her imagination, but like those ghost stories she did not know if she could bear to sit down at the desk with it, or what it might unleash.

4.

TILLY NOW WENT to school in Kelvin Grove, the next suburb over from Paddington. She wore a uniform with a hat and blazer, just as she had at Burford, even though this school was a public one, and she caught the bus each morning from Given Terrace. There were boys at the school too, though they were friendlier than those back in England, and didn't disrupt class all that often. After her first few days, Tilly had made a handful of friends. Amber, Keiko, Georgie. They were good, earnest girls, tall and rangy as greyhounds, and unlike her old friends in Swinbrook were committed to their studies. Squares, JoBeth would have called them. Sucks.

Tilly was glad to be in school. To be busy. She didn't like being in the house on Central Avenue, especially with Laura buzzing around with the preparations for her grandparents' memorial at the local community hall. All week Laura had been on the phone, pacing the pine-hoop flooring as she tracked down as many contacts as possible in Eliza's address book. Old colleagues from the university, long-lost friends. Around fifty people had confirmed they were coming, though the only people Tilly would know on Saturday were her own parents. *The whole thing is going to be excruciating*, she thought on the walk home from the bus stop on Friday afternoon. It wasn't like she could ask anyone along. How weird would that be.

Tilly unloaded the mail from the letterbox and headed to the foot of the steep stairs leading up to the house. Adjusting her backpack, she looked out across the front garden. The house next door was concealed by the fig tree, and the fat clutters of a wattle in the untamed yard. Strange, she still hadn't seen the neighbours.

Tilly clumped up to the front door. With a sigh, she pulled off her school shoes and tossed them on the rack beneath the window. The security door handle felt slippery in her grip. The smell of the cedar rose to greet her. Dust had already begun to work its way up her nose. As she stood on the threshold, she felt herself being tugged inside—whether by the house itself or by the urge to get out of the heat she could not tell. The house seemed to breathe out, alive to that tension.

'Hello?' Tilly walked inside and closed the door. 'Mum? Dad?'

Though she often came home to an empty house, today Tilly felt a flutter in the pit of her stomach. It happened from time to time, this worry for her parents. It was anxiety, she supposed, or some other kind of animal instinct that came with the death of close relatives.

It was sweltering in the house. She propped open the casement window. The hinge was stiff, but the wood finally gave, and she pegged the snib into place. There was no respite, however, from the heat. These timber places had no insulation, and air crept in through the gaps in the boards. She could see mosquitos fluttering at the top of the stairs.

Tilly leaned against the window ledge. Somewhere down the street she heard the *clock* of a cricket ball on a bat. The sound of afternoon traffic drifted from the main road. A car drove slowly by. Raising her eyes to the ceiling rose, Tilly wondered what her mother saw when she looked about the house. How many times had she stared at that same spot as she lay on the floor, the Test match crackling on Bruce's radio, the ply-panelled Fisher air-conditioner on wheels gurgling away in the background, the steady drip from the mesh vent landing near her head? Tilly imagined it would be comforting to be inside this memory.

She still had the mail scrunched up in her left hand. It was all glossy brochures and a couple of leaflets from the church on the corner. Tilly was halfway to the recycling bin in the kitchen when a postcard of an old-fashioned Queenslander fluttered to the floor. She reached down to pick it up. *Charleville Historic Home* was printed in a yellow banner along the bottom. Intrigued, Tilly turned it over, and the breath caught in her throat.

Dear Tilly, we are staying at the Hotel Corones here in the centre of Charleville . . .

It was her grandfather's handwriting; she would know it anywhere. The thin, almost illegible scrawl, spiky loops, severe punctuation. But he could not have sent it. Unless. Tilly's arms broke out in goosebumps, and she glanced behind her, towards her parents' bedroom, as if it might know the origin of the postcard. It was dated *12 December*, with a sticker over the address box indicating redirection from the UK. Of course, she breathed with queasy understanding. It had gone to the Swinbrook house first.

Tilly flinched at the slap of the security door behind her. Andrew stood by the front window, unclipping his toolbelt.

'All right, Til?' He hung his backpack on the rack and walked towards her. 'You don't look so great, darling.'

Tilly handed him the postcard, which he examined then made a sad face. He handed it back.

'Oh, honey.'

'It gave me a fright. For a minute I thought . . .'

Andrew pulled her towards him, the sharp tang of sweat rising from beneath his old Sex Pistols T-shirt.

'I might regret organising that mail redirection service,' he murmured. 'Come on, I brought home a few cans of Coke and a packet of those cheesy Doritos you like. Don't tell Mum.'

Tilly rested her head on his broad chest, comforted by the sturdiness of him as he wrapped his arms around her back. Eventually, she untangled herself, stuffing the postcard inside the pocket of her school dress.

'I'll have them later,' she said. 'Can I borrow Mum's bike?'

'Look at you.' Andrew smiled. 'My adventurous Australian.'

'Half,' Tilly said. 'Anyway, I'm only going to the pool. I want to get there before closing time.'

It took Tilly around ten minutes to cycle down Given Terrace. Nestled beside a playground covered in the blooming shade of enormous figs, the Ithaca Pool was empty. There was a swimming carnival in March and every Kelvin Grove student was expected to compete. Though she could swim, Tilly was by no means accomplished. If she started some training now, however, she might not be upstaged by too many of these Australians.

Tilly paid her entry fee and went to change in the bathrooms at the top of the metal stairs. Muggy, chlorinated air filled her nostrils as she fixed the Speedo straps over her shoulders, her skin bristling at the unfamiliar feel of Lycra, the flats of her feet stinging from the rough asphalt floor. Draping her towel over her wrist, Tilly caught a glimpse of herself in the float glass mirror—or rather the shape of her, like a shadow, at once warped and indistinct.

The water was delicious. Tilly did a lazy lap of breaststroke, keeping her head above the surface. To the left of the pool was a tall embankment, traffic from the parallel road rushing past. Behind the pool, at the back of the changing rooms, was a skate park, the distant slap and crack of wheels striking the concrete, the grind of trucks against the metal handrail. Tilly closed her eyes as she reached the deep end, her chest growing tight. She couldn't stop thinking about the skate park in Burford, and how she and JoBeth used to watch the boys do tricks on the ramp after school.

Tilly gripped the ledge, her toes grazing the greasy floor of the pool. She missed home desperately, and lately often found herself on the brink of tears. She felt like a small child again, and it was an awful state of mind, one in which she couldn't control her emotions, or how her thoughts were laid out one at a time. She couldn't talk to her mother about it; Laura was still in her own manic form of grief, careening around the house on some call or other, scribbling endless lists, leaving Post-it notes all over the place, while her father was always outside on the pretence of 'working', only willing to manage the practical aspects of this experience.

Tilly stayed like that, treading water, until with a surge of fury she launched herself from the tiles, flinging her arms over her head, making a great, cantankerous splash. She had longed for more independence, and now that she had it she wished her parents would take better care of her. To show they cared. She bit hard on the inside of her cheeks, more anger unspooling inside her. What if things stayed like this? Her mind turned to that postcard from her grandfather, and how for a terrifying moment she had believed it came from some place beyond the grave. It was a sensation she had never experienced before; like slipping through sand to some upside-down world.

A shriek cut these thoughts in half. Two little boys in UV suits bombed the lane next to Tilly, and the attendant told them off. Tilly began to swim again. And though her eyes felt tight behind the goggles, her skin stretched across her forehead, the rest of her body slipped easily through the water, gravity dispersed. Midway through her lap, she tipped on to her back and lay there, bobbing on the surface, her head filled only with the droning silence of the pool.

On the ride home Tilly's phone pinged with a text from her father, asking her to pick up some dinner ingredients in Rosalie Village. It wasn't really on her way, but Tilly replied with a thumbs up, and rather than turn into Central Avenue took the hill past the creche, and left around the roundabout with the Japanese maple, its ancient branches hooped like crinoline. Oddly for rush hour there was no one about, nor any cars or other bicycles, though there was a charge in the air, an anticipation of more rain, despite the sky being an unbroken swatch of blue. Near the op shop Tilly stopped in the shade for a drink, and as she chugged on her water bottle she noticed among the stumps of flailing native grasses and woodchips a small dead bat, wings wrapped around its twisted little body, black eyes dull and unseeing.

At the delicatessen, Tilly stood at the freezer section with the door open, savouring a few precious moments of cold on her face. Then she began to fill her basket with the shop's overpriced wares: prawn dumplings, free-range bacon, butter sourced from a local dairy. The bread on the shelf was a few days old, but she took a loaf anyway—they never had enough for toast. The bell at the front door occasionally chimed with customers coming and going, until after a while the shop fell quiet.

Perhaps it was the effect of her bike ride in the heat, but Tilly suddenly felt dazed standing under the shop's lights. She headed along an aisle lined with organic soaps and detergents but could not recall what else she needed to buy. Eventually she gave up. Throwing a jar of marmalade into the basket, she headed towards the front counter, only to find the boy who had been at the till a few minutes ago had disappeared.

Tilly paused by the fruit. She felt even more peculiar now, like she had taken a knock to the head. Her sandalled feet swam before her, the chipped red of her nail polish, the patch of hair on her knee she had missed shaving. She took a few deep breaths, but this didn't help, so she set down her basket on the floor. As she did this, Tilly sensed someone behind her, and she turned, expecting the shop boy. Instead she saw a woman standing at the top of the aisle. She smiled at Tilly. A few gold fillings glinted.

'Hello, Laura.'

The woman was old, with a wiry build, and thick, steel-grey hair. Though it was sweltering, she was dressed in a navy-blue tunic, white apron and grey moccasins. She had such a weird, intense expression on her face that terror began to vibrate in the balls of Tilly's feet; there was something otherworldly about the woman, she had no other way to describe her. And then, as if confirming it, the fluorescent lights overhead flickered, crackling, while the temperature in the shop plummeted.

'Bread any good today, Laura?'

Tilly gaped at the old woman. She wanted to say, 'I'm not Laura,' but for some reason her mouth had fastened around the words.

'Miss?'

Tilly spun around. It was the boy from the front counter. He stood by the apple cart. In one hand he held a spray bottle, and in the other a cloth. He was staring at her, eyebrows raised interrogatively.

'Everything all right?'

Tilly glanced down at her feet. A watermelon had rolled off the stand and cracked, spilling pulp and juice and seeds all over the floor. She shifted her sandals, revolted at the wet, sticky feeling of flesh between her toes. The boy went down on all fours and began cleaning up the mess.

Tilly knew she should help, or at least apologise, but she couldn't. Her heart was squealing inside her chest. What had just happened? She looked around, urgency rising. The old woman had gone. Tilly hopped over the squashed fruit and hurried to the next aisle, but she wasn't there. She wasn't by the fridges or the organic chocolate display either. In fact, Tilly couldn't find her anywhere in the shop. She darted towards the entrance and flung open the door to a shower of dazzling light. Tilly scanned the footpath one way, then the other. But the old woman was nowhere to be seen.

That night Tilly couldn't sleep. Every time she drifted off, a banging sound jolted her awake, and she'd find herself half out of bed, one hand pressed against her racing heart. After the third time this happened, she sat on the edge of her mattress, staring across the bedroom towards the white door, which was slightly ajar. She could hear the dim noise of the laptop coming from Laura's study. Perhaps she was finishing a speech for tomorrow. That's what you do at memorials, isn't it?

Eventually she tiptoed out of her bedroom. The living room was very dark, the slightly luminous outline of the couch and the television like a mountainscape. Tilly went to the kitchen and stood at the sink, eyes fixed to the window that overlooked the small bricked courtyard. From next door, a yellow square of light shone at the laundry window. Then it went out.

Tilly poured herself a glass of water. The hum of the old fridge was incredibly loud. Tilly leaned closer to the window, trying to make out the shape of the thick, wiry grass still growing near the back fence, but she couldn't see past her own reflection. She examined her face with curiosity; she did not look like herself. Outside came a distant bark. The trees next door rustled with bats.

Wiping her hands on a tea towel, Tilly suddenly longed to speak to JoBeth. She glanced at the microwave in the corner. It flashed *1:17.* JoBeth would be at school. They were off-kilter, out of sync. Tilly drank the rest of her water. It was lukewarm, slightly metallic-tasting. The fridge had stopped humming. The night-time quiet had once frightened Tilly; it seemed endless, like a black hole. Now she had been primed to understand it could be filled with other things, awful things that had been better left unknown. She placed her empty glass in the sink and headed back towards her room.

On her way, however, some instinct made her stop outside Laura's study and put an ear against the door. At first only silence echoed back, and Tilly was about to walk on when she heard what sounded like whispers, and the tap of fingers on a keyboard. A cool ripple broke down Tilly's neck, and she pressed her ear more firmly to the door. It couldn't be Laura—her mother had gone to bed hours ago. Hadn't she? Tilly waited, her pulse flicking queerly in her throat. But it had all gone quiet again, as though the room itself was somehow aware of Tilly's presence on the other side of the door.

5.

IT WAS OVERCAST on Saturday morning, an unusually chill breeze working up and down the hills of the inner-west. Eliza and Bruce had requested no funeral before their joint burial in Toowong Cemetery. This had surprised Laura: although she knew they held no religious convictions, she still expected the formality of a service. In the end, Laura had decided her parents would have still liked their friends to convene to remember them over coffee and sandwiches at a gathering afterwards.

As she stood on the edge of the plots, Laura gripped Andrew's hand, the wind shaking at nearby canopies of thick green fig leaves. What a lonely spectacle this was. The caskets set side by side looked so small, as though built for children. Laura hunched her shoulders, confused by a surge of irritation and panic. This goodbye felt wrong. The moment should have been more monumental, epoque-shaping, marked against the day, the week, the year in some significant way. Made part of the grand historical record. Instead Laura would have to bear witness with only her husband and daughter beside her, and carry the memory of this event practically on her own.

She peered down at Tilly, who looked smart in her skirt and blazer, and wondered how she was taking all this in. Tilly's face was impassive, only breaking its neutrality when she caught Laura's eye and seemed to wince. They watched the casket-lowering devices begin their work, the hearse driver standing off to the side, hands clasped in front of him, head bowed. Andrew sniffed. A few tears rolled down his cheeks and Tilly put her arm around his waist. The sun came out from behind the grey sky, shone weakly. Laura stepped forward, reaching for a clump of soil next to some tufts of grass. It had not been her intention to do so, but it seemed like the proper thing to do. A hedging of bets. A safety net. With her eyes set wide to stave off her own tears, Laura sprinkled the soil on her mother's casket, then her father's. 'By the sweat of your face you shall eat bread,' she murmured. 'Till you return to the ground, for out of it you were taken.'

Close to sixty people had gathered in the community hall on Hale Street around the corner from the Ithaca Pool. Laura joined

Andrew at the doors to greet arrivals, though she had trouble recognising many faces. Some men and women she hadn't seen for more than thirty years; others she had never met. The whole thing made her feel like an imposter, as though at any moment someone in the hall would turn around and demand she leave.

Thankfully, she did know one woman, Jenny, a colleague of Eliza's from the university. She looked remarkably unchanged, dressed as Laura remembered her in a black turtleneck skivvy and neat slacks, and red-framed glasses with matching lipstick, a handbag slung over her shoulder.

'Laura, dear,' she said, giving Laura a firm hug. 'Aren't you good to have organised all this.' She stepped back, admiring Laura with a light shake of her head. 'I can't believe how much time has passed. Literal decades. You were hardly more than a girl when you left.'

Jenny had often dropped by to see Eliza, and though she had several children of her own always had time for a chat with Laura. Jenny was different from Eliza's other work friends; she had an easy way about her that Laura had liked, attentive to Laura's responses about school or plans for the weekend, and curious about her opinions.

'I wonder, Laura, could we have a quick chat later?' Jenny now said, drawing closer to speak in a quiet voice. 'I'm leaving for Stuttgart tomorrow for a conference, and then travelling through Germany and Austria, so I don't want to miss you.'

Andrew made a gesture. It was almost two o'clock. Things were about to start.

'Yes, of course,' Laura said, giving Jenny's arm a quick squeeze. 'I'll come and find you.'

A few more people arrived, among them Meredith, a friend from Laura's university days. Laura took a deep breath, watching her go to Andrew first, even though she had only met him the once, at their wedding in London nearly twenty years ago.

'Andrew,' Meredith cried, her voice bouncing around the cavernous hall. A few guests turned to stare; Meredith did always know how to make an entrance.

'*Lore*,' she exclaimed next, as if surprised to see Laura. She mushed a cheek against Laura's. 'Oh, hun, I'm so, so sorry.'

Since moving to Oxfordshire Laura had kept in touch with Meredith first by letter, then by email, and more recently via Instagram, which she had begrudgingly joined a couple of years ago and scratched up eighty-two followers. Meredith, who had in the time since university been married twice and recently had twins, all the while making partner at a corporate law firm, managed to post at least four life-affirming stories each day. Cafe-quality Bircher muesli after a workout, view from the CityCat travelling to the office, after-work drinks on Eagle Street Pier. Soft filters, flattering angles. The twins didn't rate much of a mention, nor did her husband Graeme, who Laura knew was approaching seventy and was also a lawyer, with grown-up children from his first marriage. Meredith's job had something to do with competition law. Laura wasn't sure exactly what that meant, but she did remember Meredith had been competitive about almost everything, so it made sense she had forged a career out of it.

'Just a small gathering, is it?' Meredith said, tipping her sunglasses down her nose to peer into the hall. 'That's nice. More intimate.'

'Yes,' Laura replied. 'Mum and Dad would have preferred that. And thank you for coming along. You must be so busy.'

'Frantic.' Meredith made a penitent face. 'But I wouldn't have missed this, Lore. Not for anything.'

Andrew motioned for Laura to join him inside. Groups mingled, talking and occasionally smiling, but there wasn't much festivity. Two enormous percolators had been set up on tables for tea and coffee, and half-a-dozen trays of sandwiches and cakes. Andrew went up on stage behind the lectern to introduce himself, thanking everyone on behalf of the family for coming. He invited Laura to join him on the stage. She walked up the steps, shoulders rigid, her jaw set. She had picked a Tennyson poem she had always liked but never imagined she would recite in these circumstances.

> But such a tide as moving seems asleep,
> Too full for sound and foam,

When that which drew from out the boundless deep
Turns again home.

As she read, Laura felt oddly calm. She was aware of a noise inside her head that wasn't really a noise. It was the sound a noise makes when it abruptly ends and in its place is nothing. Emptiness. Absence. All the while she felt the eyes of her parents' friends settling on her before darting away, their expressions sympathetic yet curious, all no doubt entertaining a form of the same thought: *Thank God it's not me standing up there right now.*

Bruce's oldest school friend spoke next, a rather rambling and not all that interesting account of the years he'd known Bruce, and the regret at his sudden passing. Two women, both former students of her mother, spoke last, each remembering Eliza's wise counsel, the value of her research into tropical diseases, and how she would be missed by those at the university.

Afterwards these same men and women lined up to express their condolences as if receiving an indulgence. Laura stood by the scones and nodded and smiled like a demented cleric, Andrew at her side, while Tilly sat in the corner of the hall, scrolling through her phone. Meredith was nowhere to be seen, and Laura was relieved. She would call her later, arrange an after-work drink. A few flies buzzed about the food. The stainless-steel jugs of milk beside the percolators sweated. Eventually the crowd started to thin out, and only a small handful of friends remained, Jenny among them. She came over to Laura.

'You've done so well today,' she said. 'It's no easy task, organising this—and for the both of them. They would be proud of you.' Her gaze drifted for a moment past Laura, settling on Tilly. 'Oh my. That is your daughter, is it? She's the very spit of you.'

Laura made herself smile. Her face felt tight. The beginnings of a headache throbbed behind her left eye.

'You think? I've always thought she looked more like her dad.'

'Oh no. But then we can't see much of ourselves in our own children, can we? It's a kind of wilful blindness.'

Jenny fidgeted with the sleeve of her turtleneck. Laura had never seen her look that way—furtive. Again Laura recalled all those visits Jenny made to the house. How the friends would disappear to Eliza's study to discuss feedback on papers, or simply have a cup of coffee and a natter. Their amiable murmuring behind the door had formed its own soundtrack to Laura's childhood. She pictured the reading couch, a Parker lounge with avocado-coloured velour upholstery, and how through the crack in the doorway she would sometimes glimpse her mother's bare feet dangling from its end.

'You wanted to talk to me, Jenny?' she prompted. 'Was it about something in particular?'

'Yes, yes.' Jenny bit her lip. 'I hope you don't mind, but it's been on my mind since it all . . . you know. It's to do with your mum the last time I saw her, which turned out to be the day before your parents left the house.'

'Okay.' Laura crossed her arms. 'How was Mum that day?'

'Well, that's the thing. She was her usual self at the start. A little tired, maybe. But that's normal at our age.' Jenny gave a short laugh. 'Anyway, we talked about this and that on the patio outside. University gossip, really. Your mum had stopped visiting campus so she was out of the loop. Normally we'd exchange new article ideas, but I don't think she had been writing much either. I told her about my upcoming trip, and she asked me to bring back some *schwarzbrot*.'

'That awful brown bread?'

'Yes, she loved it.' Jenny dabbed at the corner of her eye with a handkerchief. 'We usually spent about an hour together, but that morning I didn't have a lot of time—I was due to meet my son in the city. Your mum got a little agitated when I told her I had to leave. If I hadn't known better, I'd have thought she was cross. Anyway, she walked me to the front door, and that's when it happened.'

Laura frowned, pushing some hair behind her ear. Her heart had gained pace, thumping unpleasantly against her breastbone.

'What did?'

'Well.' Jenny breathed out slowly. 'It all happened so fast, I find it tricky to remember the exact sequence of events. One minute we were saying goodbye on the deck, the next your mum was lying on the driveway below the house.'

'What? What do you mean?'

Jenny gazed back at Laura. Her eyes were round.

'She fell off the front deck.'

Laura blinked. She was struggling to process what Jenny was saying. Maybe she hadn't heard right.

'You mean, she fell down the stairs? Because that front railing has always been a bit dodgy—'

'No.' Jenny was fidgeting again with her cuff. 'And I suppose it's not right to say she fell, either. It would be more accurate to say she jumped. Eliza jumped off the deck.'

'*Jumped?*' Laura found herself smiling. It was ridiculous. Why on earth would she do that? 'I'm sorry, Jenny, but that doesn't seem possible. It must be a four-metre drop on to solid concrete.'

'Oh, I know how it sounds.' Jenny pressed her lips together. 'But I saw it with my own eyes. Eliza dragged a chair over to the railing, climbed up on it.' She gazed at Laura, then looked away, clutching her handbag to her chest, as though it might protect her from something. 'I said to her, "Eliza, you take it easy up there," because at first I thought she was reaching for a bit of cord, or wiring or whatever. But she didn't hear me. It was like she was in a trance. I'll never forget that look on her face . . .'

Jenny paused to give a theatrical shiver. Then she continued.

'Anyway, I bolted down those stairs faster than I've moved in decades. Luckily, your mum didn't appear too badly injured. Physically, I mean—just what looked like a sprained ankle, and a nasty bump on the head. But she was delirious. As though the fall had knocked her senseless. She was raving.'

Laura wiped her hands on her trousers. Her palms were clammy, and her mouth watered, like she might be sick.

'About what?' she asked.

'It's all a bit of a blur. But yes . . .' Jenny paused, gazing at Laura, her round eyes narrowing as she tried to recall. 'It was something about the house. And then something about you.'

'Me?' Laura repeated. Her voice sounded croaky now. She concentrated on the community hall's scuffed flooring, which seemed to warp and judder beneath her feet.

'Your dad came home then, and he helped her back inside,' Jenny went on. 'I told him Eliza needed to see a doctor, but he wasn't listening to me either. To be honest, I should have twigged something was up that day as soon as I arrived. The house had been a tip—cups and plates everywhere, piles of unwashed clothes. And the backyard looked like it hadn't been tended to in months.' Jenny smiled in a sad, lopsided way. 'Your mum was a neat person, to a fault some might say. That should have been a warning bell. That they weren't coping. That everything had become fraught.'

Laura felt her eyes burn with tears. She blinked rapidly, keeping her gaze trained on the floor. 'You couldn't have known what would happen,' she said quietly.

'No, but I do wonder if I should have got in touch with you somehow. Maybe if I had phoned you up . . .'

Jenny let that possibility hang in the air. Laura looked up.

'Did the police ever speak to you?' she asked.

Jenny nodded. 'Yes, some fellow with a lisp called me up soon after the news broke. I told him what I've just told you. I don't think he believed a word of it. I reckon he thought I was as mad as Eliza.' She looked wistful for a moment, then gave an unhappy shrug and brought out her sunglasses from her bag. 'Anyway, I've said my piece. I hope it isn't too much, especially today. But I thought you ought to know.'

'Thank you,' Laura said. She stepped forward and kissed Jenny's papery cheeky. 'I'm glad you told me.'

After she said goodbye, Laura watched Jenny walk down the steps of the community hall, reeling from the story. Jenny looked smaller, frailer in the shadows of the drooping sun. Eventually Andrew came over with a cup of tea. He watched Laura take a paltry sip and rested a hand on her waist.

'You look completely done in,' he said. 'Why don't you make your escape?'

'Are you sure?' Laura wilted against him. The force of Jenny's revelation had shocked the last of her reserves. There was so much she needed to process. The image of her mother's reaching hands flashed through her mind.

'Course. Tilly and I can finish up here.' Andrew squeezed her wrist. 'Hardest bit is over now.'

Laura glanced across the hall to Tilly, who had been watching her from the corner, solitary, bored. She gave Laura a pale smile that felt like consent.

Laura hardly registered the walk up the hill, or entering the house. Heading into the study she immediately opened the desk drawer and removed the coroner's report. She scanned the document until she found it, on page three. Jenny O'Neil's brief testimony that on 9 December Eliza had fallen in the house. This testimony had been recorded by Detective Inspector Anthony Sandretti on 16 December. There were no further details, or notes from Sandretti on the veracity of this claim.

But Laura knew it was true. Something had happened to her mother in the house that day. Something inexplicable. Laura slumped into the chair, shivery and a little dizzy. It was after four o'clock, and apart from that cup of tea at the hall she hadn't had a bite to eat since breakfast. She managed to stand up and go to the fridge, but had soon closed it again. Eating was too much effort. Instead she went to the kitchen sink and slapped cold water against her face. *Wake up*, she told herself. *Keep it together.*

A knock sounded at the front door. Laura remained by the sink, willing the Jehovah's Witness or the discount mechanics touting for business to leave. The house was unusually still and quiet, as if it were listening too. Laura heard another knock, and the rattle of the locked security door, followed by the shuffle of feet. Then she heard her mother's voice:

Laura?

The high, clear tone was unmistakable. For a moment Laura stopped breathing. She gripped the corner of the benchtop, her eyes fixed to the pastel-toned clothes hanging from the line next door. The arch of the church peeked from behind an oak tree. Then she turned and took a few tentative steps across the kitchen, peering around the pantry towards the front door where the outline of a figure loomed, hands pressed against the pink frosted glass.

You home, Laura?

Laura pinched her eyes shut. Blood was moving at incredible speed through her body, making her chest vibrate. She felt light-headed—perhaps she might faint? But after another beat, a voice somewhere in the recesses of her mind broke to the surface reminding her this was impossible, that her mother was dead. Laura let this reality wash over her, and suddenly she was furious. The rancour seemed to flick some switch inside, the mechanisms of her body shuddering violently back to life. *Who dares to play this trick on me?* she wanted to bellow, like a character from a fairy tale. And then, before she knew what she was doing, she had charged along the length of the house and wrenched open the front door, a wad of rolled-up Woolworths catalogues brandished at her assailant like a cosh.

'Whoa, careful!'

The figure on the doormat reared back, hands flung before their face to ward off the attack. It was a woman, about Laura's age. She huddled in the patch of light shining through the balustrade, face hidden beneath a Nike visor and a pair of aviator sunglasses. Dressed in a black short-sleeve shirt, black jeans and an old pair of Blundstones.

'What do you want?' Laura snapped, still enraged at being given such a fright while at the same time overwhelmed with relief that it wasn't her mother.

'You don't recognise me.' The woman stepped forward and took off the visor, pushing the sunglasses into her hair. 'It's me, Anita. From next door.'

Anita gazed at her, something almost amused in her eyes. Her arms were very brown, with whispers of hair in the crease of her armpits.

'Oh.' Laura rested her fingers on the security door handle, astonished that she had managed to dislodge Anita from her memory so forcibly. 'Of course. Sorry, Anita. How are you?'

'Fine, fine—but how are *you*?' Anita made an exaggerated face that reminded Laura of the downturned smile emoji on

Tilly's phone. 'I was at Eliza and Bruce's afterparty just now, at the hall. I came in late. You mustn't have seen me. I was going to come over, have a chat, but then your husband said you'd already gone home. Man, that must have been so difficult. I mean, god. What an awful thing it's been. I still can't quite believe they're gone.'

Laura flicked off the security lock and opened the door a fraction. Anita peeked through the gap, taking Laura in. She smiled, dimples appearing in both cheeks. *She looks strong*, thought Laura. Her arms had definition to them, her face was ruddy and tanned, just as it had always been. And her teeth, which she flashed in another warm smile, shone like pearls, while her dark hair had been lightened at the ends by the Queensland sun.

'I'm sorry. Am I interrupting?'

Laura shook her head. There was a Country Road canvas bag on the deck, a bulging backpack beside it. She had propped the door open with her foot, and Anita, spurred on by the presumed invitation, now pulled it right open and stepped inside.

'Far out, it's *hot* in here.' She began unheeling her boots. Her socks were thick green Explorers, man's socks. These stayed on.

'The air-conditioner is broken,' said Laura—and then, as if to prove it, pointed to the unit on the wall above the dining table.

'Cooler down the back, though, isn't it? Your mum used to have the brekkie table out there.'

Laura watched her move through the house, those ugly socks sliding over the polished boards. Anita paused beneath the ornate archway where the living room ended and the kitchen began, her hands on her hips, gazing about the space frankly, shaking her head.

'You know, I thought the place would look different.' She laughed, her mouth wide. 'How mad it that?' She peered around the corner into the kitchen. 'Do you mind if I grab a quick drink? I'm parched after walking back from the hall.'

Anita didn't wait for Laura's assent, heading straight to the cupboard that contained a few old glasses, then to the fridge where they kept a bottle of chilled water. Anita poured most of it into the glass and drank it down noisily as she stood at the sink, giving a satisfied smack of her lips when she was done. Leaning against the bench, one foot crossed over the other, she tilted her head inquiringly at Laura.

'I thought I'd see you before now. Thought I might bump into you at the shops, or out for a walk. You've been back a while, huh?'

'Oh, yes. I guess we have.'

Laura brought a hand to her brow. But just how long had it been? Each day blended into the next. She moved to the kettle. As she passed Anita she caught the hint of her sweat, but also another familiar, earthy smell. It was strange; the dimensions of the kitchen felt different with her inside it, the walls tighter, something expectant in the sultry air. When Anita reached out and placed a hand on Laura's forearm, however, her fingers were icy cold.

'It must be so hard for you. Coming home to all this.' She was looking around the kitchen with an appraising expression, perhaps noting how much had gone from this room too.

'Can I make you a tea?' Laura asked, somehow hearing cordiality in her voice.

'No, thanks.' Anita checked her watch. 'I can't stay long. I've got to get home for Ava, my daughter. I'm trying to keep an eye on her. She must be a similar age as yours. Teenagers, eh? One minute you know them, the next minute they're strangers.'

Laura followed the line of Anita's arm as she pointed to the photograph of Tilly pinned to the microwave. It had been taken last year in Greece. Tilly stood on a white rocky outcrop, wearing a baggy straw hat, the sparkling ocean below.

Laura sensed the curiosity in Anita's eyes as the kettle began to shriek. She opened and closed the pantry; she had forgotten where Andrew had put the tea bags, and the thought of Anita watching her rifle aimlessly through the kitchen drawers was unbearable. Laura put a hand against the bench to steady herself—she felt giddy with Anita standing across the room from her, as though she had slipped through a shred in time. As children, they had played together almost every day. Sleepovers most weekends; squeezed into the same single bed, hot breath on each other's faces as they shared a hundred different thoughts. And now here they were, fully fledged adults and hardly acquainted.

'Listen, Laura,' said Anita, her eyes fixed now to the window above the sink. 'I'm sorry to do this today, but I guess time is of the essence. And, look, I understand it's complicated, and you're dealing with a lot right now, and it's been unbelievable, really, what happened . . .' She paused, clearing her throat. 'But yeah, I wanted to talk to you about the house and try to sort everything out.'

Laura stared back at her.

'Sort what out?'

Anita folded her strong arms across her chest, rolling back her shoulders. Her demeanour hadn't changed; she seemed just as affable as when she'd first knocked on the front door. But now Laura noticed that she had been holding an envelope the entire time.

'The thing is, Laura—and I appreciate you probably don't know this—but I spent quite a bit of time with your folks these past few years. Your mum, especially. She did some work for us at the centre, organising a community book club, helping with the archiving, building up resources for the local history collection. Even got us a council grant. And they're rare as hen's teeth. It was nice. She was nice—and something of a mentor to me. Anyway, about a year ago, she started telling me about some ideas she had for expanding the centre. We're in a demountable over there on Handy Street, but it's not suitable for our needs; doesn't allow for much planning in the years ahead. Lize wanted to change that.' Anita smiled, her eyes crinkling. 'Anyway, before she went away, your mum told me she wanted the house, this house, to go to the trust to use for new headquarters. She was planning on drawing up the papers in the new year.'

Laura poured some water from the kettle into a mug and watched the steam rise from the rim. The kitchen window fogged up for a second before fading clear.

'I'm meeting my parents' solicitor next Monday,' she murmured. 'It's my understanding that I'm the sole beneficiary of the estate.'

Anita was nodding again; her cheer still hadn't faltered.

'Mm, okay. I see,' she said. 'I did worry this might happen. Eliza forgot to tell you.' She held up the envelope and gave it a gentle shake. 'This is from your mum. She posted it the day before they . . . Well, she put it in writing for me.' Anita stepped forward, offering the envelope to Laura.

'She sent this to *you*?' Laura turned it over in her hands warily, as though it might self-combust. 'This is the first I've heard of anything like this.'

'That's why I wanted to speak to you today,' Anita pressed on. 'So you had the opportunity to talk it over with the lawyer. To honour your parents' wishes.' She stood a little straighter. 'I feel it is a kind of duty, for Lize and Bruce.' Again she paused, and her dark eyes looked glassy. 'See, I didn't get to say goodbye . . . and it kind of kills me.'

Laura frowned, and drank some water. It was scalding, but she wanted to do something else with her hands, which had started to shake. Anita watched on, her expression almost haughty, and Laura recalled all the times she would stroll through the back door and holler '*What's cooking, Mrs T*?' to signal her arrival. She had always been so brazen, yet somehow their conflicting personalities had created a vibrant alchemy, and this memory brought on a wave of deep, aching loneliness in Laura—despite everything, she had never had a friend like Anita in the time since.

Laura set aside her mug and began to peel away the flap on the back of the envelope. Inside was a single sheet of paper with the Hotel Corones letterhead stamped at the top. Laura recognised her mother's large cursive. *Dearest Anita.* A tremor passed through her fingers. She clenched her jaw. *Bruce and I have decided it is right and proper to transfer the deeds of . . .* Laura stopped, folding over the sheet. She couldn't do this. Not here, not in front of Anita. She set aside the paper on the bench and picked up her mug.

'I know this is difficult.' Anita breathed in, held it. She was toying with a loose thread on her shirt, her knuckles were thick, old-looking. 'But you can see where I'm coming from, right?'

Laura raised the hot water to her lips again. A mad vision of herself throwing the mug at Anita flashed through her mind. The silence stretched out between them.

'Listen, Anita,' she finally said. 'I appreciate you dropping over to show me this letter, I really do. But the fact is we're going to sell the property. My husband, Andrew, he's running the show. We're working on the garden, and renovating the house, and then we're selling later in the year and returning to Britain.'

Anita glanced down at her socks. 'I saw the trailer out the front. I suppose . . .' She shrugged. 'So you've started?'

'Yes.' Laura gestured to the yard. 'The plans are almost finished. The builders have been booked.'

'And the probate—it's done?'

Laura, inhaling sharply, marvelled at her gall.

'Frankly, I'm not sure that's any of your business. Can I remind you that I buried my parents today?'

'Right.' A sound came from Anita like a laugh. 'So, you don't care about their wishes?'

'It's not that . . .' Laura drank again, wincing. 'Maybe my mother did talk about all that with you, and maybe she wrote it down. But if it was never legally binding then I'm in a fix.'

Anita stared back at her, eyes glinting.

'So you don't believe me?'

'It's not that—'

'Are you calling me a liar?'

'What? No!'

How had Anita managed to twist the conversation like this? Laura couldn't quite believe what she was hearing, though Anita had never been particularly tactful.

'I'm sorry,' she finally said. 'I have to do what's right for my family.'

'Like you did for your parents?' The colour in Anita's cheeks had faded. She had one foot planted forward, which she was rocking back and forth on, then rising high like she was about to pirouette. 'How could you possibly know what they wanted? Lize said you barely spoke to each other.'

Laura sensed herself nodding. There it was, a mirror of childhood: that precision of a wound. She almost admired Anita's efficiency. Laura took a deep breath, then another. If she stayed calm and rational, she might make Anita see reason. She could hold steady, wait it out. It still might be possible to turn this conversation around.

'Let me put it another way. Would your mother just give away her house next door like that?'

Anita blinked back at her. 'Well, we've always rented, so that's not really a fair comparison.'

Laura looked out the window, to the garden, and tried to imagine the sensation of cool air flowing through the canopy of the poinciana. She felt suffocated with Anita standing here in the kitchen.

'They had been going through some things, you know,' she heard Anita say quietly. 'Your mum and dad.'

Laura dragged her eyes away from the backyard. Anita had her arms folded again, her expression difficult to read.

'What do you mean?'

'They were kind of reclusive this past year or so. Barely left the house. Rarely saw their friends.'

'Except you, conveniently,' Laura said.

'Yes, me,' Anita snapped, her eyes flashing with fresh emotion. 'I did help them, you know. I set up their online grocery delivery, got someone around to help with the garden now and then. They had no one else. I'm not saying that to make you feel bad, Laura. It's just the truth.'

Anita was watching Laura more intently now, a shifting and mercurial look in her eyes.

'Why did you disappear like that, Laura?' she asked quietly. 'Back when we were kids.'

A memory surfaced, sudden and unbidden, from a long-ago summer. That year, when Laura was around twelve or thirteen, she had lain in the shade of the poinciana with Anita for hours, staring at the sky, talking, laughing, teasing. It had been a period in her life when she had an abundance of time; when she had enough freedom to be bored. But she had never been bored with Anita. She seemed to occupy all the space in Laura's imagination. That was the same year they found that old typewriter stashed beneath the house. Funny, Laura hadn't thought of it for decades. She wondered what had become of it—it had been a real beauty, a Royal, with gleaming keys.

'I didn't disappear,' she finally said. 'I just moved away. It happens. People . . . drift.'

Anita shook her head unhappily.

'Yeah, but it was like you fell off the face of the Earth.'

A noise came at the back door. Andrew and Tilly, returned from the hall. With a sigh, Anita hoisted up her trousers by the belt loop. She looked at Laura, nervous all of a sudden.

'Anyway, I better go. Thanks for the chat,' she said. 'At least I know where I stand with the house. By the way, you can keep that letter, it's a copy of the original.'

'Anita, hang on . . .'

But she had already turned and stalked the length of the house, the security door at the front slapping shut on her way out. Laura ran her hands through her hair, tugging painfully on the ends.

Andrew came into the kitchen, turning on the tap in the sink. He began cupping water into his mouth, most of it splashing against his suit jacket.

'Who was that?' he said.

Laura pushed past him and went down to the annex, standing at the glass.

'Anita,' she said. 'From next door.'

'What did she want?'

Laura watched the honeyeaters nesting in the tree, the branches bowing each time they jumped or swooped. There was a carpet of dead fruit lying around the trunk like a pool of blood.

'To talk about the house. She says Mum and Dad wanted to leave it to her.'

'She *what*?' Andrew stood at the top of the steps. 'Is she taking the piss?'

Laura rested her forehead against the glass.

'I don't think so. She's got a letter from them and everything.'

'Letter, my arse. Jesus Christ, does she not know what we had to do this afternoon. What a fucking nerve.' He blinked at her. 'Are you all right?'

Laura was trembling all over. Andrew hurried down to the annex and wrapped his arms around her, and Laura put her head against his shoulder. She felt calmer like this, but she couldn't stop shaking. It must be exhaustion. The stress of the day. Low blood sugar. 'You need a cup of sweet tea,' Andrew pronounced, coaxing her back to the kitchen where he flicked on the kettle.

'Don't think about it, darling,' he said, bringing down two mugs from the shelf. 'She's obviously mad. Why the hell else would she come around claiming all that garbage?'

'She's not mad,' Laura said flatly. 'Maybe she's telling the truth. It sounds like my parents weren't coping. My mother's old friend Jenny spoke to me this afternoon. She said Mum had a fall, a bad one, right here at the house. She thinks . . .' Laura swallowed. Opaque images of her mother falling from the deck flickered across her mind like a zoetrope. 'She thinks she did it on purpose.'

'What?' Andrew poured boiling water from the kettle into the mugs, the steam for a moment concealing his face. 'No. That can't be right. You'd have known about it.'

Laura passed him the carton of milk from the fridge.

'Would I?'

'All sorts come out of the woodwork at times like this,' Andrew said. 'Meddling. People like to be involved in the drama of it. Feel more important than they are.'

'Maybe . . .'

'Listen.' Andrew's voice had grown sharper, almost irate. 'There is no way we're giving Anita this house because she *says* your mum wanted to. Come on. How stupid does she think we are?'

'What about the letter?'

'Who says it's even authentic? And if it is, it won't be legal. So, really, she can go whistle for it, as far as I'm concerned.'

But it wasn't that simple. Anita's visit had prised open feelings Laura was struggling to articulate. She could identify some emotions as she stood with Andrew in the kitchen—envy, contrition. But there was also rage sprouting wildly inside herself, fury at Eliza and Bruce. Standing there at the sink overlooking the garden, Laura remembered all those mornings with her mother, weeding the pumpkins in the plots near the back fence, the collapsed tomato vines and some kind of spiky fruit Eliza claimed was a pear. Laura had always enjoyed watching her mother hack away at the tall grass with an old scythe her father brought out from beneath the house. There had been something cathartic about the *whoosh* and whip-crack of the slain stems, the clippings raked into a pile in the middle of the yard, which her father had burnt off in the late afternoon as the three of them stood beneath the poinciana, her parents drinking box wine and watching the sun streak pink across the fading sky. To her, that had seemed like the almost perfect way to spend a day. The house was resplendent with these memories. Eliza would never want to just give it all away. Forget that this history had ever happened. Forget Laura's inheritance. Forget that Laura was her daughter, and the house belonged to her too.

Laura waited for Andrew to disappear to the bathroom to shower, his tuneless singing resonating around the annex. Then she found her mobile and telephoned the solicitor, leaving a message with the request for an appointment as soon as possible.

6.

ANDREW DROPPED TILLY and Laura off on the corner of Coronation Drive opposite the Milton ferry terminal. The sun blazed high in the sky, flaring off the road, the concrete embankment and the identical office complexes. The air was heavy with the pong of mangroves, the river lapping at the smooth breaker.

With a few minutes to spare before the next CityCat, they sat on a bench and stared over the flat brown water towards West End. Cyclists made their way along the stretch of shared pathway backdropped by a few cranes. Tilly pulled out her phone and scrolled through Instagram, her chin squished against her fist. It was steaming hot, more summery than ever, though it was now approaching autumn. Her legs felt glued to the metal;

her top lip was beaded with moisture. It had rained yesterday, a tropical downpour that began in the late afternoon and had the stormwater drains overflowing. She searched for the record shop on Google Maps, and then double-checked the store in Queen Street Mall had her size in the Keds. Laura's promise of some shopping after the appointment with the solicitor had lured Tilly from the house on a teachers' strike day.

Tilly turned to study her mother, admiring the shape of her back, the wiry tendons on her arm. Grief was playing curious havoc on Laura. She was especially pale today, with dark blushes beneath her eyes. Last night she had only picked at her dinner before scraping back the chair and lumbering off to her study. 'Those writers, eh?' Andrew had scoffed. But Tilly knew it wasn't work—or, if it was, then Laura had embarked on a very different project. Her mother always talked about her stories, even when no one else was interested, and she never worked in the evenings. Something else was up. So while Laura had a bath Tilly had slipped into the study, hoping to find some explanation for her mother's behaviour.

What she discovered was a manila folder containing photographs—dozens of them. Of eerie waterholes, the rusty-red mounds of earth on the edge of the desert, desolate one-pub towns, and a single, dark figure trailing along the road. The terrifying place into which her grandparents had disappeared. Sifting through them, Tilly had experienced a disturbing sensation of cool silk slipping over her arms. Not from the images of that scorched, sandy pit where her grandparents would eventually lie dead. But from the understanding that her mother, who had been so afraid of those ghost stories, had been tormenting herself with these pictures night after night on the other side of the study door. Why did she have them? Was she planning on writing about Eliza and Bruce? The idea made Tilly feel light-headed.

The ferry arrived. Tilly led Laura towards the seats at the back. Apartment buildings, as uniform as box cut-outs, lined both sides of the river. Tilly gazed at them for a while, bemused. The wind whipped around her and Laura, a lashing of diesel. The catamaran passed under a bridge. The conductor spoke over loudspeakers, informing commuters of the adjacent sites. The glittery green building on the right was a library, a modern art gallery behind it. Further up was a place called the Cultural Centre. Everything was beige.

A plump seagull landed on the ferry's railing and stared at Tilly belligerently. The shadows of a bridge were flung long across the river's surface. It all looked so benign, but these bodies of water hid tree trunks, jagged scrap metal and broken bottles amid the ebb of the taut currents. Tilly thought about the sixth former back home who had jumped off the bridge beside the Swann Inn and drowned. They said Madison had been drinking; that her friends had dared her. Tilly had been drunk before, she had lived in those brief moments of outlandish confidence. She peered up at the concrete bridge. It was a long drop, but would it kill her? Tilly heard that when Madison's body was fished out of the water the girl's arms had been dislocated from both sockets.

Tilly and Laura got off the ferry at Eagle Street. The grand-looking entrance to the skyscraper was glass and dome-shaped facing onto the street. A line of white cabs was parked in the rank. Inside, they were ushered through a metal detector and made their way towards the lifts. It was busy in the foyer, women in pencil skirts and white blouses streaming past. Tilly, whose stomach suddenly rumbled, guessed they were heading out on their lunch break, heels clapping like applause across the cool marble floor.

The firm's reception area overlooked the river, Story Bridge and the northern stretch of the city. A few planes hung low in the air; this far up the airport seemed close. Tilly was thirsty and wanted to ask her mother for a drink but she could see Laura was preoccupied, biting at the corner of her lip. Still, a flush of colour had returned to her freckled cheeks, while her hair, normally fine and almost wispy, looked voluminous after the ferry ride, as though it had soaked up moisture from the muggy Brisbane air and returned to life.

'Laura?' A huge man in his mid-thirties lumbered towards them, a paw outstretched. 'So good to finally meet you in person.'

So this was Brad. Before, Tilly had only made out a subdued version of his Zoom conversation through closed doors, but with this new proximity she could hear the deep lawnmower rattle of his voice. He was dressed in a suit that looked expensive, though it strained across his chest and wide shoulders. Tilly stared at his bulging Adam's apple and a few hairs escaping from his tight collar.

'This is my daughter,' Laura said. 'Matilda.'

Her mother was looking at her as she said this, her voice raised, and Tilly's face grew hot. It felt like a rebuke to be introduced so formally. Brad nodded, his bath-tile smile gleaming.

His office had a view to the west of Brisbane and the swathe of river they had just travelled along from Milton. An acrid tang of new carpet hung in the air. Two chairs had been positioned in front of his desk, which Brad pointed at when he came through the door. He sat heavily in his own, the leather giving a satisfied hiss, before he wheeled across the great expanse of floor towards a filing cabinet. He fossicked around until he found what he was looking for and extracted it with an '*Ah ha!*'.

'Laura Townsend. You know, I could have sworn I'd already met you when we first started corresponding. Your name was so familiar. Then I remembered I had met you. Well, sort of.' He pointed to the bookcase in the far corner of the office, built from matching oak. 'One of yours, I believe? My husband's favourite novel. Insisted I have my own copy. He can't get enough of World War Two, you see. Sometimes I think he wished he'd been born a century ago.'

'Oh yes?' said Laura with a small smile. 'That might have caused some problems.'

'I know, right?' Brad laughed, shaking his large head. 'Funny what obsesses some people, isn't it?'

Tilly shot a look at Laura, but her eyes were fixed to a glass of water in the middle of the desk. When she glanced back towards Brad, he winked.

'Must be all right having a writer for a mum. How are you liking Brissy?'

Tilly gazed past him to the solid blue sky. Her sunburnt shoulders blazed in the air-conditioned office.

'It's okay,' she said. Then, unnecessarily: 'It's hot.'

Brad smiled again, but she could tell he didn't care. He probably saw a dozen clients each day. It was a curious situation to find themselves in, weirdly intimate, him knowing so much about her family's circumstances while at the same time not knowing them at all. He must witness all kinds of emotion during his work hours. Tears of disappointment, ecstatic grins, flashing dollar signs in people's eyes. But mostly, Tilly imagined, the ugly sides of grief—gnarled and twisted, like lesions or burns.

Brad was flipping through the client folder. When he got to the end he snapped it shut and tossed it down on the desk.

'Look, it's all straightforward, really. Your parents' estate. They had a decent whack of cash, around five hundred thousand, tied up in term deposits, which haven't done much in the past decade, as well as a modest shareholding. The superannuation death benefit is sizeable, too. Nearly two million dollars.' Brad grinned. 'Gotta love those generous university retirement provisions.'

Tilly's eyes went wide. It seemed like an impossible amount of money. Surely there was some mistake.

'And then there is the house, of course. Owned outright by your folks, no mortgage.'

'Right,' said Laura, who appeared unfazed by these wild figures. 'Well, that tallies up with what I'd been expecting.'

'And then, of course, we have the issue of Anita Bilson. Living next door to you on Central Avenue.'

Laura shifted in her seat. Tilly could see she was trying to work out how to arrange her expression. It was almost like her mother was lining up pieces of the past in her mind, weighing them against one another, testing which would best hold.

'Anita came in for an appointment last week,' Brad explained. 'She claims she'd been close to your parents for years. Especially the last few. Helped them. Groceries, some odd jobs around the house, the garden. Said they socialised. Talked most days. Shared time together. Were you aware of this?'

Tilly watched her mother. Her face, which had assumed that healthy sheen just a few minutes ago, had lost some of its colour.

'I didn't know about that until recently,' Laura said at last.

'And now we have this letter.'

Brad stared across the polished desk before threading his fingers behind his head. It was not a flattering pose: damp stains were seeping through the fabric of his suit. When he spoke again the jocularity in his voice was gone.

'Of course, *legally*, it holds little currency. But I do feel obligated to tell you that shortly before they died your parents had themselves scheduled an appointment with me.'

Tilly watched Laura sit forward, her hands clasped together as if mimicking a prayer.

'What appointment?' she asked.

'About their wills. I believe it was their intention to make changes—your mother had spoken to me on the phone about it—but we didn't go into the particulars. She called on the ninth of December. I had in the calendar a meeting scheduled for early January.' Brad picked up his expensive-looking pen, made a squiggle on the nearby notepad. 'Obviously it never took place.'

Tilly closed her eyes. Even though she didn't fully understand the implications of this conversation, she was horribly aware that it should not have taken place in front of her; that her mother had suffered a grave indignity at the hands of this Anita woman, and by extension Brad. When she opened her eyes again she directed her gaze at the carpet, wondering if she focused enough energy at it whether the floor would open and swallow her like some freak sinkhole, funnelling her through an intergalactic vortex all the way back to England. But no amount of will or wishing would transport her from the lawyer's office, and when she dared to glance up at her mother she found Laura had crossed her arms, a small but defiant smile tugging at the corner of her mouth.

'So nothing has changed substantively in the current will.'

'Well, no . . . But this woman may lodge a claim.'

'A claim to what—the house? For her community centre? Surely she has no right to it?'

Brad tilted his chair, blinking.

'It still might be prudent to talk this over with her, Laura. We see this a lot. Friends of the deceased trying to insert themselves into the probate. They can be a nuisance and decide to make life difficult for you.'

Laura was nodding, something mechanical about the gesture, her eyes glittering.

'As I said, from a legal perspective, I'd be surprised if she had a basis for any claim,' Brad continued. 'But you never know how far people are willing to go.' Here he faltered, looking for the first time uncomfortable. 'May I ask: *did* you ever discuss with your parents their wishes for the house in the event of their deaths?'

Tilly watched her mother. She was staring into her lap where she had gripped her index finger, squeezing so tight her knuckles had gone white. Tilly had never seen Laura look so angry, or bewildered.

'How many of your clients talk about death with their family, Brad?'

The lawyer smiled. 'Surprisingly few,' he conceded. 'It's never an easy topic to broach.'

They gazed at each other for another moment, then Laura turned to Tilly. There was a curious nakedness in her expression that sent a hot rush through Tilly's body. When her mother spoke again, her voice had a faint, almost intimate quality, as though she were speaking to Tilly directly and Brad was no longer in the room.

'My mum and dad . . . It's difficult to explain. They had grown distant this past year, not quite themselves. I suppose that's why we hadn't kept much in touch, and how time managed to slip away.'

Tilly steered her eyes away to the window and that blue sky. Her mother seemed to be admitting to something, though she wasn't sure what. The adult world was mysterious to Tilly. She thought about the brown river seething beneath them, dredging up all that debris, and how three days after Madison died her missing school shoe had come bobbing to the surface, the laces still tied up. *Odd*, Tilly mused. She couldn't remember Madison's face, but the image of that shoe had been lodged in her mind ever since.

Traffic roared along Eagle Street. Buses, taxis and motorbikes thundered by, whipping up exhaust fumes and grit. By now it was nearly two o'clock, but Tilly could no longer contemplate any shopping. Eager to get away from all the heat and noise, she suggested a stroll down Queen Street towards the mall where they found an arcade peeling off from the main shopping thoroughfare.

It was cool inside, a jazz track filtering through overhead speakers. Tilly and Laura trailed along the smooth walkway, admiring the ornamental stained glass set into the high panelling and the bright five-globe brass chandeliers. Eventually they settled at an outside table at L's Fine Food Espresso Bar and ordered orange juices.

'What was all that stuff about with Brad?' Tilly asked when the waitress brought over their drinks. 'About that woman next door . . . Anita, isn't it?'

Laura wiped her hands on her dress. She shrugged.

'We were friends as kids. We went to school together.'

'But you didn't keep in touch?'

'No.' Laura sighed. 'I haven't kept in touch with many people.'

'And she knew Grandma and Grandpa? Was friends with them?'

'Seems like it,' Laura replied. 'Mum always liked Anita, for some reason. Thought she was *spirited*.'

Tilly watched her mother grind tiny granules of sugar beneath her thumb and sweep them to the floor.

'But would they have wanted the house to go to her? That's pretty huge, right? A whole house.'

Laura stared back at Tilly.

'Of course they bloody wouldn't have.'

Her voice came out like a hiss. Tilly pressed her fingertips to the frosted glass. She could feel her pulse in her throat. She drank some juice, frowning. She wasn't sure how to navigate this conversation with her mother. They had always been good at talking about feelings, but lately Laura had become so remote it often seemed like Tilly was trying to communicate with her in another language.

Eventually Laura sat back, folding her arms, and studied the chandelier hanging further into the arcade.

'You know this place is haunted?' she murmured. 'The wife of Patrick Mayne, they say—Mary. The Maynes were a wealthy Brisbane family in the early days of the colony. They had a lot of influence.'

Tilly surveyed her surrounds, unimpressed.

'If I was a ghost, I would *not* be hanging around here.'

'No?' Laura's brow twitched. She took a sip of her drink. 'And where would you haunt? H&M?'

'Hardly. More like the Bodleian.'

'You and Morse.'

'Who?'

'It's changed, of course,' her mother continued. 'The antiques store's gone, so has the lovely teashop I used to visit sometimes with Mum. Room with Roses, it was called. I always had the Devonshire tea, Mum ordered a black coffee, every time . . .'

Laura's face had gone very pink, her bottom lip trembling. She had still not cried about her parents—at least, not in Tilly's presence—though she cried often enough at other things. Dogs dying in television dramas, UNICEF brochures, Ludovico Einaudi ballads. Once about five years ago Laura had even cried with relief when Tilly had been found near the creek after getting lost for a few minutes off the trail through Widley Copse. Tilly knew she should feel some resistance to her mother's pain, some fear of it even. It was selfish, but amid all the upheaval and uncertainty of the past few months Tilly needed to see her mother's grief to believe it. She needed to know her mother felt her parents' loss in order to understand how she would one day deal with loss of her own.

But Laura didn't yield. Instead she balled up her serviette, blinking her eyes clear. 'Anyway,' she went on, 'Patrick Mayne bought the land way back in 1849 for his first butcher shop. He's a notorious figure now, of course. Completely mad, and a killer too. The legend goes that he murdered a timber mill worker, and the few hundred pounds he stole from him was used to set up the business.'

'So a good bloke, then. Let me guess—he became premier of Queensland?'

Laura smiled.

'It's prime real estate today. Worth a fortune. But Patrick Mayne's children, who had no children of their own, had by the end of their lives donated all the family land and property.'

'Huh.' Tilly considered this. 'They just gave it all away?'

'They had enough money of their own, I suppose,' said Laura. 'I think they wanted rid of their father's legacy. The blood will out, that sort of thing.'

The couple sitting behind them had finished their coffees and were paying the waitress. The sounds of the city tolled through the cool tunnel, and Tilly found herself admiring the arch of the arcade entrance where the sun struck the pavement in a solid block of light.

'It's not your typical setting for ghosts,' she murmured. 'Like, back home, we've all those ruins and old manor houses and awful weather. Perfect for some haunting.'

'Ghosts live in the sunshine too.'

Tilly looked at Laura. She was sitting rigid in the chair, her hands clasped together. Tilly could make out the tiny blue veins in the pouches beneath her mother's eyes, almost sparkling, as if her blood had been spiked with shards of crystal.

'Do you think you could ever write about what happened to Grandma and Grandpa?' she asked. 'Turn it into fiction, like your other books.'

Laura said nothing. The jazz on the speakers peaked and then dipped, the arcade falling into an eerie silence until someone dropped a fork on the tiled floor and they both flinched.

'I have thought about it,' her mother finally said. 'Writing about them. Writing about what happened. Where it happened.' Laura's voice was quiet, almost a whisper. 'I suppose I'm afraid.'

'Afraid?'

Her mother took in a long breath, gazing back at Tilly steadily.

'Of putting it all into words. What most people don't understand is the power of it. Of creating that story. You see, everything takes on new life on the page. After a while, you no longer have control of it.'

'Wasn't it the same with your other books?'

Laura shook her head.

'Nothing was at stake for me. I took events from long ago, occurring in a country that isn't my own. Writing about Mum and Dad, about this place, it carries risk, it carries danger. I don't know what might come next.'

'In the story?'

'Not in the story. To me. I've preferred to live with that part of myself closed up, like a locked box. It's just . . . easier.'

Tilly sat back in her chair. She would never admit it, but until recently she had given little thought to her grandparents and the relationship Laura had with them. As far as Tilly knew there had never been a noisy falling-out like JoBeth's mum had with her sister about their dad going into a care home. She knew Laura had tried to arrange a visit over Christmas, and her grandmother had said no. When Tilly asked her father about it, he had replied that 'Some people, even our closest family, are stuck in their ways. Don't take it personally.' But, seated across the table from her mother, Tilly finally understood the peculiarity of this estrangement, and the damage it had caused. Because Laura had altered since they arrived in Brisbane; she had grown ragged, her usual even temper now moody, unpredictable. As though the events of the past few months had altered the plaster cast of her and she had taken on new, unsettling form.

Tilly stared at her mother's hand resting on the table, longing to reach for it. She considered her father's advice. Andrew had the strong belief that simple explanations bear simple emotions, and probably forgot the conversation had ever taken place. But for Tilly, it had planted a seed of terrible knowledge: that your family was not constant. That there were some conditions to a parent's love.

7.

THE NEXT MORNING, Laura walked to Dr Leong's rooms in Red Hill. It was the same clinic she had visited as a child. Her old family physician, Dr Vucic, had retired several years ago, and judging from the smiling welcome board at the reception the new doctors at the practice were all much younger than Laura. Still, Margaret Leong appeared gentle and diligent, and made lots of sympathetic noises when Laura explained she had made the appointment to discuss her parents' medical records.

Dr Leong scrolled through her notes. 'Right,' she said slowly. 'Ah, yes. I see you received authorisation from the department.' Her fingertips hovered above the keyboard. 'And now you've questions about the coronial report?'

'Yes, of a kind,' Laura said. 'I was actually hoping to have a clearer sense of my parents' health before they died. Their mental acuity, really. Some things have come to light these past weeks that don't make a whole lot of sense to me.'

Dr Leong folded her hands in her lap. A small, silver crucifix glinted over her blouse.

'Anything in particular?'

Laura sat back. She could hear the drone of a distressed fly caught behind the venetian blinds.

'Well, to begin, the report mentions you had started making house calls. Was that usual?'

Dr Leong nodded. 'It wasn't unusual. Since Covid, many patients, especially older ones, have preferred home visits. It's something we do a lot at the practice. But I saw your parents infrequently. Once every couple of months.'

'But enough for you to think they'd become reclusive? That's what the detective reported you had told him.'

'Well, it's a bit of a loaded term, isn't it?' Dr Leong picked up a biro, started to fiddle with it. 'Perhaps it would have been more accurate to say they had retreated a little. Again, it's not uncommon in patients who are getting older. Leaving the house less often, not as social as they once were. It wasn't enough to trigger any major concern. But I did notice this change in them. One to watch, if you understand.'

'Did they ever mention the desert to you?'

Dr Leong blinked. She set down the pen.

'I beg your pardon?'

'The desert. The Outback. My mother's study was full of pictures of the place. The arrangement seemed . . . manic.'

'I see.' Dr Leong pressed the tips of her long fingers together. 'No, I don't recall them ever talking about it.'

'What about their capacity to make other decisions? Around their estate, the house. That kind of thing.'

'How do you mean?'

Laura's eyes strayed to the model skeleton by the door.

'Would my mother have been able to make informed choices about her legal affairs, for instance?' she asked.

'Yes, I think so. Let's put it this way, I don't think she or your father had become in any way mentally impaired.'

'Okay.' Laura took a moment to digest this opinion. She realised she was disappointed, and following this feeling was the swift rise of terror, as though the pathway to understanding had just vanished. 'And what about other injuries around the house? Falls, that kind of thing?'

Dr Leong frowned.

'The detective asked me that same question, but I don't have a record of any events. Did you also hear that something happened?'

Laura stared at the carpet. She tried to concentrate on the line of orange and pink running through the charcoal, but it suddenly seemed a long way away. She wanted to tell Dr Leong about Jenny's story, but she knew how it would sound. Preposterous. Like Laura herself had taken leave of her senses. She straightened in the chair and let out a long sigh.

'No, I didn't,' she finally said. 'It's just, well, I've started to wonder. It's awful to say, but I'm beginning to think they both might have gone a little gah-gah. All this obsessing over the Outback, the hiding away indoors, shutting themselves off from the world. It's so unlike them. And then the other day I found out they were considering giving away the house, like it was a second-hand book or something. Does that sound healthy to you?'

'Not particularly,' said Dr Leong. 'Cognitive decline in older patients can be swift. They can develop obsessive patterns of behaviour, make rash decisions. It is possible they were both in worse shape than we thought.'

The surgery smelled pleasantly of essential oils filtering quietly from a diffuser in the corner. A few heavy medical textbooks were stacked on the desk, one raising the height of the computer's screen.

'I feel terrible for not knowing any of this,' Laura murmured.

'The death of loved ones always raises complex emotions—guilt often among them. But your parents were, at least we assumed until recently, in pretty good nick. Your dad's heart condition should have been detected earlier, but it's often the case with men his age. They are reluctant to get things checked out for fear of what may be found.'

Laura studied Dr Leong's unblemished face. Somewhere in the building a baby mewled.

'Since they died, I've had so many questions that no one seems to have answers to,' she said quietly. 'I suppose I may have to face up to never really knowing what happened.'

Dr Leong reached out and placed a hand on Laura's forearm. It wasn't much, but it was a comfort.

'You know how they died,' she said. 'As painful as that is, at least you know the cause. Given the condition of his arteries, I'm not sure your father could have escaped that heart attack, no matter where he had been. And your mum, in the end, it was just awful, awful luck . . .' Trailing off, Dr Leong sat back, scrutinising Laura afresh. 'How are you, if you don't mind me asking? In yourself, I mean.'

'Oh, well . . .' Laura blew out her cheeks. 'All right, given the circumstances.'

'You're able to do basic things for yourself? Get up in the morning, have meals, have a chat with the family?'

'Oh yes.'

'And your husband, your daughter? How are you getting along with them?'

Laura hesitated. She pictured Tilly, the soft fall of her fringe. For some reason that image had sharp edges.

'It's been a big adjustment, of course, for my daughter especially. Moving here, leaving her friends.'

'Mm.' Dr Leong was frowning, real concern etched in her otherwise smooth forehead. 'And what's it been like for you, coming back?'

Laura swallowed again. The balls of her feet were tingling. She could feel tears pressing behind her eyes, threatening to break.

'It's been fine,' she managed to say. 'I didn't really have a choice.'

Dr Leong held Laura's eye, her frown deepening.

'And have you seen someone professionally about what happened to your parents? A grief counsellor, or a psychologist?'

Laura shook her head.

'I don't go in for all that. I guess that makes me a proper Brit now, right?'

Dr Leong didn't laugh.

'It's a big trauma, Laura. To lose both of them like that. A very big trauma. There's no shame in asking for help. Let me know if you'd like to talk further.'

Laura smiled back, but her mind was drifting, like a balloon carried away by the wind. Up the stairs and through the front door. Past those white walls. The dust floating in the afternoon light. The raw heat. The blank screen.

'Actually, I'm thinking of writing about it,' she heard herself say.

'Oh yes?'

Laura ran a fingertip over her bottom lip.

'The thing is, I have such resistance to it. A mental block, I suppose. It's never been like that with other projects. But this—I can barely think about it. It's such a strong feeling that I wonder if it's a sign. That I should. That I must.'

Laura was aware of a steady hum of calm, like the vibration of a printer warming up for a new job. *I have to write about it*, she realised. Because right now it's all I have. To add order, cohesion and plausibility to the chaos of their deaths. To find meaning. *If I don't, I think the whole thing will send me mad.* Laura waited for the wave of dread to hit, but nothing came.

'Sounds like a great idea,' Dr Leong said, her eyebrows twitching as she typed another note into her computer. 'It couldn't hurt to try.'

The next day, after Tilly had left for school and Andrew drove off to visit a supplier in Darra, Laura settled at the desk with a coffee and raisin toast, shirtsleeves pushed up. Starting was the hardest, like trying to raise a spark from only a piece of dull flint and steel. She swivelled in her chair, gazing across the room towards the space where the couch had once been, and pictured her mother, the stern line of her nose contrasting with the uptick of the right corner of her lips, as though she was caught in a humorous thought.

Laura spent some time looking through her mother's photographs. She drew her own map of Hell Hole Gorge, marking the camping site, the creek, the escarpment and the waterhole where Eliza had been found. She made some notes on the landscape. The native trees, the wildlife, the ancient rockface. It felt good, this planning. She sensed a building of momentum, some potential for the project.

As she continued work on these notes, Laura's bare foot stubbed against something hard. Peering beneath the desk, she saw it was a cardboard box. She dragged it out. Inside she found more of her mother's old books, about two dozen of them. Laura perused the spines—a Glenda Adams, early Peter Careys, Christina Steads and several Patrick Whites.

She sat back, puzzled. The study had been emptied of books during their first week in Brisbane. Andrew must have brought them up from under the house, though it was odd that he hadn't mentioned it. Or maybe Tilly salvaged them when Laura hadn't been looking, worried about second thoughts. Laura shook her head, dazed by the intense light penetrating between the gap in the study blinds. She reached down to burrow through to the bottom layer where the books looked older and more worn than the others. From here she eased out a hardback copy of

Barbara Baynton's short stories. She had read them during her Australian Literature subject as an undergraduate. Laura flipped open the pages to a story she remembered, tracing her fingertip over the title. 'A Dreamer' was about a girl who returned to the malignant Australian bush pointlessly searching for her mother, who is in fact dead.

Laura closed the book abruptly. She sat very still in her chair, eyes closed. A faint whistling had started up in her ears. Eventually she returned the hardback to the box and slid it beneath the desk once again. Then she clicked on the laptop to resume work, waiting for the device to hum back to life. Putting on her headphones, Laura opened a new Word document and stared at the blank screen. The cursor winked at her. *Go on*, she told herself. *Start.* But she had lost the thread. She glanced at her notes, to remind herself, then twisted back to the laptop. She gaped at her fingers poised above the keys. It was like she had forgotten how to type. *Come on.* Grinding her teeth, a line from Baynton vaulted through Laura's mind: *What mattered the lonely darkness, when it led to her mother.*

As she tried again to sharpen her attention, Laura sensed the books at her feet, almost as if they were vibrating. It was ludicrous, but she couldn't concentrate with them in the room. She would have to take them back downstairs, or better yet bin them. No, she couldn't throw them out like garbage—Laura had to draw a line somewhere—but perhaps she could leave the box on the side of the road one morning with a 'Free to a Good Home' sign. There was something restitutional about that. Something circuitous and cyclical. A return to a natural kind of order.

'Mum?'

Laura jolted in fright. Tilly stood behind her. Her dark hair clung to her forehead; she smelt of coconut oil and sweat. The room had grown dimmer, the sun hiding behind some low cloud. Laura sat up, her neck giving a painful click. The headphones had slipped off her ears but she could make out the dim narration of a YouTube advertisement promoting a book called *The Divine Matrix*.

Tilly adjusted the weight of her backpack on her shoulder.

'Were you . . . asleep?'

'No, no.' Laura pushed back her chair, shaking out her arms, which had pins and needles. She put a hand against the desk, running a fingertip along the underside, seeking certainty in the wood's grain. 'I was just thinking about something. Sorry, I didn't hear you come in.'

She checked her watch. It was nearly five o'clock. Laura stilled. That couldn't be right. Several hours had—what—disappeared?

Tilly remained in the doorway, watching her. 'Looks like you had a productive day.' She pointed to the laptop. 'Nice one.'

Heat radiated from the computer screen, the dull whirr of the machine loud in the study. Tilly was talking again, but Laura barely heard her.

'. . . and I've got some homework for photography. I wondered if you might help me?'

Laura stood up, her stomach undulating with motion sickness.

'Uh, maybe not tonight,' she murmured. 'I'm a bit busy . . .'

'It won't take long. We could do it now if you were free.'

'I said no. *Okay*?' she snapped.

Laura still had her back turned as Tilly stalked away, her school shoes heavy against the floorboards. Soon music started up from somewhere, and Laura heard the slap of the back door. She closed her eyes again. She wanted to call out to Tilly, apologise, explain. But how? The schism was growing between them, had been for weeks. Laura didn't know how to stop it. She clicked on the mouse tracker and saw the open Word document—and ten new pages of text. She checked the file in the Documents folder. The .doc had been created at 2.58 p.m. She scanned the opening pages:

Laura sits at the desk, her laptop open. She types. Through the window the sun sets behind the trees. There is a light on next door. She can see an outline against the frosted glass, the warp of the light, then the growl of the washing machine. Above that sound, Laura thinks she hears talking. Noise travels oddly around the house; sometimes she thinks she can hear voices in the next room that are in fact coming from people on the street.

Resuming her work, Laura soon hears another noise. This time more distinct. A bang, followed by another. It continues in a steady rhythm. Laura pauses her typing. She feels disquiet, the tingle of fear, though she can't say why. Eventually she stands up and strides the length of the house towards the back door. From there she makes her way to next door's fence and mounts an ornamental boulder to better view her neighbour's garden.

The moon has bathed the balding lawn in pearly light. The yard backs on to the sprawling and unkempt garden of the church centre on the corner. It is unusually cold outside; Laura's breath comes out in a fog as she calls, 'Hello?' But the reply is silence. She is alone.

Laura is about to return to the house when she senses movement beneath her. The head of tight grey curls, followed by the dark eyes of an elderly woman, rise to her line of sight, though Laura can't quite make out her face. The woman holds a broom out like a jousting stick and proceeds to bang it against the fence.

'No,' she moans. 'No, no, no!'

The shock sends Laura reeling, and she falls back into the shrubs beneath her. The old woman continues to bang the broom against the wood, the boards shuddering with the force of it. 'Where's the other one?' she incants. 'Not you. Not you!'

When Laura manages to scramble back to her vantage point, she discovers the woman has gone. The wind stirs. Laura's attention is drawn to a large shadow fluttering by the Hills Hoist as a cape would hang from the line, morphing into a dark profile, ink spilt across a blank page. Laura grips the fence post, splinters lodging in her palm. She's aware of a low rumbling coming from somewhere, and she brings her other hand to her chest where she feels a dense pressure, like the weight of a book resting there. She wants to close her eyes, block her ears, but she can't move. So it really is possible to die of fright, she thinks as her heart convulses . . .

Laura slammed the laptop shut. This was not possible. She didn't write this, couldn't have. How had it ended up on her computer? Laura pressed her knees together, willing herself to breathe normally, to stay calm. But her chest ached. The room felt smaller, the air inside it grating against her lungs. Laura stared at the laptop, her head now hissing with a weird, high-pitched static. There had to be another explanation.

She went to retrieve the box of books beneath the desk, determined to be rid of them, but as she crouched down beside her chair she saw they had disappeared. *I must have already taken them outside*, she thought. But when she went out to the front deck and looked about, Laura couldn't see the books anywhere. The sky was grey, dark clouds building behind the figs. The bats were growing agitated in their canopies. Laura watched a few cars drive past. She longed for Andrew, for the comfort of their Swinbrook house. For the first time, she regretted her return to Brisbane, felt it deep in the marrow of her bones. Some mechanism inside her was rotating of its own accord. She wasn't quite sure how to stop it, and that was beginning to frighten her.

As Laura turned to go back inside, she sensed a flash of colour in the corner of her eye. The shrubs next door shook with promise, but it was only a bush turkey building his nest.

8.

TILLY CLIMBED THE poinciana, still fuming at her mother. She settled on a thick branch, her legs dangling on either side, and brought out her phone from her back pocket. She was enrolled in a photography elective at school, and the teacher had sent them home with the instruction to take a snap that captured changing light. Tilly wanted to catch the low sink of the sun behind the church near the corner, the creep of the shadow across the car park, and had hoped Laura might help, but no matter; she'd do it on her own. Lining up the frame, her eyes drifted to the grey space between the obscure bleed and the bright grassy verge. She took the shot, then a few more. She would play with the settings later, adjust the filter, the gradients. The house grew dark behind her.

Up in the tree, Tilly listened to some music on shuffle, picking away at the tacky bark. The sun was sinking fast, insects starting a dusky racket. Beneath her, the backyard had been gutted for the impending build, the lawn clawed apart and gaping like it had been shelled. Still, the design was taking shape, the bones of the extension sturdy in the gloam. The new part of the house would be tall, its imposing shadows cast over the clothes hanging on the line next door. Following the pattern of the patio's brickwork, Tilly noticed in the last sliver of sun on the elevated terrace a woman seated in a camping chair, drinking from what looked like a bottle of beer. Somehow she spotted Tilly in the tree, and raised a hand to call, 'Good spot you've got up there!'

Tilly guessed it was Anita, the neighbour who made that dubious claim over the house. Anita sat straighter, her face scrunched up to better make out Tilly through the branches. Her legs were planted wide beside the chair legs, as if she were about to spring to her feet. It was an inelegant pose, reminding Tilly of her PE teacher, Mr Noor.

'How you guys getting on over there?' Anita called.

Tilly glanced towards the back window, worried her mother might hear. She paused Spotify on her phone.

'Yeah, fine. Thanks.'

Holding up her bottle in a kind of salutation, Anita took a swig and ran the back of her hand across her mouth.

'Looks like you're making good progress on the renos. Going to be a big house when you're done.' Anita made her way across the terrace, her face appearing above the fence line. '*Oof*,' she exclaimed. 'Bit of a tip back here! Hey, your dad going to sell those bricks?' She nodded towards the old pavers stacked in the corner.

'I'm not sure.' Tilly frowned. 'Would anyone buy them?'

'You betcha. Marketplace. I sell everything on there, it's great. I even met a bloke that way once.'

'Like, romantically?'

Anita laughed. 'Don't know how much romance came into it.'

It was starting to get cool. Tilly eased herself to the branch beneath her, then leapt to the ground.

'There's a bunch of stuff still under the house,' she remarked. 'Books, mainly, a cricket bat, some old paintings and photos. Collectors could be into that?'

'Yeah, for sure. I love vintage stuff. Maybe I can have a look one day.' Anita brought up the plaid sleeve of her shirt and rubbed at her nose. 'Ever seen a typewriter down there?'

'Oh, um . . .' Tilly's mind wandered beneath the house and to that bench where she had left the typewriter under the tarpaulin. The faint glimmer of the keys, the outline of the chrome lettering that spelled *Royal*. 'I'm not sure,' she murmured. 'I'd have to check.'

Anita stepped away from the fence, giving a shrug. She had pulled a beanie over her hair and she smelt sweetly of beer. From the street, the bats in the trees were going crazy.

'No worries.' She sighed. 'It was mine, originally. A birthday present about a million years ago. I think your mum may have forgotten to return it . . .' She gazed at Tilly, something shrewd and almost calculating in her expression; it made Tilly's spider senses tingle. 'But hey, if you find it, maybe then I can write the great novel too. Show Laura it's not so hard. What do you reckon?'

'Yeah, maybe.'

Tilly shoved her hands in her jeans pockets. Behind Anita, she could see a shadow at the back door, the glow of a cigarette end. Then the figure stepped into the flush of the security light. It was Ava, from school, scowling across the yard.

'Mum?' she called. 'Come on. I'm hungry.'

Tilly stared back, a hot flush creeping up her throat. Ava held her eye, then tossed her cigarette on the paver and ground it out with her boot. So far Tilly had not had much to do with Ava. She moved among a circle of girls that seemed older and harder than others in their grade, wearing eyeliner, Doc Martens and black nail polish. They weren't Goths as such—Tilly had known a few of them back home—but they did keep themselves distant from everyone else, hanging about by the gates at recess and smoking at the back of the bike shed during lunch. In French,

Tilly sat behind Ava, and the other girl always had a wireless earbud hidden beneath her long dark hair.

'There in a sec, love,' Anita called over her shoulder, then turned back to Tilly. 'You know, I used to be jealous of your mum's house,' she said in a low voice. 'All those books, and Bruce and Eliza being so clever. I suppose that's where Laura got it from, the writing.' Her face creased with a sad sort of smile. 'We used to make up stories together. Me and your mum. Did she ever tell you that? During the summer holidays. We'd punch out a few pages together on my old typewriter. They were good, too, as I recall. Spooky. There was one, still gives me chills thinking about it. "The Package", we called it. About a girl who keeps getting books delivered to her front doorstep. She doesn't know where they keep coming from, and finally she goes off her head.' Anita laughed. 'Symbolic much? The mad genius and all that.'

Tilly studied Anita's scuffed work boots and sturdy calves. She didn't understand this idea about writers. She had met some of her mother's boring author friends—they didn't seem to know how to talk about anything other than themselves. It was for this reason, perhaps, that she found it difficult to imagine Laura writing a story with Anita; they seemed to be activated by different energy forces.

'What kind of job do you have?' she asked Anita.

'Local council. Special projects. Heritage, environment, culture. It's just part-time, but I'm always working on something new. Your grandmother helped with a local history project last year; she knew how to do the research, work the library, access archives.' Anita smiled again, faintly. 'The truth is I couldn't have done it without her.'

Tilly wondered what Anita saw as she studied her in the gloom. A reflection of Laura, or Eliza—or an unsettling amalgam of the two? Maybe neither. Ava didn't look much like her mother, despite their shared swarthiness. Anita was too bronzed, too healthy-looking. If Ava was her mother's reflection, Tilly thought, watching the girl stalk back inside the house, it was a wraithish one, like the outline of a discontented soul projected to a screen. She returned her attention to Anita.

'Did you know my grandparents well? It's weird, but after everything that happened, I still know so little about their lives in Brisbane.'

Anita did not seem surprised by this admission.

'Your mum doesn't talk about them much, hey? Yes, we were close. Me and Lize, especially. They both were good sorts, I can tell you that. Intelligent people, but not snobs about it, you know? They always had time for a chat. Your grandpa used to dress up as Santa for the annual street party and hand out the pressies. They were respected in the neighbourhood.'

Tilly smiled. She would have liked to see Bruce in that suit. Her other grandparents back in Cheltenham were always bah-humbug about Christmas, and stingy with their gifts. It was a good year if Tilly got more than a card with a ten-pound note taped inside.

'It's a shame you never got to spend a Christmas with them,' Anita murmured. 'But that's the price you pay for living so far apart, right?'

Tilly shrugged. 'I guess,' she said.

Now cold, Tilly zipped up her hoodie. She could feel the presence of the house at her back, and all that cavernous, empty space, until a light went on in the kitchen, throwing a pale beacon across the dusty lawn. Tilly stepped away from the fence, wincing at her unguarded talk with Anita; for being disloyal to her mother, of whom she had always been so proud. She swiped angrily at her nose with her sleeve, all of sudden wanting to cry.

Anita continued to watch her with a level expression and ran a breezy hand through her hair.

'But hey,' she said. 'Ask your mum about that typewriter, yeah? And "The Package".' Anita winked. 'She'll remember it, I know she will. A copy of it is probably still floating around somewhere under the house.'

But Tilly didn't ask Laura about the typewriter, or the short story. In fact she hardly saw her mother for the rest of the week. Laura spent all her spare time shut away in the study, and when she did emerge it was often with a shifty, distracted expression, her eyes darting over Tilly's face like she was trying to read something indecipherable on it. Andrew didn't seem to notice, but then he was consumed with the renovations. Tilly didn't understand how they could all exist alongside one another and yet so much remained unsaid.

School continued. The routine grew familiar. Long, hot days inside the classroom, half of which had no air-conditioning. Tilly began to wonder how any real work could be done: by the afternoon she was dazed from the heat, barely managing to drag herself back home from the bus. The swimming carnival had been and gone, with Tilly placing a respectable fourth in her backstroke event, and her relay team came second. During the events Ava sat in the bleachers with a couple of other girls. She hadn't changed out of her school uniform, earphones still in, though every now and then when Tilly caught her eye from the side of the pool, Ava seemed to smirk.

One afternoon Tilly and Andrew wandered down to Rosalie Village. It was a small T-intersection strip made up of Thai restaurants and a burrito joint, a bottle shop, a few cafes, an optometrist, a florist and a tiny supermarket. The footpath was cluttered with titanium-frame bikes locked to signposts and supervised by stern, Lycra-clad men drinking coffee in tall glasses on their weekend ride.

After buying some ingredients from the delicatessen, Tilly and Andrew stopped at an ice-cream shop where they sat at the plastic table and chairs on the pavement and watched the street. A few cars drove by, SUVs parked alongside the kerb. Andrew's face was very red as he sucked on his sparkling mineral water. Tilly thought about her mother lying beneath her linen bedsheet back at the house, the lazy circles of the ceiling fan beating out a steady rhythm as she had a nap.

'Do you think Mum's okay?' she asked.

Andrew shooed away a fly.

'How do you mean?'

'Like, in herself.'

'I think so, pet, yeah.'

Tilly stared at her iced chocolate. The cream had melted into the ice-cream, turning the milk viscous.

'I feel like I hardly talk to her these days. She seems so . . . distracted.'

'She's busy, that's all. There's been a lot to organise with your grandparents' affairs.'

'Yeah, I get that.' Tilly blew out her cheeks. 'But it must be so weird for her, living in the house where she grew up with Grandma and Grandpa. Them being gone. It must do something—to your state of mind, I mean.'

Andrew leaned forward, planting his elbows on the wobbly table. He looked tired; there were new lines under his eyes, and his lips were chafed from the heat.

'Listen, Tilly,' he said. 'You've got to remember we're only here until December. It's hardly any time at all. Once we're back in England, life will resume as normal.'

'Will it?'

'Of course. This is an adventure that most kids would dream of. Living in another country, day after day of sunshine!'

'That's not what I mean. Mum's changed and—'

Andrew let out a loud sigh. 'Your mum is sad, that's all. It came as a shock for all of us. It takes time—to grieve. I know it's difficult seeing her like this, with the stuffing knocked out of her, but it's our job to be patient.' He sat back, rubbing at the end of his nose. The bottom of his short sideburns, which had started to grey, were damp. 'What your mum needs is some rest and a bit of space. Everything else will get better from there. I want you to be a little more grown-up. Do you think you can do that?'

Tilly folded her arms and looked away. *He's project-managing Mum*, she realised. *He's project-managing us both, and just running down the bloody clock until he can sell up and we can all go home again. It's his only setting. What would happen if real catastrophe struck?* Tilly pushed away her milky drink.

Never had she seen in such stark light the limits of her father's capabilities. It made her queasy with disappointment.

'I spoke to Anita, you know,' she continued, now spoiling for a fight. 'The other night. She told me stuff. About Grandma and Grandpa.'

A bus grumbled by, billowing out a great hot cloud of grit. Andrew squinted back at her, blotting the sweat on his forehead with a serviette.

'That woman's a troublemaker.'

'She hardly seems—'

'You stay away from her, you hear me?'

The viciousness in Andrew's voice made the hair on Tilly's arms stand on end. He had never spoken to her like that—his unflappable nature rarely faltered.

'Okay,' she said quietly. 'Understood.'

They dawdled home, Tilly careful to hang back a few paces behind, still smarting. Some kids on bikes streamed past, a couple of Ubers, a maroon bus called CityGlider. Andrew paused at a real estate agents' display window, tapping on the glass and making noises of wonder. 'The prices,' he hissed in Tilly's direction. 'They've lost the plot, these Australians, they really have. No house should ever cost *this* much!'

On the corner Tilly stopped at the op shop. It looked like a regular worker's cottage from the outside, with two large framed windows overlooking the pavement. Tilly peered in at the display of crockery, the suede brogues, the leather satchel. She glimpsed a counter, and a man with wispy white hair standing behind it.

'Dad,' she called. 'Won't be a second.' She didn't wait for his reply.

Tilly pushed open the heavy door, a bell chiming above her. The man looked up from the magazine he had been flicking through and gave Tilly a tight smile. His plastic name tag read 'Clive'. Bay City Rollers played from the record player.

Tilly wandered through each room, fingertips brushing over the racks of corduroy jackets, tatty paperbacks, Kenny Rogers cassettes. The floorboards creaked beneath her feet. The store smelt of old coffee grounds. She stopped in the alcove near the front to study the dolls perched on a stand. There were a few Cabbage Patch kids, a Winnie the Pooh and, extraordinarily, a golliwog, *something you'd never see back home*, thought Tilly, glancing about with nervous incredulity.

'After something in particular?' Clive had closed his magazine to watch Tilly with greater attention. Perhaps he thought she might shoplift.

'Just looking, thanks.'

She wanted to find something for Laura. Something to cheer her up, to bring back some of her old humour. The shop was unbelievably hot: Tilly's T-shirt clung to her back. The music warped on the turntable, the needle working its way over a scratch on the record.

Tilly was about to head back out the door when she spotted the row of framed paintings hanging on the wall behind the cash register. They were mainly watercolours. The Bungle Bungle Range, the Opera House, a gritty lane somewhere. But on the end of the row was a black-and-white photograph of a house—a Queenslander, just like her grandparents'. Tilly took a step nearer, craning her neck.

'Excuse me. Could I see that one please?'

With a sigh, Clive trudged out from behind the counter. He disappeared into an alcove, returning with a small stepladder. It seemed to require astonishing effort to hoist himself up the two steps, grunting and muttering as he performed this activity.

'This one?' He tapped on the glass.

'Yep.'

He passed it down to Tilly before commencing his strenuous descent. She clasped the frame in her hands, which now felt numb with cold. The song playing on the record player skipped, stuck on the eerie loop of '*Sha La La La*'. Tilly took a deep breath, her heart thudding as she examined the photograph. *Was* it her grandparents' house? Everything about the house looked the same. The balcony, the frosted-glass panelling, the concrete drive, even the enormous boulder next to the letterbox. Tilly had no idea when the photograph had been taken, but as she turned over the frame she saw the scribble *Laura Townsend* in black marker.

'No way,' she breathed.

Tilly felt a tremor in her hands, a thrill deep in her gut. She looked up and met Clive's gaze across the counter.

'How much?' she asked.

They arrived back late to Central Avenue, tacky with sweat. Along the street, the nesting bats in the fig trees chittered. Laura emerged from the study to greet them. Her hair was damp from the shower. She had changed into a cotton dress and sandals.

'Ooh,' she said pleasantly. 'What have you got there?' She pointed to the package wrapped in old newspapers under Tilly's arm.

'It's a present,' she explained as the three of them sat together on the sofa, before immediately springing to her feet again. Tilly could barely contain her excitement. The occasion felt weighty, significant, as though she were about to bestow upon Laura a family heirloom previously mislaid for generations.

'For me?'

'It's something that once belonged to you,' Tilly said as Laura began tearing away the sticky tape. 'I thought you might like it back.'

As soon as Laura glimpsed the granular monochrome, her face went still with curious recognition, her cheeks colouring.

'*Ta-da!*' Tilly performed a magician's flourish and bowed as the last of the wrapping fell away. She pointed to the back of the frame where Laura's signature had been scribbled at the bottom. 'It's you, isn't it, Mum? This is your photo?'

'Yes, it's mine.' Laura swallowed, her eyes shining. 'Where on earth did you find it?'

Tilly clasped her hands together. This wasn't quite the reaction she had been hoping for.

'At that charity shop at the bottom of the hill,' she said. 'Weird coincidence, hey?'

'Yes,' Laura agreed. Her voice had risen to a flaky pitch. 'I gave this to Mum and Dad when I was about your age. A Christmas present, if I remember right. They must have got rid of it.' She tried to smile but her mouth sagged in a strange wobble. Tilly clenched her hands tighter, battling her own emotion. She didn't understand. Why wasn't Laura happy?'

'Well, I think it's a real find,' Andrew said, admiring the frame. 'I mean, what are the chances?'

'Hm,' was all Laura said.

Tilly watched her father frown, though he pushed on regardless, giving Laura a tap on the thigh as he rose to his feet.

'Right!' he cried. 'Let's get this chap up before I order some dinner.'

'Oh, are you sure?' Laura stood up too. 'I mean . . .'

'Come on,' Andrew said, already halfway across the room, holding the frame aloft. 'A beauty like this should be restored to its rightful place.'

Tilly followed her mother's gaze, which idled on the photograph. Cocos palms loomed large to the right of the shot, skimming a long, thick shadow across the deck, while Laura's bike leaned against the banister beneath the carport. The pink frosted-glass windows of the master bedroom had been edged open.

Andrew found a spot on the wall beside the piano where a picture hook was still lodged in the timber. Tilly and Laura joined him, standing together by the stool. Laura remained agitated, biting at the corner of her thumbnail. After some shouted instructions and to-and-fro, Andrew finally loaded up the frame and managed to hang it straight on the twine. The photograph projected an austere, imposing impression, its scope distorted against the blank, white wall.

Stepping away to admire his handiwork, Andrew declared, 'Not bad.'

Laura folded her arms. Standing at her side, Tilly could sense the heat radiating from her bare shoulders. She peered closer at the frame, having noticed a whitish smear on the print on the corner beneath the front bedroom window where the photograph had been overexposed. *That's odd*, she thought. *I don't remember seeing that in the shop.* Tilly waited for Laura to say something, but after a while her mother gave only a loud sigh and walked away towards the kitchen. Tilly dropped her head, her eyes blurring.

Across the living room, Andrew gave an encouraging smile.

'It was a nice thought,' he said. And then, frowning slightly as he turned back to the frame, 'But it is strange that it ended up in that old shop, isn't it?'

9.

THEY ARRIVED RIGHT on seven o'clock, with Meredith crying '*Yoo hoo*' from the deck, her husband Graeme in tow. She didn't wait to be invited inside; as Laura emerged from the kitchen she saw Meredith yank open the front door and charge into the house. They had brought wine. Two bottles of Josmeyer pinot gris, which Meredith thrust into Andrew's hands—'I'd get them straight in the freezer, Andy, we want them *crisp*.' Then she turned in a circle, taking in the living room, its ceiling rose, the long stretch of hoop pine flooring, the timber screen hinting at the small kitchen. 'Well, isn't this just lovely.' She sighed. 'The place really breathes.'

What she meant was, the house was sparse; they had very little furniture. Laura could see that; Meredith's presence, large and inundating as it was, made the absence all the more conspicuous.

She took them on a tour of the house, pointing out the areas for proposed renovation. Meredith and Graeme made all the right noises. Tilly slunk out of her room for introductions, and submitted to Meredith's gushing ('Isn't she the spit of you, Lore!'). After that, they talked about Paddington, how it had changed in recent years, and the skyrocketing property prices across all of Brisbane. ('It's Melbourne and Sydney buyers!' Meredith exclaimed with glee. 'You can't get a place for less than a million and a half anywhere these days. Anywhere half-decent, that is.') Andrew offered to take Graeme out into the yard to more closely inspect the renovations, leaving Laura and Meredith by the windows in the annex. Meredith watched them, her face settled into something like calm, then gave a toothy smile. Her lips were fatter than Laura remembered. She must have had work done.

'Show them a digger and they're like small boys again.' Meredith tapped a lacquered hand against the glass. 'Next they'll be playing in the sandpit.'

Laura glanced towards Graeme, who was gripping the ladder as he peered up at the extension, his other hand pressed against his lower back, his wrinkled face caught in a grimace. He didn't look all that boyish to her. But he seemed a gentle, obliging man, someone who would accommodate Meredith's energetic demands.

'Now tell me, Lore. How are you holding up since the memorial?'

Turning from the window, Laura was met with a hungry expression, one that made no attempt to conceal Meredith's true motivations for coming to dinner: to study Laura and assuage some sordid curiosity. It was no surprise—Laura had always known the limits of their friendship. But what could she say that would possibly contain the feelings of the past few months? Laura didn't understand them herself.

'Oh, you know,' she replied. 'Soldiering on, like you have to.'

The house stood silent around them, a cool presence rising from the tiles beneath Laura's bare feet. At her back, she felt the beat of the sparse annex, empty except for a wooden table with a wilting succulent in the corner, and she gripped her hands together, fighting at a surge of fresh, startling emotion. For a moment she seemed to hold it at bay, but when she saw how Meredith peered at her with such genuine concern Laura could not stop the small, pathetic whimper escaping her.

'I don't—'

Meredith held up a ringed finger. Then she pulled Laura to her bust and held her there, murmuring and stroking her hair.

'Oh, Laura. Poor Laura.'

Her voice was quiet, almost tender, and Laura allowed herself to give in and sag against Meredith, cushioned by her enormous breasts. Being held and fussed over was exquisite. Laura could not remember ever being coddled like this, and longed for the feeling to stretch on. But after a moment Meredith shifted her stance, forcing Laura to step away, and the luxury of their union was gone.

'Do you know what I did when my mum died?' said Meredith, her bright eyes avoiding Laura's in favour of the backyard. 'I got my townhouse repainted. Remember the place on Hampstead Road? Well, the day after the funeral, I flew back to Brisbane and went straight to Mitre 10 around the corner. I bought what I needed, and then I went home and painted around the clock for three days straight. I guess I just needed everything to be clean and clear and empty to move on . . . But look at me,' she complained, wiping a fingertip beneath her eye. 'You've made my mascara run.' With a temperamental scowl, Meredith turned back to the men in the garden.

Laura could hardly remember when Meredith's mother died. She had been ill for many years, Laura managed to recall that, along with the certain inevitability to her death, an attitude that now seemed callous. Meredith had been young, barely into her twenties. It was an incredible loss, and Laura felt a sting of shame for having not made more of an effort to talk with her about it, to have not offered more support. But Meredith had never been one to interrogate feelings, and if she had not been hardened before, Laura mused, a glossy shell had certainly grown around her since her mother's death, deflecting sentimentality, corroding weakness. Perhaps that is how some people managed to survive.

The twins had been left with the au pair back in Hawthorne—'I'm too old for toddler-wrangling!' Meredith screeched. At first Laura was disappointed at their absence. One less thing to talk about over dinner. But Meredith had no trouble making conversation. Once the men had returned from the garden, it was one long stream of dialogue: about the house and the renovations, about her house, about work at the firm, and then the dilemma of where the twins would attend primary school. She kept stealing sly glances at Laura as she scooped kamaboko dip onto a carrot or poured more wine, waiting for an opening to the real discussion she wanted to resume. But when it became clear one wouldn't present itself, Meredith simply launched back, apropos of nothing, into the story of Laura's parents herself.

'It was a big deal here,' she said. 'Wasn't it, Graeme? A very big story.'

'It was,' Graeme confirmed. 'All over the TV news. Papers, radio.'

'Mm.' Laura tried to chew on a dry cracker. 'We have been told. It sounded horrible.'

'I even had a call from some journalist digging about, did I tell you?' Meredith shook her mane of dark hair. 'Trying to get the dirt on the family, on you. But what could I tell them?' She laughed.

Laura sipped at her wine. She didn't want to talk about any of this tonight. She had hoped for some easy reminiscing with Meredith, journeying back to her younger, carefree university days. From across the table, she was aware of the sceptical gaze of Tilly, and Laura realised that in organising this dinner she had wanted to show off this past to her daughter. It seemed pathetic, really. But lately Laura had felt so rigid, as if recent events had remoulded her into a new and unalterable version of herself, and that, surely, had been part of the reason she had grown so distant from Tilly. *Here!* she wanted to shout. *Look! I used to be fun.*

'Well, the press worked themselves up about nothing in the end,' said Andrew. 'Well, not *nothing*,' he added with a grimace. 'But nothing sinister. The coroner made her determinations. Death by natural causes. Case closed.'

Meredith nodded sympathetically, and turned to Laura.

'But you never discovered why they went out there? I mean, it was so strange, wasn't it? Driving all that way for no apparent reason.'

The candlelight for a moment dipped, as if battling against a sudden breeze, their shadows elongating across the tablecloth. Laura toyed with her fork. She didn't know what to say. She didn't want to reveal to Meredith that she still didn't know the answer herself.

'I think they just wanted to get away,' she finally said. 'They had become interested in the landscape of the desert, the history. That kind of thing.'

'Strange place for a holiday,' Meredith remarked.

Laura frowned. 'Yes, it was. But the police didn't think much of it in the end. They put it down to some fit of eccentricity . . .'

She trailed off, staring at the photograph of the house hanging on the wall behind Meredith. A cool feeling rattled down her spine, fingers over piano keys. She wished she had arranged the seating at the table differently—she didn't want to spend all night staring at that damned thing. As soon as Laura had peeled away the wrapping paper she had known it was her print; as familiar to her as her own face in the mirror.

Laura had taken a photography subject at school, using the Minolta her parents had given her one birthday. She had spent several afternoons on the nature strip, waiting for the light to strike the front windows, creating that glowing effect in the air that she had never seen elsewhere. And she had spent even longer in the darkroom, developing and re-developing the negatives.

It had been a fine photograph—Mrs Hughes had said so. The house appeared humble and grand; aged and contemporary. A timeless Brisbane afternoon caught in black and white. Her father had agreed. 'Very good work, Laura,' he said as he admired the frame. 'You've captured the spirit of the house perfectly.'

But when it had been Eliza's turn to view her present she had flinched away from it, only to ask in a troubled voice, 'What's this?' Examining the photograph, Laura had seen what looked like a smudge in the corner of the front bedroom window in the shape of a person, a woman in fact, and above it was a whitish smear as though the print had been overexposed.

'I . . . don't know,' she stammered. 'But it shouldn't be there.'

'You can see it too? See *her*?'

Laura had pinched up the corner of her sleeve, rubbing at the glass. It wouldn't lift.

'Of course I can!' She had snatched away the frame, glaring at the blemish. 'Something must have gone wrong with the inks or the processing. Or got inside, under the glass . . .'

'What are you two on about?' said Bruce, peering over the top of his specs. 'I can't see a thing wrong with it.'

Laura sat back, close to tears. Her mother had been staring at her, an odd, wary look in her eyes, although when Eliza studied the photograph once more she announced in a brighter voice, 'You know what? Dad's right. I'm sorry. It must have just been a mark on the glass because it's gone. See?' And when Laura bent over the frame again she saw that the smudge had indeed disappeared.

The controversy was not mentioned again, and soon after her parents had begun to cook the Christmas lunch. The photograph, however, was never hung in the house. Laura always assumed it was because her mother didn't like it, yet even a book she didn't care for sat on the shelf. And now, all these years later, the scene had been repeated, with Tilly standing before Laura, waiting for some recognition of the serendipity, some gratitude even, her eyes growing wider, her shoulders dropping in confusion. Laura had felt a piece of her heart shrivel. How could she explain that she was thinking of her own mother's anguished face as Eliza had first laid eyes on the print?

'And the probate—that's clearly gone off without a hitch,' Graeme said, drawing Laura's attention back to her guests. 'Who did that work for you?'

She pictured the shimmering office tower, the serpentine curve of brown river.

'Brad Agnew.'

'Oh yes, everyone knows Brad,' said Meredith. 'Nice man. His firm did Graeme's mother's estate. That wasn't easy, let me tell you, with four squabbling sisters and their offspring. A word of warning, Tilly. You know who your real allies are when a couple of million's on the table.'

Tilly blinked back at her. 'I guess it's lucky I'm an only child,' she said.

Meredith glanced at Laura, then burst out laughing. 'Oh, I like her. Very dry, like you, Lore.' She leaned towards Tilly and tapped at the tabletop. 'Now tell me, young lady. How do you find our Australia?'

Tilly shrugged. 'It's okay.'

'*Okay*? I would have killed to be a Brissy girl at your age!'

'Really? Why?'

'Well, I grew up in Townsville, which made Brisbane a beacon in the tropics, like London or Tokyo! Mind you, my scope of what constituted lively was small back then.'

Tilly studied Meredith. 'And now?'

There was, Laura was disturbed to recognise, some amusement in her daughter's eyes.

'Well, I'm still here, aren't I? Haven't left since I was at university with your mum.'

Tilly turned to Graeme. 'What about you?'

'Oh, don't ask Graeme!' said Meredith.

'Why not? Weren't you a kid here either?'

'I was,' said Graeme in a serious tone. 'About a hundred years ago!'

'Before the internet,' quipped Andrew.

'Before electricity, more like!' Meredith squawked. 'Graeme is very decrepit.'

'I am,' Graeme agreed. Some parsley had caught between his front teeth. 'But I had a terrific childhood in West End.'

'It was a slum back in those days,' Meredith apprised the table. 'You wouldn't want to be caught dead there.'

'It has changed in recent years, that is certainly true,' said Graeme. 'Then again, everything does and—'

'Of course, you couldn't live there now if you wanted to,' Meredith interrupted. 'Graeme's mother's old dump in Drury Street. Flooded twice. Mould everywhere. Only two bedrooms. Tiny yard. Not an ounce of charm to it. Sold for over two and a half million last year. Can you believe it?' She pointed a finger at her husband. 'I told you we should have held on to it. Your sisters should never have got their way.'

Graeme stared at his wineglass, eyes rheumy.

'I have a lot of fond memories of that house.'

'Not me.' Meredith shuddered. 'I can't say I miss Sunday afternoons at Una's with Graeme's ghastly family. I'm telling you, you really get the measure of someone when a house is at stake. The white-anting, the manipulation, the threats. You'd have thought you were in an episode of *The Traitors*. It taps into something savage in people.'

'Blimey,' Andrew said.

'It has been unpleasant,' Graeme agreed, looking wistful. Meredith reached out and patted his wrinkled hand. Tilly glanced between them, and sank back in her chair.

'People in Australia are obsessed with houses,' she muttered. 'I don't get it.'

Meredith pursed her lips. 'Well, you don't need to, sweetie. Your parents have made good choices, and now they're going to improve this house to make a greater return when it's sold. I imagine you will benefit from that.'

'How?'

'Because generally the children benefit from the prosperity of their parents. It's called inherited wealth.'

'Sure. But what about all those people who don't own houses?' Tilly continued. 'What can they pass on to their children?'

Meredith smiled tightly. 'That depends on the parents themselves. My mum and dad, they didn't have much, but they did teach me if I wanted something I would need to work hard for it. I was young when I decided I wanted my own place, maybe twelve or thirteen years old. I worked part-time jobs as soon as I could, and bought my first property when I was twenty-one. That's how I've got on in life.'

Laura could see Tilly was not satisfied. She set down her fork with a clatter, and when she raised her eyes, Laura saw something imperious in her expression, which made Laura feel both proud as well as afraid of what her daughter might say next.

'But if everything is so expensive now, how can people afford to buy a house in the first place? They could work hard like you did and still not have nearly enough.'

Meredith sighed. 'I see you've raised a socialist, Laura,' she said. 'Though you always were a little left of centre. I guess that comes of having an academic for a parent.'

'And growing up under Joh,' said Laura, folding her arms. 'What's your excuse?'

'Army brat, of course!' Meredith crowed. 'Blue, blue, blue.'

'All kids are socialists,' Graeme said cheerfully. 'I probably was myself at Tilly's age. You must have something to be angry about.'

'I'm not angry,' Tilly said mildly. 'It's just what I've noticed.'

'Well, isn't it the same in Britain?' Meredith protested. 'Come on! Class is way more entrenched in your society than ours. Look at how you lose your minds over the royal family.'

'Maybe,' said Andrew. 'But I think the conversation about it is a little different.'

'Oh give me a break, Andrew!'

'Well . . .' Andrew wasn't going to quibble; he didn't care enough about politics to stake a claim for any position. 'I certainly can't complain about the hand life has dealt me.'

'You make it sound like you had no say in the matter. Like you didn't work for it.'

'That's not what I mean—'

'I'll tell you what I think,' Meredith went on loudly. 'I think everyone wants something for nothing these days, and there is always someone else to blame when they don't get it. Now, don't get me wrong, I didn't like the last government any more than the next guy. I mean, everything they did wrong on women, on integrity, on the environment. Appalling. Unforgivable. But they got one thing right: hard graft pulls you up in this country, it always has done. That's success—what it boils down to. That is the truth.'

Laura stared tiredly at the tablecloth flecked with pasta sauce. She was ashamed of the conversation, and ashamed of Meredith's venal nature. She wished that she had never invited her old friend over to the house. But she was angry at Tilly too, smirking and slouching there as if she had proven some oblique point. Laura had the sudden urge to reach over the plates and slap her across the face.

Oddly, Tilly must have detected her anger because she twisted in her seat and pulled out her phone, and the insolence of the gesture made her look like a small child again, like that toddler who never slept. Hour after hour of crying. Refusing to let Laura leave the room, making herself almost ill with hysteria if she did. And that period of time, which had been in reality only a few months but felt like years, when Tilly would only fall asleep if Laura held her. Some nights, when she managed to keep her rage and exhaustion at bay, Laura relented, crying her own silent tears as Tilly's weight finally grew heavy in her arms. Her innocence was unbearable. But other times Laura sensed her fragile hold of her temper loosen, and her anger lashed out, wild and unbridled, like Scylla. She would push Tilly down on her mattress and menace over her in the dark, pulling ghoulish contorted faces, hoping to frighten her into submission. Hoping to scare her to sleep. It only happened once or twice, but Laura loathed herself for days afterwards, shuddering at her dreadfulness. She doubted Tilly would even remember it, but it had snared in Laura's mind like an insect in a spider's web. What she was capable of.

Meredith poured more wine. She was already tipsy, on her way to being drunk. This could have been a prelude to one of her parties at Highgate Hill, thought Laura, recalling the sloppy dancing, Meredith grinding up against some boy in the backyard, the vomit and the tears, and how the next morning Meredith would always make her guests breakfast, with no trace of a hangover.

Meanwhile, darkness pressed against the windows. The night fell fast in Brisbane; dusk never lingered. A halo of orange candlelight hung above the dining table, giving the impression they were bobbing about on a treacherous sea.

When Andrew finally offered to make coffee, Laura was relieved. It meant the evening would soon be over. All that talk about her parents, and the renovations, had left Laura wired. She brought out the dessert from the kitchen—chocolate molten babycakes from Nigella Lawson's website and a bowl of whipped cream—and watched the others demolish it. Afterwards Andrew, by now quite drunk himself, poured everyone amaros while staggering back and forth from the drinks cabinet.

'Has Laura told you about our problem with the neighbour?' he called.

Meredith narrowed her eyes at Laura with revived interest. 'What's going on?'

Laura pressed her fingertips against her temple, nudging at the pulse. *Don't*, she wanted to say, and almost did, except she was aware of Tilly watching, her scrutinous gaze like a peeler over Laura's skin.

'It's nothing,' she said. 'Just a misunderstanding with Anita from next door.'

'How so?'

Laura looked towards Andrew, dismayed. Couldn't he change the subject?

'Anita's been making a nuisance of herself, that's all. Contacting Brad. Telling him all sorts of silly things about my parents.'

'She *what*?' Meredith took an indignant swig of her digestif. 'What exactly has she been saying?'

'She told the lawyers Eliza and Bruce intended the house to go to her "community centre",' replied Andrew, making air quotes. 'A donation. It would mean the centre could relocate and expand.'

'The cheeky bitch.'

'But what about your parents' will?' Graeme inquired more soberly. 'Did they indicate any of this?'

'Well, no. But there was a letter, from my mother, to Anita . . . And Brad did say my parents were thinking about changing their wills. They had scheduled an appointment before they died. So you can see my problem.'

Laura reached for her amaro and took a small sip. From the corner of her eye, she noticed at the kitchen's bifold windows what looked like a shadow passing behind the frosted glass. Soft light projected across the living room floor. It was pointless talking about any of it: she would never get Meredith to see the complexity of the situation, or the complexity of Anita, who Meredith had met several times when they were younger but clearly did not remember. Her loyalty was the dogged variety, hard-edged and uncompromising.

'I don't see any problem,' Graeme was saying. 'Except your neighbour thinks she can take you for a ride.'

'What a grasping, insensitive cow!' Meredith hissed. 'Imagine, after all you've gone through, for her to turn around and do this.' She signalled to Graeme. 'We should put her in touch with Lynnette. They sound like kindred spirits.'

'It's not like that . . .'

Laura waited for Andrew's intervention, but he just sat there with arms folded, a silly grin on his red face, and this demeanour stunned Laura for a moment, fixing her to her seat. The feeling reminded her of that night in the Swinbrook house, when she first received news about her parents, and how she had believed she could absorb all that pain like an enormous sponge. What had she been thinking? It was almost laughable how wrong she had been. At last she recognised how vastly her atomic properties had transformed, hardening her so profoundly that when an entity as powerful and compact as grief had come at velocity, the shock of its impact had been catastrophic.

Laura felt the full force of this as she clutched her amaro glass. She hadn't held together but splintered, and all that had been left behind was dust and debris flittering about the disaster zone.

Eventually Laura stood up and began to clear away the plates, hardly hearing Meredith's new loud and obnoxious story about some work colleague and a sexual harassment suit. After stacking the dishwasher, Laura washed her hands at the kitchen sink, gazing as she did through the window. In the yard, the poinciana was still; there was no wind tonight. The moon was a cuticle, hanging low. Laura stared at her strange, tired reflection, waiting for some shadowy contour to rise up behind her. But nothing materialised. She was alone.

She flicked on the kettle and brought down the mugs from the shelf. It had been a ritual all those years ago for Laura to make the first cup of tea for her parents before school. As a family, they drank gallons of the stuff. And so, every day, year after year, as habitual as breathing, Laura performed this task. 'Don't forget me,' her mother used to say each morning, coming up behind her. She would then rest her hands on Laura's shoulders before bending down to kiss her cheek, as quick as a bird, and make them both laugh.

Laura closed her eyes, summoning that entreaty, and for a moment there was an undeniable press of cool fingertips against her shirt. She stood like that, encased in an unlikely calm. Then came Meredith's laugh from the living room, a high grating sound transported direct to the kitchen, and the feeling vanished. Laura poured the boiled water into the mugs. When she glanced back to the window, Laura was aware of a hollow sensation, as though she were being pulled towards the night on the other side, towards the tree and a place that enabled a dark communion with the house.

10.

TILLY WALKED BACK from the bus stop a few metres ahead of Ava. They had started work together on a joint history project. Ava liked Tilly's idea about the Toowong Cemetery—or, at least, she had consented to it with a sullen shrug. Ava rarely took notes in class or showed much interest in what they were learning, so Tilly knew she would be doing the bulk of the research. She didn't mind. Something about being in Ava's proximity thrilled her; there was an undercurrent of danger and volatility to the girl, a bit like what Tilly imagined handling a nerve agent inside a glass bottle would feel like.

'Hey,' said Ava, now sidling up beside Tilly. 'How gross was the bus just now. Mitchell *stinks*!'

'Totally,' Tilly agreed. She longed for a shower, to wash the day away. 'I wish they'd let us put the windows down.'

'Health and safety.' Ava swung her arms as they strolled along the footpath. 'You know our mums were friends back in the day. They probably walked home together like this too.'

'Yeah, it's freaky, isn't it?' Tilly tried to keep her voice casual. 'I can't imagine my mum as a teenager.'

Ava rolled her eyes. 'That's a good thing, trust me. Most of the time my mum acts like the kid and I'm the adult.'

Tilly glanced at Ava, taking in her deep frown and smudged eyes. She didn't know how to calibrate her conversations with the girl—when to be honest, when to play it cool. Ava was prickly about everything. They had paused to cross the road near the entrance to the creche. Ava pulled out a stick of gum and offered Tilly a piece. It was strawberry-flavoured, but after turning it over in her mouth a few times the taste disappeared.

'Does your mum have other friends in Brisbane?' Ava asked. 'Like, from when she lived here before?'

Tilly shrugged. 'One or two. No one comes over much. I don't think she wants other people in the house.'

'Huh.' Ava considered this. 'Is she weird? No offence, but she's a writer. They're all a bit weird, aren't they? Stuck inside their own heads?'

'She's not weird,' said Tilly, but it was not a convincing defence. She thought back to the awful dinner with Meredith and Graeme, and how towards the end of the night Laura had disappeared into the kitchen for what felt like ages, leaving Tilly trapped at the table, Meredith honking about interest rates and how much her weekly shop at Woolworths now cost, as though she couldn't afford it.

'Well, this thing with the house, with Lize and Bruce, *that*'s weird.' Ava chomped furiously at the gob of grey gum. 'I mean, it's even making my mum act strange, and she's usually pretty chill.'

'Yeah,' Tilly said unhappily. 'It's messed up.'

They had stopped outside the house. Tilly raised her wide-brimmed straw school hat to relieve the damp heat pinching at the back of her head; the days were still astonishingly warm. She sensed movement on the front deck and saw her mother shrink away from the balcony. How long had she been standing there?

'Do you miss them?' she heard Ava ask. 'Lize and Bruce, I mean.'

Tilly hoisted her backpack further up her shoulder. 'I didn't actually know them all that well.'

'Really?' Ava smiled, a gleam of white against her pink lips. She had very straight teeth, unlike Tilly's which protruded slightly on top. 'But they're family.'

Tilly stared at the fig tree, and the shadow it slung over the adjacent houses. The tree was old; probably already established in the middle of the street when her mother was a child. Something about that brought comfort to Tilly, a permanence to the hazy mirage of Central Avenue.

'Lots of people don't hang out with their relatives,' she said. 'They might live far away, or not get on, or be dead. I mean, what about your grandparents? Do you see them regularly.'

'Yeah, but I was always closest to my gran. Mum's mum.'

'What's she like?'

Ava hesitated, biting at her bottom lip. She had stepped nearer to share the shade, so close that Tilly could smell the Daisy Love clinging to her shirt collar.

'She died. About a year and a half ago.'

Tilly felt the blood rush to her cheeks.

'Oh. I'm sorry,' she said. 'That's really sad.'

Ava stared back, her expression inscrutable. A blast of humid air wafted up from the fetid drain by the kerb, and Ava crinkled her nose, dropping her eyes to the asphalt.

'Anyway, my mum keeps asking if you wanna come over,' she said quietly. 'For dinner one night, if you're free. She's going to cook her chicken parmis. We could finish the work on our project afterwards. Look up some pictures on that archive Ms Petrovic was talking about.'

Tilly wondered how her parents would react to this invitation. Anita was clearly a touchy subject, practically taboo. It was probably best not to say anything; she could just pop in next door and send a text saying she was out with friends in Rosalie Village.

'Sure, sounds nice,' she said.

A few bush turkeys lurched across the road and crashed into some foliage. The sky was darkening, rain clouds building up in enormous clusters in the west; it was wild how capricious the weather was here.

'I don't think I've had chicken parmis before. Is that an Australian thing?'

This, finally, elicited a toothy grin from Ava. She stepped away from the verge and teetered on the kerb, legs lean against her lace-up boots.

'Catch ya,' she said.

Tilly watched her skip ahead and duck beneath the low-hanging branch, her backpack rattling as she climbed the steps towards her front door. Tilly's own bag hung heavy on her shoulder, loaded up with textbooks for her weekend homework. She clumped up to the deck, glimpsing her mother in the hammock by the corner swinging idly from side to side, a book in her lap.

With a smirk, Laura pushed back her sunglasses. 'You've made a friend.'

She had deep, angry bruises beneath her eyes and dry, gnawed-at lips. She looked awful. Tilly pulled off her school shoes and tossed them on the rack at the door. 'She's not really a friend,' she said. 'We share some classes. We're doing a project together. History.'

Laura frowned at this, snapping her book shut.

'She looks like Anita. That same cocky, I-don't-give-a-fuck stride.'

Tilly turned away, swallowing thickly.

'Mum, you sound like a nutter,' she muttered.

'Yeah, well, her mum's a liar, so I'd take whatever she says with a pinch of salt.'

'What do you mean?'

But Laura wouldn't answer. She simply settled back in the hammock and resumed her reading.

After making herself a peanut butter sandwich and a Milo, Tilly went to her room and FaceTimed JoBeth from her laptop, hoping to catch her friend in England before she left for school. They spoke for a couple of minutes, JoBeth munching on a piece of toast as her mother drifted past in the background with the instruction to *hurry up, you'll miss the bus.*

'So, do you like it yet, Tils? Australia?'

'I don't know. Not really.'

JoBeth slurped some tea. 'Why not?'

Tilly gazed at JoBeth. She did not know how to begin to explain to her friend what was happening in the house. So much had changed in a few short months.

'It's my mum,' she said eventually. 'She's . . . different here, I guess. It's all a bit weird.'

'You're fighting? Oh, man. *Same.* My mum is driving me fucking mental right now. Do you know what she said when I got my nose pierced?'

Tilly let JoBeth rant, her own attention attracted to the square of light at her bedroom window, muttering, 'Yeah, what a bitch,' at intervals. Meanwhile, at the bottom of the screen, she could see JoBeth tapping away at the keyboard, probably chatting with others online. It dawned on Tilly that she may not be friends with JoBeth by the time she returned home—a likelihood that didn't much bother her. She thought about Ava's green eyes; her small, straight teeth. Tilly felt drawn to the other girl, though she didn't quite trust the instincts creating this magnetism.

Later that afternoon, when lightning flashed at the front windows and rain poured down the side path like a theme-park slide, Tilly wandered through to the back of the house to inspect the garden, standing at the oily-looking windows for a while, transfixed by the flow from the back fence triangulating around the poinciana. A mass of brown water was building against the glass, some leaking through the seal. From the living room, a news bulletin played on the television, the drenched presenter in a yellow anorak warning about dam levels and levees across south-east Queensland.

Fetching a towel from the bathroom, Tilly recalled the terrible floods from a couple of years ago. They had watched the reports about it on an evening BBC update. The aerial shots showed most of Brisbane's CBD underwater, while further out, on the plains south of the city, thousands of properties had been destroyed, only a few dwellings on stilts left bobbing about in a grey ocean.

'Are you going to call your folks?' Andrew had hollered to Laura from the couch. 'Check they're okay?'

Tilly had observed her mother in the kitchen, her face creased with worry. Laura picked up the cordless phone, stared at it, then put it down. For the first time, it had occurred to Tilly that her mother's emotional fortitude had limits. It was an unsettling realisation.

Eventually Laura had looked over to Tilly and smiled, an attempt at comfort. Tilly had seen that look before: it was the same expression her mother adopted whenever she had a migraine. She was struck down by them every few months and Tilly, alarmed at the incongruity of her energetic mother in bed in the middle of the day, liked to check on her, somehow getting it into her head that if she didn't Laura might die. Her mother always opened one bleary eye, squeezed Tilly's hand and croaked: 'Don't worry, darling. I'm not going anywhere.'

When she finally made her way to the living room, Laura had said, 'They'll be fine.' But there had been no hand-squeeze for Tilly, no further reassurance. Laura simply perched on the couch and stared at the television screen, as if her parents' safety would be confirmed by the news anchor.

The rain sleeted against the slick pavers of the patio. Tilly loved the rain back at home, cut-glassed and gritty as it was, often blasted in from the arctic, with fairy-tale names like the Beast from the East. She would often wander down to their stream after a storm and sift through the rubbish flattened against the old wooden footbridge: dead toads, a few small trout and shoes among the detritus. Once she found a filthy Paddington Bear, which she took back to the house and cleaned up, then stashed at the back of her wardrobe in case her mother found it.

The annex had grown humid. She could feel the sweat on her face and chest, and moved away from the windows to open the French doors. The rain was louder, with a deeper, reverberating bass, and she took in a long breath, feeling it at the back of her throat. It was still warm outside and the glass panels in the door soon fogged up. Surveying the soaked garden, her fringe dampening against her forehead, Tilly was about to close the door when she caught a flicker of movement in the corner of her eye.

It was Laura. She had come up the side path and was heading towards the poinciana. Her feet were bare. She threw a look behind her, in the direction of the annex, but she did not see

Tilly standing in the doorway. The rain continued to fall in warm, fat drops, and her mother was already drenched. When she reached the low-hanging canopy, Laura raised her face to the sky, and kept it turned that way, squinty-eyed. Tilly watched, aware of the skip in her own heartbeat, as her mother sprinted across the remaining lawn and grabbed at next door's fence, gaping into Anita Bilson's yard. Then she started yelling, her long arm flailing about.

Tilly stepped into the rain, her blood moving astonishingly fast through her veins. The air around her plumed, flushing a current simultaneously hot and cold, making her skin tingle.

'Mum?'

Her voice caught. What if Ava saw? Tilly imagined her recounting the scene with her friends the next day behind the school bike shed; she pictured the girls' disdain as they sucked on their cigarettes, the way their kohl-lined eyes would narrow in cruel mirth, their mouths forming into the shape of a single word: *Freak*.

'*Mum*!'

Laura gazed across the stretch of verdant grass, smearing hair from her eyes. It took her some time to focus on Tilly through the rain, and once she had she shook a wrist at her—a wave, or was it a dismissal? But her mother was wearing such a weird, vacant expression that, in another burst of fright, Tilly stormed across the patio and shouted, 'What are you *doing*?'

The rain was cold, soaking her in seconds. By now Laura had dropped down from the fence and had begun to walk back to the house. Tilly followed her, watching Laura head inside, grab a towel flung over a chair and begin to dry herself with the vigour of an iceberger. Spread across the tiles were the mud, grass clippings and leaves Laura had traipsed in.

'Mum?'

Laura paused her work.

'I wanted to bring in the washing,' she said, 'but it was already drenched. I'd forgotten how heavy the rain gets here. What's the matter?'

Tilly raised a hand to her mouth, afraid she might laugh. It was a deflection, feeble armour against the knowledge that something was terribly wrong. Suddenly Tilly's chest ached at the memory of the weight of Laura's hand in hers as she crouched beside the sickbed, her breath muggy against her mother's face. How easy it had been back then to ask if she was all right.

'I meant, what were you doing over there at the fence?'

Laura handed Tilly the towel; she hadn't registered the pool of rainwater at her own feet. She began to dry her legs, still waiting for her mother's reply, aware of how much she needed Laura to clarify her motives, to explain away her behaviour.

'I thought I saw something,' Laura finally said. 'Someone, actually. It was Denise Bilson. She was out there in the rain. I was trying to tell her to get back inside before she slipped over.'

Tilly finished drying herself. Her mother had her eyes on the back windows, gazing towards the poinciana. There were two vivid spots of colour in her cheeks.

'Who is Denise Bilson?' Tilly asked quietly.

'Oh, you know.' Laura bristled. '*Her* mother.' She made a thumb gesture towards next door.

'Anita's?'

'Mm.'

The rain had stopped and the windows overlooking the garden turned lustrous behind the fog. Andrew called out from the front deck. He wanted to show them the power line that had come down across the street. But Tilly did not reply. She was fixed to the chilly tiles.

She watched Laura march up the steps and across the floorboards towards the study. She only stopped once her hand was on the doorknob, her eyes finding Tilly's along the length of the house. She raised her other hand, pushing a finger against her lips, and in this action seemed to want to defer, or perhaps transfer, an explanation that shut down all the terrifying possibilities pinging through Tilly's brain. She waited for the osmosis, but none came. Laura entered the study and shut the door, leaving Tilly alone in the annex, locked in the knowledge that either her mother was lying, or she really had seen Ava's dead grandmother in the yard next door.

11.

'We've timed it well,' Andrew remarked. 'This project.'

It was late, nearly midnight. Tilly was asleep. Laura and Andrew had been looking over the designs as they lay in bed: the treated bamboo, the new garden deck, the separate set of stairs at the back leading to a new master bedroom, the lap pool running like a sleek culvert down the side of the house and feeding into a square-shaped basin built into the courtyard. Laura turned to face him.

'How's that?'

'The boom. Prices are off the charts. It's overtaken Sydney increases, I read today.'

'Oh yes?' She ran a hand distractedly over his arm. 'So what does that mean for us?'

Andrew slid down the pillows, pulling Laura with him. He kissed her tenderly.

'It means in a few short months we're going to make a packet!'

Once he had flicked off the lamp and began to gently snore, Laura stared up at the white ceiling, her mind turning once again to Denise Bilson. She wasn't aware Anita's mother still lived in the house next door; until yesterday, Laura had not seen the old woman for more than twenty-five years. She had hardly aged, though she had not seemed to place Laura across the line of the fence. It may have been the rain, or maybe Laura herself had simply altered beyond recognition.

Laura settled her cheek against the cool satin of her pillow. She had spent many afternoons at Anita's house, running through the overgrown backyard while Denise baked packet meat pies and dished out Uncle Tobys Roll-ups. Laura had enjoyed these playdates, mainly for the treats—the only sweets she was allowed at home were carob buds and orange juice frozen into plastic icy-pole moulds. Denise didn't have a husband, as Laura recalled, or a job of much standing—she did a bit of cleaning at the school, and sometimes worked a shift at the tuckshop—which was perhaps why Eliza didn't make much effort with her. Her mother could be snobby like that. Still, Eliza had liked Anita. Laura remembered that from childhood: her mother's gruff approval.

When the girls weren't playing at Anita's house, they spent their free time at Laura's, often lying in the shade of the poinciana, swatting flies and telling stories. Anita had a vivid imagination; she inhabited other characters and their points of view with a mix of vitality and ease. She conjured scenarios of high jinks, drama, emotional intensity. *She's a born storyteller*, Laura thought wryly. But she had none of Laura's dedication or discipline, for it had been Laura who had taken the fragments of these ideas and worked them into fully fledged narratives in her old Spirax notebook, refining night after night. Most of these drafts came to nothing, but there had been one story that Laura had submitted for an assignment at school, and the teacher, so impressed, had invited her to read it out to the class. Laura could not for the life of her remember what it had been about, but she did recall that feeling of pride as she stood above her seated classmates, the power of holding those boys and girls suspended inside the tale. And then the look on Anita's face as her friend realised the story's provenance. It had been the same expression she had worn when Laura told her about the sale of the house. One of bemusement, and rage.

At some point she closed her eyes and must have slept, and quite deeply, because when she woke again it was abruptly, and she felt stunned and uncertain for a few moments, trying to recall where she was and what she was doing there. The house seemed still, and Laura wondered why she had woken. The bedroom was very dark. But when she sank back into her pillow she heard another noise, like cutlery clattering against a plate, followed by a footfall and the distinct groan of the timber floorboards.

Laura sat up, strangely calm, wondering if she was still half-asleep. She strained her ears in an effort to identify the noise, then decided to get up and head to the kitchen. She turned on the light. The dishwasher hummed quietly through the last few minutes of a rinse. Laura gazed out of the windows. The wattle lining the back fence shook; then, a second later, came the clock of nuts and a small branch falling on the tin roof. Laura smiled. *Case closed, Columbo*, and with a yawn she rested a hand against the stove.

The burning feeling was instant, searing her skin. Laura spun around. All four of the hotplates raged with electric red.

'Jesus fucking *Christ*!'

Laura dashed to the sink to run the cold tap over her hand, shaking and clutching at her wrist, but the tepid water did little to assuage the incredible pain, so she side-stepped to the freezer for a bag of peas. This worked better. Fastening a tea towel around the bag like a tourniquet, Laura edged back to the stovetop and swiped her good hand over the rings, measuring their heat. But the air above the plates was unchanged, and when she put a wet fingertip to the smallest ring the ceramic felt cool. Laura took a hasty step back and shook her head, as if trying to dislodge the stubborn understanding stuck there. Had she somehow turned on the hotplates and turned them off again? Or had she left them running after dinner? Laura rubbed at her brow, trying to recall what they had eaten. Cold stuff—a salad, some rotisserie chicken—so that couldn't explain it.

Her thoughts were interrupted by more footsteps, hurried this time, and the click of Tilly's door. Laura strode from the kitchen and headed straight to Tilly's bedroom. But when she tried the handle, the door was locked. Laura put her ear against the wooden panel, yet all she could make out was the dull whistle of a breeze moving through the weatherboards, the damp scent of beneath the house rising like mist. Then came a childish giggle. The back of Laura's head prickled. It was the middle of the night. Who on earth would Tilly be talking to? Probably Ava, from next door. Laura didn't want the girls spending time together anymore. She had resisted this decision, not wanting to play disciplinarian, but she had reached the end of her patience. They were already too entangled with Anita; the girls being friends was just another complication. Laura gave the door handle an angry rattle, then banged on the wood, once, twice.

'Tilly,' she cried. '*Tilly*!'

A second later the door quietly opened and Tilly poked her scrunched-up face around the jamb.

'Mum?'

The room was dark and smelt of old socks.

'It's late,' Laura said. 'You need to stop talking on your laptop and go to sleep.'

Tilly padded over to the desk and flicked on her lamp. In the orange glow, she reached for her water bottle and had a few swigs before collapsing back on the bed.

'I *was* asleep,' she groaned. 'You woke me up.'

Don't lie to me. Rage coursed through Laura's body. This was a feeling she did not recognise; the violent force of it was bracing.

'I heard you, Matilda. Laughing. There's no point pretending. You can talk to whoever it was another time.'

As Laura turned to leave, Tilly sat up, cross-legged. Her gaze fell on Laura's hand wrapped in the tea towel.

'What happened?'

Laura paused by the door.

'Let's just say, if you're going to cook for yourself, I'd appreciate you turning off the stove when you're done. I nearly burnt my hand off just now.'

'Mum, I was asleep.' Tilly spoke slowly, deliberately, but she could not conceal the waver in her voice. 'I haven't been cooking.'

'I suppose the stove turned on by itself, did it?'

'I don't know!'

'And how many times do I need to tell you—don't lock this door,' Laura snapped. 'It's not safe.'

Tilly was staring at her, her face contorted with the threat of tears. She wiped a hand across her nose.

'You're the one who needs sleep, Mum, because you're not making any sense. I did not lock that door. It doesn't even *have* a lock!'

'Oh for fuck's sake, Matilda.'

Laura threw up her arms, and as she did Tilly shrunk away, clapping her hands over her ears and cowering on the bedspread. It was such a pathetic gesture it took Laura right back to those nights she had loomed over her cot. She glared at Tilly, sickened with remorse. But Laura was more indignant at how Tilly had dredged it unsanctioned from her memory.

'Just do as you're told,' she muttered, and closed the door behind her with a bang.

She slept again until nearly midday, an unbroken sleep that left her groggy and listless. She hadn't heard Andrew get up or Tilly leave for school. Laura only rolled out of bed when the builder, Jon, parked in the drive, and at the slam of the van door she hurried into the bathroom to hide. She couldn't face anyone today. Soon the noises of destruction eddied around her: the earthmover gauging out great clumps of lawn, the jackhammer attacking old concrete, the whip-crack of nail guns.

Eventually Laura had a shower and dressed. This made her feel a little better, her head clearer, more capable of taking on the afternoon. Her burnt hand felt a little better too, though she still kept it wrapped in a dressing. And when Andrew's voice sounded from the backyard, she decided to buck up and make coffee for everyone. She brought out a cafetiere with mugs on a tray, along with a tin of panettone from a shop in Rosalie.

'All right, hon?' said Andrew, stubbing out a half-finished cigarette. He'd started smoking again, though he never managed to do it well, puffing away solemnly, the B&H wedged down as far as it could go between his thick fingers. 'Jon was just talking about the deck for the new bedroom. Turns out there's been some pushback from the council after all. Issue around weight distribution.'

'Oh yes?'

Laura smiled up at Jon. He was a tall, loping sort of man, with spindly arms—she imagined him as a basketballer in his youth. He was never without his Broncos cap or his stubbie shorts, which showed off surprisingly hairless legs. Scratching at the whiskers on his chin, he pointed to the sky where the sun dangled like a lazy orb.

'We can build up, but we have to build out,' he said.

Laura held her hand against the glare. The men watched her, waiting. She kicked at a dry twig, heard it snap.

'And what does that mean?'

'Well, we'd have to extend, like in the design, but further out,' Andrew explained. 'Eating more into the paved courtyard and the unique L-shape of the pool . . .'

'Wouldn't really be much of a pool, then.' Jon smiled without showing his teeth. 'More of a gutter, hidden off to the side of the house.'

Laura frowned. 'Right. That doesn't sound like what we're after, does it?'

Jon glanced at Andrew, who in turn nodded towards the poinciana, the lush canopy, and the dead fruit on the garden floor.

'There's another option. I know we're still waiting on the arborist's opinion, but Jon thinks the tree may have died. It's probably from poor pruning. See?' Andrew approached the tree and indicated one of the lower-hanging branches. 'It's been cut out from the trunk, which has killed it, basically. Soon these branches will fall off.' As if to prove this claim, he tested his weight against one, bowing it. 'When they do the borer can get into the soil and make its way to the house.'

Of course, Laura thought dimly. The one thing she wanted to keep had to go. Her single request. She could see Andrew anticipated some protest, but she was too tired for anything like that today.

'So we might need to think about getting the tree removed,' Andrew continued, encouraged by her silence. 'And then we could think about building out that way instead.' He shot a look at Jon, as though hoping the other man would confirm this, but Jon had begun picking at his fingernails, flicking the grime into the grass. 'Anyway, Laura, we don't need to decide now, I just wanted to let you know.'

Laura could feel the rapid crawl of an ant up her bare leg, then another. It was torture, standing there, not swatting them away. She gazed out across the yard, once again picturing her mother in the garden. All this had been enough for her parents, why couldn't it be enough for Andrew? The sharp sting from a bite followed, and she thrust out her leg like she was kicking an invisible ball. It was impossible to precisely describe the feeling that had taken root in her, an emotion or desire or perhaps simply a certainty that they were doing something very wrong. Andrew and Jon would think she was a lunatic.

Laura looked at the soft paunch where Andrew's T-shirt had been cinched into his khaki shorts. Once this would have triggered a painful tug of love for him but now she only sensed the gritty weight of a stone inside her chest. Back in England, she had been relieved at the prospect of a project to keep him so thoroughly occupied; Andrew was a man who needed constant vocation or he started to brood. Recently, however, she had begun to hate the way he spoke about the house. *Her* house. These modifications meant nothing to him, all part of the renovation process, forgetting this was the place she had grown up in and been shaped by. The place that contained her childhood. The site that preserved the untarnished memories of her parents.

'Whatever you think best, darling,' she said to Andrew. 'You're the expert.'

Laura left him standing there in the backyard. She went to the kitchen, running tepid water over her hands, and listened to the scrabble of birds nesting on the roof. Jon's voice droned through the window, but she couldn't make out what he was saying, then came the shrill ring of a mobile phone. The back door opened and Andrew came inside. Though not before leisurely dusting off his boots on the mat, something he never did, and this action stilled Laura by the sink, bracing for what might come next.

'Do you want tea?' she called.

Andrew padded up the steps and stood at the entrance of the kitchen, his feet planted wide; it was a stance that made him appear taller and broader than he was. The end of his nose was peeling. His eyebrows looked singed.

'No, I don't want any bloody tea,' he said.

'Something cold, then?' But when Laura went to move past him for the fridge, Andrew stuck out his arm.

'You could *try*, you know.'

His mouth was near her face; she felt the warm tickle of hair at her ear, and along with it the stirring of some feral danger—Andrew was rarely angry, but when rage visited it was usually explosive. She gazed back at his grey eyes; the same benign colour as Tilly's.

'What do you mean?' she asked.

'This.' He hissed the word. 'All *this*.'

'What—the renovations? I've told you, do what you think is best.'

'So you don't care? About what the house will look like when it's done? All my time and energy—that means nothing to you?'

Laura's arms and legs grew heavy, her shoulders sagging as though she was about to fold in half. *Take me away*, she wanted to say. *Take me home*. But home would never be home again. She was trapped in between, liminal. Panic beat at her breast, and Laura shut her eyes, forcing herself to conjure the calm of their garden back in Swinbrook, mist rising from the porter-coloured stream at the bottom of the lawn. But the image wouldn't come. All she could register was a scuttling from somewhere in the house, the study perhaps. Yes, the study. And it wasn't scuttling so much as scraping, the sound of a finger tracing a line of text, the turning of a page. It was so noisy—how could Andrew not hear it too?

'Laura?'

There was exasperation in his voice. He was tired too; he had been working every day for weeks. Laura opened her eyes.

'It's not that I don't care,' she said. 'I know you'll do a good job, you always do. I'm just . . . Right now, it all feels wrong somehow. I can't explain it better than that, I'm sorry.'

Andrew made no reply. He stood a few paces away from her, blinking. He was still angry, she could tell by the mottled colour in his cheeks, but there was something perspicuous about his expression now. His face had softened.

'It's for you, Laura. This work. Only for you.'

He sniffed, looking at the floor. Laura took a step towards him.

'But it's for you too, Andrew,' she said evenly. 'The house, the sale, paying off all our debt. It was to help you too, remember.'

He was shaking his head. 'It was your idea. You said that it would be good for all of us. And now we're here, you don't give a fuck.'

Laura balled her fists, squeezed, on the verge of unleashing a scream.

'I just can't seem to get a handle on anything since I've been back,' she said. 'I thought the dust would settle after the coroner's report, the memorial, but no. Then I thought the writing would help—but that just seems to make it all worse.'

Andrew made a face. He gestured about the kitchen.

'We still need to keep on with this project. We're working to a schedule. I need your input.'

'But it feels wrong. All this work, all this change.'

'Is this about what Anita said? Because if you've let her inside your head—'

'It's not that.'

'It's just a house, Laura,' Andrew snapped. 'Not a living, breathing person.'

Laura glared at him. *As if it's that easy*, she wanted to shriek. *As if I can turn off that part of myself like I'm a set of steel pipes.* She picked up the kettle, set it down again. Jon had finished his phone call. The backyard had grown quiet. Laura looked over her shoulder, down the passageway, and rubbed at her eyes. *Where was Jon?* she wondered—there, in the middle of the backyard, gazing up at the poinciana. There was nowhere to talk to Andrew, even if she wanted to, and nowhere to escape to, either.

'Maybe it's time we spoke to someone else about your mum and dad,' Andrew continued. 'A professional. The shock, you know, no one can cope with that. The grief. It's clearly been too much . . .'

'What would be the point?' Laura said. 'They can't change what happened.'

'But they can help with other things. At the very least, you need more sleep.'

Andrew reached out to touch her, but she was too far away. A space had flourished between them. He didn't look angry anymore but scared. A scared little boy.

'All right,' Laura said. 'I'll make an appointment.'

'You will? Really?'

Laura stared back at him. If she agreed, it would buy her some time, some space.

'Yes. I'll do it tomorrow.'

Andrew nodded, his face clearing. He was a practical man, who sought practical solutions. In his mind, this was a problem that could be solved if it was approached rationally. Spheres of influence. Blue hats.

'I'm going out,' Laura said, grabbing her keys from the stand. 'I need a change of scene. I won't be long.'

'Sounds like a good idea.' Andrew raised his hands to his head and ran them through his hair, smiling with relief. 'Give yourself the chance to think.'

Laura walked towards the border of Paddington and Bardon, taking the track around Norman Buchan Park. It was just before the end of the school day; the roads weren't busy. She went slowly. The run-in with Andrew had depleted her. He was right—she needed more sleep. Yet sleep never came easily here; the sky was too bright, too urgent; every time she lay down in that bedroom, no matter how carefully she drew the blinds, a strip of precocious light crept in. But when had Laura actually last slept soundly? Night after night of good, solid rest? If she charted it backwards, surely it took her to the time before all those midnights she'd spent pacing up and down the house with newborn Tilly.

She thought about that period of her life when a deep, peaty exhaustion had taken hold. At first, things had been on track. She had done well during the first couple of weeks of Tilly's life. Once the immediate shock of giving birth had worn off, and she was home and starting to establish the punishing routine of broken sleep and feeding every three hours, some normality had resumed, some calm. Laura had begun to believe motherhood might be something she could do. That she might even be good at it. But everything went downhill about a month in after Laura developed mastitis.

At first, she could hardly get out of bed. It took enormous effort to shower or brush her teeth. The infection made it too painful to breastfeed, so she started expressing milk with a pump and feeding Tilly with bottles. Her mood went haywire—the slightest disagreement sent her flying off the handle—and she felt constantly one beat away from full-blown rage.

Eventually the pain in her breasts diminished, but her state of mind did not improve. Andrew took the brunt of it. She simply couldn't stand the sight of him, and it wasn't long before this morphed into the belief he wanted to take Tilly away from her. This progressed to Laura waking in the middle of the night shouting at Andrew, convinced he had been about to maim her with a knife under a pillow, or strangle her. She started sleeping on the living room couch. After a while, Laura wished he would leave and take Tilly, and once or twice she wished he would actually kill her. Just for it all to stop. But when he didn't, she plotted running away herself, and even booked an EasyJet flight to Tunis.

Laura crossed the road and walked up the footpath towards Government House. It was strange to have not thought of it more often, this postnatal depression, which had lasted about six or seven months in the end. At the time, it had felt inescapable, as though Laura had been dropped to the bottom of a deep well. During the day she had sat on the couch, watching Tilly playing on the mat, and felt nothing. No love, no affection. Just a numb obligation. Laura had told herself it was down to having to express milk during the mastitis, and the bond between them had been stunted, but she knew it was more than that.

Still, it had been easier to be alone with her daughter than trying to parent together with Andrew. Back then, Laura began to think she and Tilly had a kind of agreement: mutual indifference. Until that point, Tilly had not smiled at Laura; she always stared back with a coy twitch of her mouth. But every now and then Tilly would grip Laura's little finger, and it was like opening a valve of her heart, releasing a torrent of pent-up emotion. Laura began to live each day for this breach of the dam wall.

She suffered through all this almost silently. Andrew had known something was very wrong but was too tired and preoccupied and incapable to do anything about it. Laura didn't blame him; she had been good at masking her illness when she wanted to. But that period had left an indelible mark on her psyche, and she came out the other side of it terrified of something like that happening again.

And now it is, Laura thought dimly. *I am on that couch again, stunned. I pass her each day in the house and I feel nothing. Only she's not a baby anymore, she's a teenage girl. I am causing her harm. I am that monster in the dark.*

When Laura returned to the house, she didn't seek out Andrew, or Tilly. Instead she went to her study. She would sit at the desk and write for the next hour. She must, or else how would she ever begin this project? Since she had decided to write about her parents, a kind of veil had grown around her practice that she had failed to draw back. This had never happened to her before.

When she strode into the room, she discovered the remaining books lining her mother's old bookcase were scattered across the floor. Laura didn't take much notice of it; the workmen had been shaking the foundations of the house all day, while a sledgehammer had been propped against the kitchen steps, ready to massacre the tiles. She proceeded to collect the books and restack the shelf, face turned away from the spines, which smelt of rot. The last book was *Voss*; in the fall it had somehow made its way beneath her desk. Laura went to crouch down for it, but something made her hesitate.

She remembered reading once that Patrick White came up with the idea for the novel during an air raid in the midst of the London Blitz, and it seemed as extraordinary to Laura now as it had back then that such creativity could be borne at a time of chaos and uncertainty. And while the character of Voss had been based on the failed explorer Ludwig Leichhardt, White had seen something of himself in his creation.

Laura traced a fingertip over the bright yellow title on the old dust jacket. Why had her mother hoarded all these books? Had she decided to seek out some lessons in fiction? It was a curious title to choose; Laura would be surprised if anyone read it these days. But perhaps Eliza, like the novel itself, wanted to explore the role of misery in finding enlightenment? This concept was antithetical to the woman Laura knew, who was rational, scientific, unsentimental. Eliza had never encouraged Laura's creativity or her yearning to fill that space in between things, and Laura felt a sudden flash of irritation, fresh anger even, at her mother. She would have valued talking about these ideas with Eliza. She might have been better equipped to deal with what she had inherited. She might have been better able to make sense of the mess left behind.

Laura turned the book over in her hands and let the spine fall open at a dog-eared page. *It is only human sacrifice that will convince man that he is not God . . .* She glared at the shelf. How much she wanted to be rid of them all. But it wasn't possible. Of course she could tear the jackets from the binding, rip the pages to shreds, but the text would still live on inside her, as though the ink moved its way through her veins. She could bury them under the house, but they would still find a way of clawing their way through the floorboards and back onto this bookshelf. They were indestructible.

From the fig tree, the bats chittered. Wood smoke from someone's burner drifted on the afternoon breeze. Laura returned to the desk and dropped into the chair. She flicked on the lamp and rebooted her laptop. The screen opened to a new passage of text:

A monster lives beneath the house
Hear it whisper, hear it scratch
It lies asleep throughout the night
And visits in the brightest light

A monster lives beneath the house
Hear it whisper, hear it scratch

Don't wake the beast from this sleep

Else find your bones buried in the deep . . .

On it went for another page, all formatted in typewriter font. Laura couldn't believe what she was reading. It was the poem her father had made up at bedtime when she had been a little girl. He used to turn off the lights and raise the lampshade to his face while he recited it, his brow stretched long and ghoulish from the white light, before tickling Laura and giving her a sandpapery kiss on the cheek. She had loved that time with her dad, and the deliciousness of fear mixed with longing.

Laura sank back in the chair, her head spinning. From outside came the low rumble of the bus on Given Terrace, and then another sound, familiar and strange. Laughter, and the low timbre of a voice that sounded exactly like her father's. Laura began to shake—first in her hands, then right down to her feet.

She found them at the cast-iron table on the patio. A bottle of white wine in a chiller positioned on the steps, Andrew's head bent in towards Anita seated beside him, an arm slung over the back of her chair. She said something under her breath and they both cackled.

'Hello, love.'

Andrew was tipsy—Laura could tell from his limp wave. In one compartment of her mind, she registered the acute pain of his disloyalty, but she could deal with that later. For now she concentrated on the way Anita peered into her lap, the flush in her cheeks perhaps brought on by something other than the wine.

'Laura, I popped around with a peace-offering,' she said. 'But unfortunately your man and me have gone ahead and drunk most of it!'

Anita looked at Andrew, and they both laughed again. How long had they been sitting out here? Laura clenched and unclenched her fists, trying to extinguish her outrage. But it wasn't working. Laura strode to the border of the patio but didn't come any nearer. Her fury had drained away as fast as it had arrived, leaving behind a residue of confusion. Like everything to do with Anita, she felt unsettled.

'What's going on?' she said, glaring at Andrew.

His response seemed to reflect back to Laura in slow motion. He took forever to meet her gaze, and when he did his eyes looked empty. Finally he said, 'Laura, why don't you sit down with us?' but with little eagerness. No one moved. After another moment, he stood up and came over to Laura, bringing with him an old shoebox that had been balancing on an empty terracotta pot. 'Anita wanted to give you these,' he said.

Laura peered inside. She saw herself aged around eleven or twelve, buck-toothed and lank-haired, smiling back.

'They're old photos. Us as kids, some of your folks.' Anita pushed away a few curls from her forehead. 'I thought you might like them.'

Laura didn't say anything. Instead she studied Anita; she wasn't dressed in her usual work shorts or a singlet but in a sleek black jumpsuit, which clung flatteringly to breasts that were perter than Laura remembered. She could smell her deodorant. Could it have been Impulse, the same spray-on they had used as girls, Mysterious Musk? She fought the urge to gag.

Andrew returned to the table though did not sit down. He picked up the wine bottle, stared at it, and seemed surprised that it was almost empty. He was still wearing a threadbare T-shirt and Hard Yakka khakis, his stomach straining at the waist. He glanced at Laura, urging her to say something, to act more like the host she had not asked to be.

Eventually she went over and sat in his vacated chair. 'You know our girls are friendly?'

'Laura.' Andrew's voice was low, cautionary.

'Excuse me?' said Anita.

'Ava,' Laura continued, undeterred. 'Chip off the old block, isn't she? Worming her way into my daughter's life, causing trouble. Well, I don't want it, Anita. I don't want her anywhere near Tilly.'

'Maybe,' Andrew said, wringing his hands together, 'maybe it might be easier if we take the heat out of all this. Ladies? If we remember that you're old friends?'

Laura smiled sweetly. 'Oh, I remember.'

She watched Anita take a final mouthful of wine, then push out the chair and rise to her feet, something regal about the gesture, an unexpected dignity in her posture.

'Listen, Laura, I know you're dealing with some stuff,' she said. 'And that's okay. But you need to understand that all I've been doing is respecting your parents' wishes as I understood them. I get that it's painful, I get that you have regrets, but at the end of the day it's up to you what you do next.' Anita tilted her head, gave Laura a sympathetic look. 'I'll take a step right back and leave you be.'

'How big of you,' Laura muttered.

'Darling, come on,' Andrew said.

'Listen,' Anita continued. 'I wasn't going to mention it, but since we're having this little chat . . . I wondered, Laura, if you might be able to keep it down a little more at night?'

She had her arms folded, the sympathy in her expression gone. Laura shook her head.

'What do you mean?'

'The noise, at night.' Laura didn't miss the look that passed from Anita to Andrew, or the way Andrew lowered his eyes, his humiliation taking a different shape. 'The crying, the calling out. In the yard. I'm sorry, I don't want to make a big deal of it, but it's keeping us up and I do need things calm at my place for my—'

'What on earth are you talking about?'

'It's fine, I understand. Grief. It's mad, isn't it? Some of us are noisy. Others bury it further down, I guess.' Anita pointed towards the poinciana. 'It's funny, though. I don't remember you ever crying when we were kids. Even that time when you broke your arm falling out of the tree. You were more scared, I think, of showing pain.' She smiled wolfishly. 'Or maybe you were just scared of telling your mum what you'd done. You were always a bit terrified of her.'

Laura didn't know what to say. She looked to Andrew, expecting to finally see some indignation on her behalf, but all she found on his face was complicity. He believed Anita. He was on her side. This understanding landed like a body blow. Anita took another step away and stuck her hand out like a salute.

'Well, goodnight. Thanks for sharing the vino.' She grinned at Andrew. 'Hey, don't forget. The kookaburra, yeah? You've got to watch him.'

Her eyes strayed towards Laura's, glinting in the last sliver of afternoon light. Laura ground her teeth until her jaw ached. Andrew stared at the ground, shoulders slumped, exhausted by an exchange he had barely comprehended. Laura walked back inside the house. They would argue about it later in strained voices, and Laura would forgive him, though this time the transgression would take longer to heal.

From the safety of the kitchen, Laura looked out over the garden, her gaze drawn towards the line of the fence next door. She thought about those strange paragraphs that had first appeared on her laptop. *Where's the other one?* the old woman had asked. Laura buttoned up her shirt, shivering—the question had yawned open a great pit of black fear. When she met her eyes in her hazy reflection in the window, Laura had to look away. Somewhere in the house Andrew closed a door. Laura moved away from the sink, to the fridge; dinner needed making. Outside the sun speckled pink across the egg-white sky.

12.

TILLY SAT ON the edge of the tombstone and stared at the end of her glowing cigarette. Smoking gave you cancer—she understood this. Not her kind of smoking, mind: a couple of times a week and hardly inhaling. Still, there was something wanton about an activity that brought you closer to death. Perhaps that was why Tilly had decided this would be her last B&H menthol. Hanging out among the graves made her look forward to all the life she had left to live.

Ava, who sat across the path from Tilly, preferred rollies without a filter, her fingers moving expertly over the Tally-Ho paper as she made another cigarette. Tilly watched her for a moment, then looked away, gazing across Toowong Cemetery. They were finalising their history project, which was due next week. In the end they had settled on the story of Patrick Mayne. Tilly had suggested the visit to the cemetery to see the family crypt, and Ava had made a sketch. Afterwards, they had wandered through the grounds together.

At first Tilly felt uneasy about Ava examining the names on the tombstones, sometimes chuckling—'Um, *Doris*?' But after a while she found some resonance in the place, a kind of comfort in learning the kink in the path where the trees grew lush, their canopies expanding across the lawn. And the knowledge, too, that somewhere in there were her grandparents' graves, though she didn't remind Ava of this. Maybe they would soon stumble across them anyway, Ava's mocking eyes growing wide at the recognition of the etchings in the stone. None of it felt real to Tilly.

'Hey, Tilly, if you were dead, do you reckon you'd come back and haunt people you knew?'

Ava seemed particularly unhappy today, Tilly thought. She had grown thinner and had deep bruises beneath her eyes. Tilly wondered if she had depression, and then wondered why she hadn't considered that before. They'd had a mental health session in their PE class last week and talked about 'dark moods' and self-harm.

'I don't think I'd hang around the cemetery,' she replied. 'If you were a spirit, you could go anywhere. Like New York. Or Paris.'

'Paris?' Ava repeated.

Tilly scratched her arm. She was still disappointed that her parents had never offered to reschedule the cancelled trip to France. 'Yeah. Wouldn't you want to go there?'

Ava shrugged. 'I guess.' She seemed annoyed now, her mouth pinched.

The sky rumbled and some leaves skittered across the path. The air felt heavy, full somehow. There had been warnings about another storm on her dad's radio that morning, and more rain, if that was possible. It had been raining on and off for nearly a week. The creeks were full, the river's tide higher than usual; the drains were all rushing with run-off, the streets were slick. Everything was damp.

'I'd like to drive around Australia for my gap year,' said Ava, fidgeting with the Zippo. 'Spend a good chunk of time in the Outback. That's real country.'

'You've been out there before?'

'Well, yeah.' Ava sniffed. 'Mum's into it. Camping, rock climbing, treks. She's got all the gear and knows all the best routes. I've started saving my pocket money, and when I turn fifteen I'll get a job at Woolies; they're always hiring. Then when I finish school I'll get a kombi and just'—she flicked her wrist—'go.'

Tilly chewed the end of her hair. It tasted salty. She thought about her mother, and how she seemed to rarely encourage Tilly in anything these days. It sent a hot, flushed feeling through her body, making her skin prickle.

'Would you go with someone?' she asked.

'Nah.' Ava tried to ignite the Zippo, but the spark wouldn't catch. 'I might meet people along the way, but I wanna be alone.'

'What about your mum?'

Ava shook her head. She was still staring moodily at the ground. 'She's good at being alone,' she muttered. 'We both are.'

Tilly had always thought Laura was good at being alone too, but now she was starting to wonder if preferring something didn't automatically make you good at it. Laura had left Brisbane just like Ava was suggesting she would in a few years' time, and as far as Tilly could tell that had caused a kind of murky, unspeakable pain between her mother and her grandparents. Tilly gazed at her red nail polish. Suddenly she longed for her mother, to see her smile again. In England, she was always smiling—and laughing, which to Tilly sounded like a bell.

The sky was closing in. A few fat drops of rain began to fall. Ava stood up, dusting off the back of her leggings.

'Come on,' she said. 'It's about to piss down.'

They collected their bikes from the *No Standing* post on Frederick Street. The rain was heavy now, the pavement lacquered with eucalyptus leaves. Tilly struggled with her D-lock; the key caught, refusing to turn.

'Hurry up!' Ava had one foot against the raised pedal of her own bike. 'I'm soaked.'

'I can't seem to get . . .' Tilly threw down her bag. 'The lock's fucked.'

Ava checked her phone. 'Shit! My mum wanted me home by three and it's nearly half-past.'

'Hang on! Can you help me?'

'Sorry, I've got to go right now.' Ava heaved off the kerb, her back tyre squelching through the water that was rushing towards the drain. 'But move it, yeah, or you won't get home.'

'What the fuck, *Ava*? Since when do you do what your mum asks?'

'See you Tuesday night at mine for dinner,' Ava called over her shoulder.

The rain was pummelling Tilly's back as she hunched over her front tyre, rattling the key in the lock. Eventually she took a deep breath, removed the key, and tried again, slowly this time, and she felt the miraculous *click* as the mechanism complied. She whipped off the bracket, shoving it inside her saturated backpack. Then she got the bike moving along the footpath. For a moment the rain seemed to ease as she cruised beneath the canopy of banyan figs.

But when she came to a clearing she was lashed again by great sheets of north-westerly rain, and almost toppled from the seat. She pushed on, blinded by the downpour, and felt the bike moving freer, faster, as she trundled down the hill. Before she realised what this might mean, however, the wheels slid out from beneath her, a swift lurch to the right, like invisible hands had reached out and shoved her. She landed in the gritty brown stormwater that was seething through the overflowing drain in the dip before the hill grew steep again.

A few cars puttered by, their headlights on, testing the depths. One man had his window down, shouting to Tilly, but she couldn't hear him. She just wanted to get home; she wasn't far, if only she could just make it up this bloody hill. She tried to pick up the bike but the water was too fast. Something flayed at her leg, a branch perhaps or a piece of wiring, and her thigh burned. The bike was tugged away, inch by inch, until all of a sudden it shot away from Tilly and disappeared down the embankment.

She was afraid then. A bright, hot fear, pounding like her wounded leg. The force of the current grew stronger, like ropes coiled around her knees. Another car drove past but didn't stop, and Tilly stumbled, careening into the brown river. She hauled herself up, panic squeezing at her throat. Somehow she made it out of the water, but her mother's bike was gone.

It took Tilly an hour to limp back to the house. She went around the back, tripping over the canvas covering the floorless ground where the annex used to be, and ducked beneath the scaffolding holding up the fresh wooden beams on which the upstairs loft would soon be built. Water cascaded from all directions around the house and eddied at the grate at the bottom of the driveway. Tilly stood shivering near the door, watching her father try to drag a tarpaulin over the building tools stacked on the clearing next to the fence.

'*Dad?*'

He looked up, startled, as he batted his way through the flaps back inside the house. He was soaked.

'It's a deluge out there. The whole yard is a mud bath. Wind's absolutely smashed the poinciana—it's on a frigging tilt.' He wiped his brow with his T-shirt. 'All the foundation soil has come loose around the roots from the renovations.'

Tilly was shaking all over—even her teeth were chattering. She wrapped her arms around herself as Andrew eased off his gloves.

'What happened? Til? Why aren't you talking?' He clocked her leg. 'You're hurt.'

'The water . . .' She sobbed. 'I lost Mum's bike. We were at the cemetery.'

'Who was?'

'Me and Ava.'

Tilly heard a noise behind her. It was Laura. Her face was a strange, sickly colour, and her eyes were red. She walked across the living room and sat carefully on the edge of the couch. She didn't seem to notice Tilly's bleeding leg as she flicked on a lamp, bathing the room in an eerie yellow hue.

'What kind of kid hangs out at a cemetery?' she muttered.

Tilly stared at Laura. She couldn't remember the last time her mother had said a kind word, or expressed a shred of concern or interest about any aspect of her life. They had become strangers to one another. Where was that person she had always relied upon? Who listened? Outside, the rain had eased and the rhythmic slap of branches against the roof had stopped.

Eventually Laura let out a loud sigh and Tilly looked away, towards the adjacent wall, and the black-and-white photograph of the house. Her gaze was encouraged towards that smudge. Only it was no longer a smudge. Tilly felt her heart slow, her blood pressure dropping, followed by the sound of a low, deep whistle. There, in the corner of the photograph, was a woman standing beside the blinds. Tilly took a step closer. It couldn't be, could it?

'What the fuck,' she breathed.

The woman, Tilly recognised her. It was the same lady from the delicatessen. Tilly reached up, grasping her earlobes, to give them a sharp tug. She used to do this as a little girl, to wake herself from a bad dream.

'What's wrong?'

Laura had sprung up from the couch, her hands planted angrily on her hips. Tilly turned back to the photograph, and the hairs on the back of her neck stood on end. She fought the cartoonish urge to rub at her eyes with her fists. To test this reality. Because the woman had now disappeared.

'Tilly?'

Tilly raised a feeble hand, shook it at the frame.

'I . . . I don't know. I thought I saw her. There. In the window.'

Blood roared through Tilly's head. She didn't know what she was more afraid of—the photograph, or her mother.

'What do you mean you saw her. *Who*?'

'No one. Okay? I got it wrong. It must have been a trick of the light or something. I'm sorry. Please, let's just forget it.'

Tilly was slipping through the floor. That was the exact sensation: like the polished hoop boards beneath her feet had parted, and she was sliding towards the dark pit under the house, with no one to catch her.

'What did you see?' said Laura again. 'In the photo—who was it?'

Tilly opened her mouth, then closed it again. She looked desperately towards her father.

'Matilda. This is important!'

Tilly shrunk from Laura, but her mother reached out and gripped Tilly's wrist, her fingernails digging into the soft flesh.

'Tell me,' she hissed.

'I don't know, Mum! There's nothing there now. Can we just forget it?'

The light overhead flickered for a moment, crackling and fizzing, as if it too were agitated by the commotion.

'Maybe we should just take the bloody thing down,' Tilly heard Andrew say. 'It's really not worth all this fuss.'

'Leave it,' Laura said. Her voice was shrill. The light gave another splutter, then went out, throwing them into gloom.

'Honestly, the wiring in this place,' muttered Andrew as he made his way across the living room floor.

'I said leave it! Don't touch it, Andrew. I mean it.'

'Laura, you're being ridiculous.'

But before he could make it to the opposite wall, the photograph suddenly slipped from its position on the hook—the old twine must have been too worn to hold the frame. They all watched the photograph hang there at an odd, slanted angle before the whole thing slipped further and went crashing to the floor. The force of it shattered the glass inside the frame, and tore the hook clean off the wall. The three of them hurried over, crowding around the mess. The photograph had come loose, bulging out of the case. As Laura grabbed hold of one corner, shaking it free from the fragments of wood and glass, they all spotted the old, slim notebook secreted inside the frame. Laura swiftly unpeeled the brown masking tape.

'Laura?' It was Andrew. 'Whatever that is, leave it alone.'

But she wasn't listening; she was halfway across the living room floor, her stride as cool and efficient as that of a lynx. Tilly watched her turn to the first page, her eyes growing wide with what looked like a mix of dread and excitement. Tilly took a few steps away, swallowing down the thick tears building at the back of her throat.

'Laura.' Andrew's voice was now weak, pleading. 'Don't run off like this. We need to talk. Tilly's upset.'

Laura stopped at the threshold to her study. She was holding the old book like it was a precious artefact excavated from a tomb. She gave Tilly one final searching look before she gently moved the notebook from one hand to the other. Tilly thought it was in order to reach out for her, inviting a hug. But Laura was only feeling about for the handle. When she went inside and shut the door with a bang, Tilly didn't flinch. She had decided not to cry, either. Instead she peered down at her wrist where the welts throbbed from her mother's fierce grip. The imprint was already starting to fade.

13.

LAURA WENT STRAIGHT to the desk and flicked on the lamp. The collage of grotesque pictures crowding the walls loomed back at her in the semi-darkness. From the living room she could make out the muffled sounds of Tilly's bewilderment, and Andrew's attempts at comfort. Then the slap of the flyscreen door, followed by Tilly's angry footsteps down the stairs.

Laura stared at the notebook. Only it wasn't a notebook as she had first thought but a diary. Strange; Laura could not recall ever seeing it. Though old, it was in good condition, the yellowing pages smelling cool and slightly flowery. She held it up to her chest for a moment, feeling the thud of her heart against the leather jacket, before she set it down and opened to the first entry. Dated 1977. Eliza and Bruce moving into the house. Painting the kitchen, building the annex out the back, visiting the local nursery, and sweltering through the stultifying heat of that first summer when Eliza needed to lie in a cold bath for any respite—*I feel like my head is made of dandelion wisps.* Woven through all this were notes on the events of the times, meetings with colleagues at the university, ideas for papers, some academic gossip. Then a few months passed before the next entry of a single line: *A girl, I'm sure of it, due in August.*

Here Laura needed a pause. She could hear the cadence of her mother's voice as though she were speaking down the telephone. The thoughtful breaks, the pithiness, the restraint. And then, as if responding to these reflections, the entries grew more sporadic, snatches of time Eliza found between work and caring for baby Laura. Gaps of weeks, months, and in a few instances years. There was a scribble about Laura's first steps, some toddler chatter, and the first day of school: *She didn't look back when I dropped her at the front gate. Not once. I cried when I got home. The house was so quiet.* Holidays up and down the coast, dinners with friends, the occasional film. Laura's leaving for London had a few pages, though that mostly concerned a trip into the city to buy a travel wallet from David Jones. There was an excitement to this change in the family, even if it was tinged with sadness: *I don't think I've let myself think about just how much I'll miss her.*

It was all quite ordinary; fleeting glimpses of a normal life captured on the page. After a while Laura felt a pang of disappointment—what had seemed like a door to something important had just as quickly slammed shut in her face. Tilly's birth was recorded with exclamation marks. Eliza and Bruce retiring within a few months of one another, the trip her parents made around three years ago to London: *Tilly really is very like Laura, not so much in looks but in demeanour. I found myself falling through a kind of time trap.*

Then a gap of a year, which recommenced with brief entries about Anita. Laura sat straighter in her seat. Now Eliza detailed some work she had begun at the centre on Handy Street, archiving old photographs, cataloguing local history. A hobby, at least to begin with. There were several entries about Anita visiting the house, and how much Eliza enjoyed her company: *She has a fierce intelligence. I am learning a lot from her. She has strong convictions.* This went on for a while, the bond developing between the women, and a weird inversion of their roles: Anita providing tutelage to Eliza, who in turn became the grateful student. Eliza grew reflective, discursive, vague: *It seems almost impossible to undo the past*, she wrote, *unless you are prepared to cede power. Afraid of this truth, we are all drawn to the outer edges of this land. What would happen if we returned to the centre of it? If we tried to reach the heart?*

Laura sat back heavily in the chair. She knew she was jealous of this friendship between Anita and her mother, but she was also curious. She had never shared this kind of thinking with Eliza. How had Anita managed to convert her?

This continued for another few entries. Anita invited Eliza to marches, bookshop talks, a tree-planting afternoon. But when Laura turned the page and read the next entry, she had to stop and read it again. The tone had changed, those leisurely reflections replaced with torrents of scrawled notes, the paper sometimes torn from the force of the pen: *Something is happening. Something in the house. I don't quite know how to describe it, except that I feel it, every morning when I wake up, every night when I try to sleep. Watching me.*

A week later: *Last night I saw someone passing by the window. It was a woman, I think, old like me, but I could not quite make out her face.*

Then, the following month: *She is outside the house, peering in. She wants something from us. From me. I don't know what, or how I can begin to give it to her.*

Laura traced the date at the top of the page: *October 2023.* A little over a year before they died. Laura ran a fingertip over the edges of the notebook, aware of a new power emanating from it, dark and destructive. She read on. The entries continued every week or so, detailing other events in the house. Unexplained voices. Missing books. Lights going out. A plague of cockroaches in the backyard as thick as a carpet, a tile seemingly flung clean off the roof. Her mother growing more perplexed, and more afraid. It was all horribly familiar yet at the same time unreal. On and on it went for a period of around six months: *This afternoon we did some work in the garden. When B went to make iced drinks in the kitchen, he found the back door locked. The front door too, as well as all the windows. We couldn't get inside. We had to ask Anita to call a locksmith. I pretended we had locked ourselves out, but I knew it was her. B and I talked about it later, discussing our options. We can't talk to anyone else about it—what would they say? B is so understanding, so reasonable. He feels it too.*

The gaps between entries grew. Laura flicked through to the final pages, hurrying now, hardly wanting to read: *Laura telephoned yesterday. She wants to visit, with Tilly and Andrew, this Christmas. I had to tell her no. I can't let that happen, not now. Not until we have this sorted. It breaks my heart.*

Approaching the end, the writing grew fainter, frailer: *She's back. Oh Christ, she's in the house again.*

Then: *I saw her again at the kitchen window. That's the third time this week. It was a warning. A message. To leave. She wants us to leave this house, or something atrocious will happen. I have talked to B, we have decided.*

Laura turned the page to what she realised was one of the final entries, dated 9 December, only a few days before her parents died at Hell Hole Gorge: *This afternoon I was saying goodbye to Jenny when I felt a switch flick inside my brain. It was like time had stopped, and I was suddenly overwhelmed by an impulse to climb over the railing and throw myself off the deck. I had no control over my body, or even my own thoughts. Jenny was screaming at me to stop, but it was like she was talking to me from deep underwater. I wasn't afraid of hurting myself. But I did hurt myself; I thought I had broken my ankle when I landed on the concrete drive, and that set me off raving. Bruce came home then and Jenny left and I don't remember much else after that . . .*

And the final entry, on 10 December: *So we are leaving. We have no choice. We need to get as far away as we can from the house—I don't know where we will end up. I'm not sure it matters. We won't come back. The house will no longer belong to us. Maybe then we can be free of this. And maybe Laura and young Tilly will be free from it too. Because I know in my bones if I don't do something it will pass on to them.*

Laura let out a strangled sob. She thrust away the notebook and sat staring at the blank white walls. She felt wretched, and ashamed. All this time she had been waiting for an explanation for her parents' distance, for their coolness. Now she had proof it was because they believed they needed to protect her. From the house, and whatever they thought was inhabiting it.

At the window, the light was turning, purples and reds in the sky. The bats were screaming, but it sounded muted, distant. Laura rubbed at her eyes, and the press of tears there. It was odd, but after all this time she could raise a perfect image of her parents loading up their old Pajero in the driveway, the slam of the boot making the backseat judder, and a soft light at the bedroom windows like a pair of eyes, as real to Laura as a person could ever be.

The police never considered that her parents may have wanted to keep driving. That Hell Hole Gorge had not been their intended final destination. Laura stood up, pushing away the chair. What if that feeling had followed them out there? What if that is what really happened out on the escarpment?

It didn't take her long to pack. She only needed a change of clothes, some deodorant, a hat, her phone charger. Her backpack was already at the front door, the manila folder with her mother's photographs safely inside it. Andrew appeared in the doorway and watched her move around the bedroom. Then he came inside and picked up the diary, which Laura had placed on the side table.

'So what is it?'

He flicked through the pages. Laura went to the cupboard and brought down an overnight bag from the top shelf.

'A diary. Belonging to my mother. She must have hidden it away inside that old frame before she left the house.'

'Why would she do that?'

Laura looked at Andrew. He was gazing at her with bloodshot eyes.

'Because she believed the house was haunted. And that she and my dad needed to leave. To save themselves, but also Tilly and me.'

Andrew gaped back at her.

'Laura, for fuck's sake. Can you hear yourself?'

She zipped up the bag and hoisted it over her shoulder.

'What are you doing?' Andrew had taken a step nearer. Sweat coated his upper lip.

'Well, I can't stay here. I have to leave.'

'And go where?'

'Out there.' Laura pointed towards the road, to that imaginary space beyond it, to the darkness. 'To where they died. To Hell Hole Gorge. The police never did a proper investigation. They just wrote it off as two old people out of their depths. But something else pushed my mum and dad out of this house. Some dark force.'

'Some . . . *what*?'

Laura snatched the diary from Andrew and clasped it to her chest.

'My mother saw it, she felt it. I think it followed them out there. I'm going to look for the clues to prove it.'

'Laura, please.' Andrew's voice pitched up in bewildered desperation; he was practically shouting. 'Your mum and dad had some kind of breakdown when they went out bush. That's what happened. That's your answer, plain and simple. And if it's in that diary, then it proves it all the more. It's tragic, it really is, but you need to stop all this because you're starting to frighten me.'

'You don't understand, Andrew. How could you? This'—she shook the diary at him—'this is my mum telling me to follow her out there. I can't believe it's taken me so long to figure it out.'

'Laura, I'm sorry, but this is crazy talk. I thought you were going to get some help for all this. Real, professional help. I'm going to call someone. The doctor, at the clinic!'

She pushed past him and headed towards the front door, reaching for her backpack, and gathering the car keys from the dining room table.

'You're going now?' Andrew cried.

He grabbed her. It was the first time Andrew had laid hands on Laura in all their years of marriage. It took her a moment to register the force of his grip around her bicep, the way her neck cricked as he yanked her back towards him. As they stood face to face, she could see him calculating his actions, wondering whether exerting physical force was a risk he was willing to take.

'What about Tilly?' he hissed. 'You're just leaving her like this? Jesus Christ, Laura, this isn't like you.'

'I'm doing this *for* her!'

Andrew glared at her, and Laura could see he knew he couldn't stop her. Eventually his grip slackened and she shook herself free, and pushed open the front door. On the deck the air was ripe, full of dew and freshly cut grass. Laura peered over the balustrade, spotting the Pajero in the driveaway. An energy came off the house like waves. It was a long drop, but she found herself suspended there, contemplating the distance, and how a fall might bring an end to it all. There was something compelling about that possibility.

'Don't worry, I won't be long,' she called to Andrew, hurrying down the stairs. 'Only a few days. I've got my phone if you need me.'

'Yeah, but will you answer it,' he muttered from behind the security door, a faceless silhouette.

Laura drove along the M2. After the urban sprawl of Brisbane disappeared, along with those swathes of industrial estates, the road inclined to Toowoomba. From there she headed north-west. It was very dark away from the city's luminous nightscape, and the highway was not well lit. There appeared to be some cattle around, but it was otherwise mostly broadacre country. The radio reception dipped and crackled. Every now and then a truck thundered by, rattling the Pajero. Enormous abandoned grain silos popped up from the roadside like mushrooms.

Laura arrived in Roma after midnight. She pulled into the first motel she saw with a vacant sign. An elderly man in flip-flops directed her to the room. When he was gone, she sprawled out on the lumpy bed and fell asleep in her clothes.

The next morning Laura woke at six o'clock, and after a shower she continued the drive to Charleville. She felt oddly calm and refreshed, her mind clear of all that static from Brisbane. Out here, the landscape was flat, fields of livestock on either side of the freeway, though quite green after the rain. Paintbrush clouds streaked across the blue sky. Occasionally Laura passed a field crop of sunflowers. After Morven, the grass disappeared and the earth went chalky red. It was dark in patches, like rust, and riven with threads of salmon-coloured sand. There were no cattle or sheep about now, though Laura did spot a couple of feral pigs dead on the side of the road. The Pajero hummed, the air-conditioner straining against the relentless sun pounding at the glass.

Although her GPS indicated it was only another forty-five minutes to Charleville, it felt to Laura like hour after hour passed by. A familiar weight of exhaustion settled over her, and Laura found herself losing her line of focus on the long stretch of freeway, the flat, unpopulated paddocks like a shifting hallucination. She had never driven this far in her life. But as she pushed on that resolution returned, an invisible string drawing her deeper and deeper towards the centre. Eventually she pulled over at a truck stop and got out of the car, squatting behind some tall boulders for a wee. Studying the drowsy movement of the withered ti-trees, she checked her phone. There was no reception. The air crackled, wheezed.

She drove on, passing an olive grove, more rocks and a war memorial lookout. There were eucalypts nearer to Charleville, as well as clusters of quinine. Laura parked around the back of the pub next to the drive-through Bottle-O. She had booked a room at the Hotel Corones in the middle of town.

'Checking in?' The concierge, a middle-aged guy with glasses, studied Laura from behind a computer.

Laura admired the lobby. The hotel had been built during the 1920s and still had some of the Art Deco trimmings: the stained glass above the saloon-door entrance, the Tapet Café-style wallpaper, tall ceilings, a formal dining room, an airy front bar. *Yes, I can picture them here*, she thought with a small smile.

'Number one,' the man said, handing over a key on a bulky tag. 'Top of the stairs.'

On the way up to her room, Laura was startled to recognise the ornaments in what must have once been the hotel's sunroom on the other side of the landing. These objects had featured in the photographs the police developed from Eliza's camera. Wooden and leather-bound chairs were on display, a chaise longue, a glass cabinet full of old crockery and vases. A chipped ceramic urn sat on an oak stand with a white lace doily. Another cabinet exhibited old tins of nutmeg and cloves, empty perfume bottles and satin gloves pulled over a wire hanger to effect a waving hand. Photographs of the original proprietor's family members lined the windowsill, their frozen faces from a lost era staring eerily straight back at Laura.

She went to her room and lay on the bed while the fan beat through the thick air. A gritty wind rattled at the door, which opened on to the hotel's large wrap-around balcony. Laura retrieved her mother's diary from her bag and held it to her chest, then sank into the pillows and fell asleep, only rousing when her stomach growled.

She wandered downstairs. By now it was approaching six o'clock, and the dining room had filled with locals. She headed to the adjacent bar, where a few couples had perched on stools, and a family occupied one of the four-seater tables dotted about the room. Beside one of the windows was a framed commemoration of the annual bilby race, four stuffed-toy marsupial mascots sporting colourful bandanas pinned beneath the glass. Laura ordered a Caesar salad and soda water and sat in the far corner, with a view of the flat-screen TVs replaying the rugby league from the weekend.

'All right, love?' A waitress with big hair came over to Laura's table. 'You're staying upstairs, aren't ya?'

'Yes, that's me.'

'You foreign?' The woman smiled; there was gold between her teeth. 'England?'

'Recently, yes. But I'm from Brisbane originally.'

'Right-oh.' The waitress tossed the towel over her freckled shoulder. 'What brings you out here?'

Laura stirred her soda water, studying the pulpy lemon swirling about the ice. She wasn't sure she wanted to answer. She glanced at the waitress's name tag: *Sue*.

'Research,' she said. 'I'm a writer.'

'Are you?' Sue pointed to the ceiling. 'Well, here's a story. That room you're staying in upstairs. It's haunted, they say. Some bloke, a cattle farmer, blew his brains out one night during a stopover to the city. Years ago. The bullet is still lodged in the wall above the bedhead. Robbo, the owner, just filled it with a bit of Selleys and painted over it!'

Laura pulled her plaid shirt tighter around her shoulders. Her face felt like it was collapsing in on itself, a crumpled aluminium can. She tried to smile.

'Now that *is* a story. I'll sleep well tonight.'

'I wouldn't count on it, love. That bloke's ghost is said to roam the hotel. Comes out at the stroke of midnight.' Sue looked about, searching for someone, perhaps this Robbo, to confirm the story. Then she laughed, the loud, serrated sound of a smoker. 'Don't look so worried! Whole town's bloody haunted.' Sue caught the eye of an old fellow slumped over the bar drinking from a bottle of dark ale. 'Isn't that right, Nev? Ghosts everywhere in this place!'

'Zombies, more like,' said Nev, tipping back his Chinchilla Bulldogs cap. 'We're all the walking dead.'

Laura joined in with their laughter, the roar of the television crowd loud through the bar. Someone had scored a try.

'Where are you?'

Andrew sounded very far away. Laura shifted in the car seat, the leather groaning. She was calling him from the Pajero parked out on the street. It was the only spot she could find phone reception, and now that bloody farmer must have been interfering with the frequency, she thought with an exhausted giggle.

'*Laura*?'

'I'm here. Charleville. The hotel.'

'How is it?'

'Fine.' Laura rubbed at her eyes. 'I'm tired, that's all.'

'The drive okay?'

'Mm. Long.' Laura exhaled slowly. 'Six, seven hours.'

'Oof.' Andrew sighed. 'Look, do you want to talk to Tilly? I thought you ought to . . . She's in her room, but I might be able to coax her out.'

Laura gripped the steering wheel. Her chest ached.

'No, leave her,' she said. 'I'll call back again tomorrow.'

A moth had got trapped inside the car and was battering against the internal light. Laura kept her eyes trained on the rear-view mirror and the three teenagers on bicycles loitering by the kerb. One of them spat on the ground.

While Andrew spoke, Laura found her thoughts straying towards her mother, and all those books lining the shelf in her study. What had drawn Eliza to those stories? What had they unleashed? Laura took in a deep, ragged breath.

There was movement behind her, but when she adjusted the mirror she saw how the teenagers were now standing in a line along the kerb, faces turned to the car, completely unmoving. Then, in unison, they began walking towards her.

'Are you there?' Andrew said.

Laura gripped tighter on the steering wheel, her knuckles whitening. She tried to concentrate on her own reflection in the mirror, the pallor of her skin, her empty eyes, as she remembered another line from *Voss*: *Everyone is still afraid, or most of us, of this country, and will not say it. We are not yet possessed of understanding.* The boys walked by, one of them bumping against the bonnet and making the car shake.

'Laura?'

She let out a slow, uneven breath. 'Yes, I'm still here,' she heard herself say, fading in and out, as though it were coming back to her from the other end of the line.

The next morning Laura drove to Hell Hole Gorge National Park. It was around two hundred and eighty kilometres from Charleville. Google Maps had indicated there wasn't much else out there: a dinosaur centre with some accommodation in Eromanga, fifty kilometres south of the park, and a general store that doubled as a pub in Adavale. Beyond the national park was more desert, then the union between the borders of the Northern Territory and South Australia. Before leaving, Laura had told the concierge at the Hotel Corones where she planned to travel. He raised his eyebrows, and fished out a key from the top drawer of his desk. 'In case we're all closed up before you get back,' he said. 'Front doors are locked at nine.'

The freeway was almost empty as Laura began the drive. She didn't want to think about what she would need to do if the car broke down, or she got herself stuck. The temperature gauge on the dash read thirty degrees. A cooler morning by outback Queensland standards. It was still early; Laura wanted to reach the national park before the full blaze of sun peaked in the sky. She had brought along a couple of water bottles, a coffee and an egg sandwich in a plastic box from the service station in Charleville.

She stopped at the Adavale general store to use the bathroom. The woman behind the counter called out a friendly greeting and carried on reading her magazine. Laura nosed about, taking a carton of juice from the fridge, another bottle of cold water, and the dry-looking pie from the oven perched above the confectionary. Somewhere further into the house that adjoined the store a television played the opening theme tune to the ABC morning news.

'I hope you don't mind me asking, but do you remember seeing these people?' Laura drew out a crinkly photograph of her parents that she kept in her wallet. The photograph had been sent to Tilly a few years ago along with a postcard from the Empire State Building. 'They came by your shop in December last year. The twelfth.'

'December?' The woman gave a low whistle, peering over the top of her smudged glasses. She made a sympathetic face. 'They're that poor couple from Hell Hole, aren't they? I spoke to the police about it when it happened. Yes, they came by. Bought a few things—some fuel, I think—and posted a letter. A postcard, too, did that go overseas? Anyway, nothing out of the ordinary.' She studied Laura. 'You a relative?'

Detective Sandretti believed this woman had been the last person her parents spoke to before they died. For some reason,

Laura felt some comfort standing across the counter from her, the oven cabinet warming her arm.

'And how did they seem to you?' she asked. 'Do you remember?'

'*Well.*' The woman exhaled. 'As you can imagine, we get all sorts out this way. Not always the most savoury, but usually all right. This couple, they seemed tired. Frazzled, if I'm honest.' She started wiping the bench, though there were no crumbs about. 'Jittery maybe describes it better. Like they were in a hurry. I remember wondering where they were in a rush to get to.'

Laura absorbed this, her gaze fixed on the glass jar of sherbet sticks, the spiral of the candy making her feel like she was coming undone.

'You retracing their steps?' The woman crossed her arms and leaned on the counter, concern in her face. 'We get folks up here from time to time. Looking for answers, I guess, especially for those loved ones still missing. It's real sad.' She sighed. 'I've lived here for twenty years. People said I was mad to come out this far. But they don't understand. It draws you to it, like a magnet, you know? And though I wouldn't trade a second of it, there is something dreadful about the beauty of this place. Something monstrous.'

Laura nodded. She could sense that in the air, the competing kinetic forces pulsing like breakers in the surf.

'At least they were found, darl,' the woman said kindly. 'As painful as that is, at least you can hold on to that. Some folks come searching out here and find nothing. As if their loved ones never existed in the first place.'

Laura thought of that painting hanging back in the living room in the Swinbrook house, the hypnotic vista. Over the years she had stared at it for hundreds, possibly thousands, of hours. There had been a reason Andrew found it, something prophetic and arcane. Those craggy escarpments and the deep basins, the gaps in the rock filled over time with all that rich, red dirt. So long and far away, though she had never really left.

Laura reached the entrance to the park a little before ten. The campground at Powell Creek was another seven-kilometre drive. She took the gravel road slowly. The landscape was pinkish and sandy, with wilga shrubs and drooping branches dotted along the route. There was no one else around. She passed a cluster of yellow-tinged acacia, and some brolga standing stock-still in a fetid puddle. Off to the right, a rusting tractor had been abandoned on an empty plain.

About five hundred metres from the campground a muddy embankment appeared. Laura pulled over and climbed out of the car. The water was high after the rain, and it did not look safe to attempt a crossing. For a moment she considered returning to the Pajero and driving back to Charleville. Back to Brisbane and her family. But then what? She would still never know what really lured her parents out here. She would have failed. Laura stared at the coffee-coloured surface then grabbed her backpack from the passenger seat.

The water was cold and gritty, with a surprising undertow. It was only a hundred yards or so to the opposite bank, but with each tentative step Laura's trainers sunk further into the silt. It seemed absurd, suddenly, that she was out here, wading through this crossing, with no one to help if she needed it. Her foot caught on a rock, and she stumbled, nearly sprawling face-first into the water. But she regained her balance and straightened. There wasn't a breath of wind out here. The back of Laura's neck tingled with burn. After another minute she had pushed her way through the remaining water and made it safely to the other side.

Laura wandered about the empty campground at Powell Creek, taking in the blackened circle of an old fire, the chunky tyre marks of departed four-wheel drives. Lolly bush speckled the site, and a few scruffy spinifex pigeons had clustered beneath a bench. There were no facilities—no toilet, no kitchen. Laura stared at the blank blue sky, taut with the rising heat. Her throat was dry, her nose filled with dust.

Unzipping her backpack, she sifted through the photographs from the manila folder, trying to match them to where she calculated her parents had set up camp. But there were no panoramas, no establishing shots, only tight-focus portraits and objects out of context. It was impossible to determine exactly where they had died.

Laura spent another half an hour searching about the campground. She found nothing except for a couple of propane canisters and an old nappy. She stood with her hands on her hips, squinting around the empty site. Heat shimmered off the red dirt. The silence hollowed out the air. 'Hello?' she shouted absurdly. '*Hello?*'

Laura felt rage and despair building inside her. What had she expected? Some kind of reckoning? Some kind of epiphany? She kicked at a cluster of stones. In a nearby tree, a small kingfisher watched her. The sun blazed on, unperturbed.

Eventually she set off on the marked walking track towards the waterhole. It was rocky and undulating, while the air around her buckled and expanded. She spent about an hour traversing the gorge, which was steep in places. The terrain was arid, the track deeply rutted. An eagle flew overhead, and Laura spotted a few water rats scuttling down by the smaller washpools, but it seemed a lonely place for wildlife.

On the way back towards the campground, she climbed a large escarpment and sat down, slipping off her backpack and staring down at the waterhole below. She was sweating, and her knees ached. Was this the last view they had enjoyed together? Laura was filled with a terrible sadness. It was a desolate, unearthly spot to die, but exquisite too, just as the woman in Adavale had said.

Unlacing her trainers, Laura peeled off her socks and stretched out her pale feet. The air was full of sarsaparilla. She closed her eyes and listened, but there was no sound bar her own breathing and the shuffle of her thighs against the gravelly ridge. She reached into her backpack and brought out the copy of *Voss* her mother had kept in the study. She flicked through to another dog-eared page, and the text Eliza had underlined: *But in this disturbing country, so far as I have become acquainted with it already, it is possible more easily to discard the inessential and to attempt the infinite.*

Laura had never much enjoyed the novel. She hadn't understood what the fuss was about—another European man hubristically ventures into the Australian bush, believing himself to be God right up until the moment of his death. But sitting here, as though stranded on another planet, Laura began to appreciate what it might mean to attempt the infinite. What it might mean to face up to yourself. Because there was no one else out here, Laura realised. No one waiting, no one following. She was alone. And then she wondered whether her mother's newfound interest in the book, in all those books, revealed something about her nature, and what her parents had come to believe during those final weeks before they died. That suffering could help illuminate a path to this wisdom. That self-sacrifice could restart another person's life. That it could rid them of an unwanted past.

Laura returned the novel to her backpack and brought out Eliza's diary. Such a flimsy thing, and yet so powerful; it practically vibrated in Laura's hands. She turned to that last entry: *Maybe then we can be free of this. And maybe Laura and young Tilly will be free from it too.*

Laura stared at her mother's handwriting, trailing a fingertip over the ink. Then she hung her head in her arms and cried out great, shuddering sobs. In the silence of this vast space, the explanation was bittersweet, a suture for a weeping wound. Eliza and Bruce had come out here for love. They drove deep into the centre of the country hoping it would banish the force from the house. Return it to its place of origin. Start again, afresh. It wasn't such a mad idea, not really. The ghosts from those novels came from this red centre, after all. They came from this land, from this bush. It had been their final act of duty as parents, their final act of devotion. Laura wiped her eyes, blew her nose on her shirt. She would probably never know what had made them believe something was haunting them, or why they decided they wanted rid of the house. Perhaps all that was bound up in another malaise. One of ageing and neglect. It was hard for Laura to dwell on this, or what might have been different had she been with them in Brisbane, if she had never left . . . But no, there was no point. She couldn't change any of that. Still, better understanding their motivations went some way to assuaging the pain of losing her parents. It had the quality of a story written in stone.

Laura stood out the front of the Hotel Corones and watched a Nordic-looking family load up their four-wheel drive. The parents were methodical in their morning preparation, the father strapping the equipment to the roof while the mother fastened the seatbelts of the white-haired children in the back. Laura admired the father's tanned, sturdy legs as he fixed the last case to the car rack, and when he called out something one of the children laughed.

Laura went upstairs to finish packing up her room. She had slept badly in the small bed, inhaling the slightly chemical scent of the linen. Eventually she had dozed off, only to be woken by scratching noises outside the door and the heavy tread of footsteps along the corridor.

'Mum?' Laura had mumbled, clawing to sit herself upright, straining to properly wake. She checked her phone—it was just after midnight—but it was not the barmaid Sue's forewarning that had set her heart galloping. It was the threat of that other force, that other darkness, that had perhaps travelled out here after all. With her eyes glued to the hotel room door, Laura waited for several minutes in pure terror. But no one arrived.

Eventually she heard the distant sound of the communal toilet flushing, a little boy's cry, and his father say, 'Back to bed, kiddo.' Then another door had closed, and the hotel was quiet again.

Laura had not been able to get back to sleep after that. She'd slipped out of bed and sat at the small table by the window, her laptop charging before her. Tipping back the screen, she began to type, and for the first time in months the words flowed readily, like a boulder had been prised loose from a banked-up stream. After an hour, she had pages of new material. Some of it good, some of it rubbish, but all of it building blocks for her story.

Laura slung her backpack over her shoulder. As she did, her mother's diary slipped out of an open zip pocket and fell to the floor. Laura retrieved it, and noticed something poking out from the back sleeve of the Moleskine. It was a photograph. Eliza, Bruce and Anita, standing in front of the Brisbane house, taken in selfie-style. Anita's lean tanned arm in shot, that crinkle in the corner of her eyes. The three of them were laughing, full of happiness, full of life. And there, at the top right-hand corner, near the edge of Anita's front garden, she saw it. The back of a steel-grey bun. The slope of an elderly woman's shoulders in a navy-blue tunic.

Laura's eyes dragged back to Anita, the glint of that smile. She was aware of her own steady rise and fall of breath. She could have laughed. Instead she bit down hard on the inside of her lip.

She's spirited, that one.

No, Mum, she's not, Laura had always wanted to reply. *She's scheming and wily, and when your back is turned she's laughing at all of us.*

Laura returned the photograph to the back of the diary, and zipped it up inside her backpack once more. After giving the room a final once-over, she ran a fingertip along the brick above the bedhead. The stone felt smooth, undisturbed. Laura shook her head. What a con. There had never been a ghost.

14.

THOUGH AVA'S WEATHERBOARD sat level with Tilly's on white timber stumps it was a smaller and plainer house. There were no window features above a deck, only a row of steep stairs leading to the front entrance that faced the street. The door opened to a cramped vestibule with a threadbare couch and a wicker coffee table. Tilly left her shoes inside the door and wandered towards the back of the house, the smell of frying butter and breadcrumbs wafting down the hall. She adjusted the heft of the Royal typewriter in her arms.

'I know Ava promised you my parmis tonight,' Anita called from the stove, 'but I ran out of time to get the other ingredients, so it's just plain old schnitties.' She looked over her shoulder and gave Tilly a wink.

It was an open-plan kitchen and living room. The walls had been painted a beige colour, which Tilly supposed made for better durability. It was all quite plain, unrenovated, with the old stove in the far corner and a gap beneath the bench where the dishwasher should have been. Inhabiting this space were two overflowing boxes of recycling, while in the middle of the dining area was a large, mug-stained table bearing a plate of apples with a few fruit flies floating above it. On the floor by the fridge was a bowl of cat biscuits, and beside it a litter tray, with a couple of old poos poking out from the grey material. Tilly couldn't see the cat.

There was an earthy smell in the house. It wasn't like the sandalwood or cedar of her grandparents' house; there was something lived-in about it, corporeal and grimy. But *real*. It was cold, though; the floor was tiled with what looked like slate, while the old analogue radio on a stand by the back door had the sound turned right down. Tilly guessed the bedrooms were off to the right.

'What have you got there, mate?' Anita asked, throwing a tea towel over her shoulder.

'It's that old typewriter you were asking about,' Tilly said with a shy smile. 'I found it under the house.'

'No way.' Anita grinned. 'You're a star—your mum didn't mind, then?'

'Uh, no.' Tilly stumbled over the lie. 'All cool on that front.'

Anita adjusted the knob on the gas stove, and added more oil to the pan.

'Put it on the table near the front door. By the bookshelf. Cheers for that, Til.'

When she returned to the kitchen, Tilly heard a sound behind her and saw Ava slink from one of the dark doorways. She threw herself across the couch, barely glancing Tilly's way as she mumbled, 'Hey.' A strong odour of pot followed her, though if her mother noticed she didn't say.

After transferring the schnitzels from the pan to three plates waiting on the bench, Anita went to the fridge and brought out a bowl of coleslaw and half-a-dozen other condiments, then took them all over to the table. Tilly felt her phone vibrate in her back pocket, but she didn't check it. Anita gestured to Tilly to take a seat.

'Food's up,' she called to Ava, who dragged herself from the couch and shuffled over. Ava sat down at the table and yawned, finally looking at Tilly.

'Told you we ate early. Eat early, bed early, wake up early.'

'*I* wake up early,' Anita corrected her. 'Then I wake *you* a little after that.'

'It's the light,' Ava said, serious now, her face set in a frown as she reached for the tomato sauce. 'The sun rises so early because we're so far north. In Melbourne, in winter, it's still dark at eight o'clock in the morning.'

'And how do you know that? You've never been further south than Coffs Harbour, my baby!'

'It's worse in Britain,' said Tilly, accepting the heaped spoonful of coleslaw that Anita held aloft, then squeezed a generous portion of tomato sauce on to her plate. 'In winter, it's dark by the early afternoon.'

'Yeah?' Anita smiled again, shaking her head. 'How about that.'

'Mm. Like, four o'clock. You leave school and it's getting dark.'

'Whoa.' Ava was shovelling food into her mouth—it was the first time Tilly had ever seen the other girl eat. 'That is crazy. It's like those countries—Norway, Iceland—where they have darkness for, like, half the year. That would make you feel pretty mental, I reckon. Never seeing the sun.'

'And then they have long stretches of no darkness at all,' Tilly said. 'Only light. And night-time is this kind of weird orange glow. Midnight sun, they call it. Imagine sleeping during the day all the time.'

Anita laughed. 'Sounds like when I used to work night-shifts at Friday's in the city. Those were some good times. BC. Before Children.' She gave Tilly another wink. 'Make sure you have as much fun as you can before starting a family, Til. Because before you know it you're waiting up for them to come home from parties.'

'God, Mum!' Ava slapped her hands down on the tabletop and pushed away her empty plate. 'No one wants to hear about your sad party stories from last century.'

'Well, yes, it was technically last century.' Anita licked the coleslaw spoon and put it back in the bowl.

'Yeah, well, they're boring as fuck.' Ava picked at her teeth. 'I bet Tilly's mum doesn't go on and on about her glory days as a grunge girl.'

Tilly chewed on the piece of gristly chicken.

'I don't think my mum ever went to a nightclub. If she did, she's never told me about it.'

'Oh no, Laura never went clubbing,' Anita said, folding her arms. 'She was too busy working, or studying. Your mum was very diligent. Still, it paid off, didn't it? Successful author and all that. Your grandmother was proud of your mum's writing, you know.' She rose from the table and headed back to the kitchen, where she flicked on the kettle. 'We often talked about your mum's books. And about history and that. I'm more interested in Australian stories, of course. Over time, your gran became interested in those stories too. Queensland has its own dark past.' Anita smiled, though it didn't reach her eyes. 'I suppose you know that already.'

Tilly set down her knife and fork. In the seat beside her, she sensed Ava, the spread of her warm arms across the table.

'All places have creepy pasts, Mum. It's nothing special.'

Glancing at Tilly with bloodshot eyes, Ava jutted her chin in search of confirmation. Tilly nodded, because she was a little afraid of Ava, but also because she agreed. She watched Anita fix the hot drinks, the window set above the kitchen sink glowing indigo. The house would soon be dark.

Tilly took her cup of milky tea through to the lounge room and sat next to Ava on the couch. When she checked her phone, she saw she had six missed calls from Laura. *Oh, so now you want to talk*, Tilly thought. She hadn't heard a peep from her mother while she had been fanging it along the dusty roads of western Queensland like a half-baked Furiosa. Her dad said Laura should be home soon, though he didn't seem to know much about her mother's movements either. Tilly ignored the calls. *See how you like that.* The TV was playing the evening news. Footage of a drought somewhere in South Australia, then sport. The couch was only a two-seater—every shift in the soft leather sent Tilly tipping closer to Ava.

'You like that, don't you?' said Ava, her face caught in the blue hue of the screen.

'What?' Tilly looked up from her phone.

'Tea.' Ava chuckled. 'Don't English people all like tea?'

'Oh. Yeah.'

It was very warm in the lounge room. Astonishing heat seemed to be coming off Ava's bare legs, which were only centimetres from Tilly's hands folded in her lap.

'I hate tea,' Ava muttered.

She pushed her feet against Tilly's thigh, stretching, and Tilly caught a glimpse of black underwear through the gap in her shorts. She wondered for a moment if she was attracted to Ava; she certainly hadn't felt like this around other friends. Troubled, Tilly set down her mug and scoped out the rest of the lounge room. There was a keyboard on a rickety stand in the corner, and another small bookshelf stacked with old copies of *National Geographic*. A wilting fern had been positioned near the back door, which Tilly assumed led out to the backyard.

'She's got all her books in her room, you know,' she heard Ava say. When Tilly didn't respond, Ava poked her leg with a toe. 'My mum. She has your mum's novels piled up beside her bed.'

Ava spoke in a way that sounded threatening to Tilly. As though by owning these books Anita had discovered a secret about Laura that Tilly did not know. She stared at the television, aware of Anita's yawning in the kitchen and the sound of the tap running over the dishes in the sink. When the news ended, Ava stood up and motioned to Tilly to follow her. Together they walked into Ava's bedroom.

It was neater than Tilly had imagined it would be, with faded lilac wallpaper and a floral trim. There were no posters on the walls or piles of washing in the corner; no dying plants on the windowsill. The single bed next to the desk had a chequered quilt cover. The mantelpiece above the fireplace was lined with old May Gibbs paperbacks which were bookended with two small ceramic bowls of potpourri. Ava went to her chest of drawers where she had some cosmetics in a box and began wiping her face with cleanser and cottonwool pads. She eyed Tilly in the mirror.

'Sit down,' she said. 'Get the computer ready.'

Tilly took the plastic chair by the desk. When Ava joined her, she smelled of aloe vera. She smiled at Tilly and took command of the laptop, opening a new browser window. Ava's face was different without make-up, Tilly thought. Her eyes weren't quite so bright, and this made her look more sincere. Tilly's phone buzzed again with another missed call from Laura, and she punched out a quick reply: *What?? Just next door, stop hassling.* Then she turned off the phone.

'So,' Ava said, tapping away at the keys. 'What's left for us to do on this project?'

Tilly glanced towards the window where the lace blind fluttered against the mosquito screen. The gibbous moon hung above the tree line and the church spire on the corner.

'I emailed you the family tree. I reckon we just print that off, and include your sketch of the crypt on the front cover, then it's pretty much done.'

Ava wrapped her hands behind her dark head.

'You never told me—Eliza and Bruce, are they there too? At Toowong Cemetery?'

Tilly nodded.

'Yeah. I haven't been back to their graves. I'm not sure if Mum has either. It kind of feels like a bad dream. It was all so bleak.

The sound the caskets made when they hit the ground . . .' She trailed off, giving her head a slight shake. 'But at least they're together, I guess.'

Ava studied her, the lamplight throwing a thin halo around her head. She reached for something in her desk drawer. As she did, Tilly glanced to the other side of the bedroom where a doll's house had been positioned next to the cupboard. She hadn't noticed it when she first came in. It was an A-frame, with three storeys, each room containing miniature furnishings. A father sat on a tiny couch in the living room, a boy stood at the sink in the bathroom, and a little girl had been seated at the dining room table. The mother, meanwhile, lay on the double bed in the third-floor mezzanine. At least, Tilly assumed it was the mother. Her head was missing.

When Tilly looked back, she saw Ava had a joint. She lit up and inhaled a few times, then offered it to Tilly.

'Oh no, it's okay, thanks. I don't—'

'Go on,' Ava said. 'It's only weed.'

'Um, okay.' Tilly had a puff, then another.

Ava shook her head. 'You need to hold it for longer before you exhale.'

Tilly followed these instructions, and coughed. She handed back the joint and reached for the water bottle on the desk. Ava smiled and had another toke, squinting at Tilly through the smoke.

'Do you believe in ghosts?'

Tilly swallowed, aware of the flicker of her pulse at her throat.

'I don't know,' she said. 'I don't think so.'

'But you're obsessed with dead people. You picked a cemetery for our project.'

'It's a history assignment.' Tilly smiled. 'There's bound to be a few bodies about.'

Ava had another drag and passed over the joint again, the tip glowing red.

'What about Eliza and Bruce? Do you think about them much?'

This time Tilly's head spun as she held the smoke in her lungs.

'Yeah, of course.'

Ava looked into her lap, picking at a thread on the hem of her shorts.

'Sometimes I see them,' she murmured. 'Sitting together on your front deck. They used to hang out there. Reading and talking.'

Tilly put a hand over her mouth, stifling a burp. Her breath smelt of tomato sauce.

'Mm, yeah. It's nice to remember them that way.'

'No, I *see* them.'

Tilly rubbed at her eyes. The lilac wallpaper behind Ava seemed to shimmer.

'It's probably shadows,' she said. 'A trick of the light. Or it's my mum. She reads out in that old hammock. Maybe you see her and think it's Grandma. They looked a bit alike.'

Ava nodded absently. 'That's one explanation.' Her face suddenly brightened. 'Hey, I know what would be cool. We could summon them. I have a ouija board. Let's talk to Eliza and Bruce!'

'Oh, no.' Tilly reached for her hair, which felt thick like spaghetti. What exactly had Ava put in the joint? For a moment the hollowed-out faces of her grandparents swam to the front of her mind, their cartoonish empty eye sockets leering back at her. 'Shouldn't we just finish our project?'

'Fuck that.' Ava was already scrabbling about beneath the desk. She brought out a black rectangular box. 'Come on. We'll set this up on the bed.'

Tilly rose from her seat and followed Ava across the room as if in a trance. Her arms and legs were as heavy as cement. She sat at the foot of the bed, near the window, where cool air undulated, and watched Ava turn off the ceiling light and dim the desk lamp before settling by the pillows, one leg stretched across the quilt.

Ava proceeded to unpack the plastic spirit board and the planchette, which in this set was a simple shot glass. An alphabet had been printed in two curved shapes running through the middle of the board, numbers in a straight line beneath. *Yes* and *No* were positioned near the top.

'Have you done this before?' she asked.

Tilly shook her head. The dimensions of the room felt out of whack; she could hear Ava's wet breathing as though she had a hand on Tilly's shoulder, mouth pressed against her ear.

'It's easy. I'll be the medium. We just put two fingers on the planchette like this'—she picked up Tilly's hand and brought it over to the shot glass—'and then we ask questions of the spirit. If Eliza and Bruce are nearby, they will communicate with us, and the glass will move.'

'Okay,' said Tilly, though she had no idea why she had agreed to it.

Ava sat forward, eyes closed, and proceeded to speak in a low, formal voice.

'Good evening. This is Tilly and Ava in the living world. We wish to speak with Eliza and Bruce Townsend. Are they there in the spirit realm tonight?'

Tilly stared at the shot glass. It stood still. She peered at Ava through her fringe, expecting to see her sneering back, the joke exposed, but the other girl had her eyes closed, brow creased in concentration.

'Eliza and Bruce, are you there?'

This time the shot glass wobbled beneath their fingertips. Ava's eyes popped open.

'Was that you?' she hissed.

'What? No.' Tilly bit her lip. 'I didn't move it.'

'Just keep your hand still.'

Closing her eyes, Ava took a deep breath and entreated the spirits of Tilly's grandparents for a final time. But the glass did not move again. Ava frowned at the ouija board, then gave a shrug—'I guess that's that.'

Tilly felt herself wilt with relief. She could go home now, and try to forget this had ever happened. Her head was still spinning after the joint, and she wanted some fresh air. But just as she was about to slip off the bed she saw the shot glass suddenly scrape an inch across the board.

'Hey!' Tilly glared at Ava. '*You* did that.'

'No, I didn't.'

The glass was still moving. It crept in a straight line across the board before making a steep curve near the far edge and steering up towards the *Yes*. Tilly's heart lurched.

'Stop it, Ava. I've had enough. Please. I don't want to play anymore.'

'But I'm not doing anything. I swear.'

Tilly stared back, panicked at the fear she heard in Ava's voice.

'I think we should stop—'

'Wait!' Ava gripped Tilly's wrist with her other hand. 'They're here. With us. I can feel it.'

'I don't care,' she spluttered. 'I don't want to talk to them. This is mental.'

The blood was roaring in Tilly's head. She was afraid she might be sick.

'Shhh! Let's just ask them if they have a message. That's all. One question.'

'Oh my god, Ava, no way . . .'

'Eliza and Bruce, this is Ava Bilson from next door,' Ava continued in a louder voice. 'I am acting as the medium, and I have your granddaughter, Tilly, here with me tonight. Do you have a message to pass on from the spirit world? Something for Tilly?'

The shot glass began travelling down the board at speed in the direction of the alphabet. Tilly's heart was thumping wildly. The glass hovered over the 'G'.

'It's working,' Ava whispered. 'Fucking hell. They're *talking* to you.'

They both stared as the shot glass continued to spell out a message across the board.

'G-O-H-O . . .'

. . . M-E,' Tilly finished. 'Goho Me?'

Ava shook her head. Her eyes shone darkly in the lamplight. '*Go home*. They're telling you to go home.'

Tilly gazed at her. Neither of them seemed to know how to grasp at this instruction. But an abrupt bang at the front door made them both jump.

'Ava!' came a muffled shout from Anita. 'Get that, will you? I'm in the bath.'

'Hang on.' Ava quickly packed up the ouija board and planchette, and returned them to their hiding spot beneath the desk. 'Wait here,' she said to Tilly. 'I'll be back in a sec.'

'What about . . .'

Tilly didn't finish. She sat on the edge of the bed for another moment, then rushed to the window, sucking in great lungfuls of cool air. Did they really just talk to Eliza and Bruce? It was all too much. She was shaking all over, and her guts were churning like she'd just come off the Gravitron. In the yard, shadows skipped about the lawn. The church spire in the next block was cast in soft yellow light, there was a faint outline of trees, and then the unyielding black of next door.

From the front of the house, she heard the slap of the wire-screen door, then voices. Ava, sullen and monosyllabic, and then Laura, growing louder and more agitated. What was her mother doing here?

Tilly stood up and crossed the room, opening the door a crack. She could make out the long corridor adorned with banksia-printed wallpaper. She could smell cigarette smoke. Ava stood with her back to the interior, her long legs gleaming.

'I've come for Tilly. Would you get her, please?'

Laura had stepped inside the house. Behind her, Tilly saw a fig tree in the middle of the road groan in the violent gust of wind, bringing down a shower of old rain. She opened the door wider.

'Yeah, okay.' Ava raised a fingernail to her mouth to nibble at. 'She's in my room. We were just finishing our history project.'

'Avey, is everything okay?'

It was Anita, wrapped in a towel. She had appeared from another room and now came to the doorway. Her cheeks were very pink, her hair wet. 'Laura? What's going on?'

Laura didn't seem to want to look at Anita. Her eyes were fixed on the tassel lampshade hanging in the hallway.

'Tilly texted to say she was here.'

'Yeah, she came over for dinner tonight.' Anita beckoned Laura to come further inside. 'It's all been low-key, don't worry.'

'She's not supposed to be here. She knows that.'

Tilly groaned. She felt dizzy again, but she knew she couldn't stay hiding away in Ava's room.

'Mum?' she called, making a slow shuffle down the hallway. 'Chill, okay. Everything's fine. Just fine.'

Laura glanced from Anita to Tilly. She shook her head with incredulity. 'Are you stoned?'

Tilly wiped her mouth with the sleeve of her windcheater, then stared at the floor. Ava smothered a laugh.

'Oh, you think this is funny,' Laura said. 'Hm?'

Anita sighed. 'Look, Laura, I'm sorry. I assumed you gave permission for Tilly to be here. It's just a mix-up.'

Laura looked about, her eyes landing on the typewriter on the table beside the bookshelf.

'Is that my old typewriter, Anita?'

'Actually, it's my typewriter. It belonged to me.'

'What? No. It was always in my house.'

'Tilly brought it over,' Anita said, voice tight. 'She told me you didn't mind.'

'Did she?'

'Mum, I'm sorry . . .' Tilly began, her cheeks burning with embarrassment. 'I didn't think you'd want it.'

'Oh, she doesn't want it,' Anita muttered. 'She just doesn't want me to have it.'

Laura turned back to Anita and threw up her hands.

'You know what, that's it. I'm done with this, Anita. This *game.* I'm drawing a line in the sand, and I'm taking my daughter home.'

Anita looked from Tilly to Laura, her mouth pinched.

'No one is playing any game, Laura. Your kid came over for dinner. Get off your high horse.'

Laura took a step forward, her jaw set.

'I know what you've been doing,' she said quietly. 'I know. You started with my parents and now you've moved on to Tilly.'

Anita's eyes went wide.

'Relax, Mrs T,' said Ava, folding her arms across her chest. 'Tilly and I just been having a harmless little séance.' She nudged Tilly's foot with her toe. 'Are you going to tell her who you spoke to?'

For a moment the girl's obnoxiousness stunned Tilly; she didn't know what to say. Laura looked just as taken aback. She watched her mother place a hand on the frame of the door, her wedding ring catching the light with a cruel glint.

'Tilly?'

But Tilly still couldn't say it. She knew it was obscene. That Laura would be wounded and confused, and that Tilly had caused it. Ava began to laugh.

'It was Eliza and Bruce. Can you believe it?'

'*What*?'

'They were there, in the room with us. It's never worked for me before. They must have wanted to talk to Tilly. And do you know what they said?'

'Ava, enough!' Anita snapped. 'This isn't some joke, you know? We're talking about real people here. Have some bloody respect.'

Ava straightened her churlish slouch in outrage. 'But it's true!'

Laura reached for Tilly's hand. When she spoke again, her voice was surprisingly calm.

'We're going home,' she said. 'It's late.'

Anita adjusted her towel. Her shoulders were speckled with damp.

'Laura, come on,' she said. 'Ava didn't mean any of this. It's just a misunderstanding.'

'Oh, I understand perfectly what is going on.'

Anita frowned.

'What's that supposed to mean?'

'It means, Anita,' said Laura in a low, clear voice, 'that your campaign against my family stops tonight. I know it was you. I'm not sure how, but I know you made my parents believe someone was haunting them so you could get your hands on their house.'

Anita shook her head slowly.

'Laura . . .'

'And then afterwards, when you couldn't get what you wanted through the lawyer, you tried some other underhand tricks on me. But it hasn't worked. Okay? So I think we're done here. Because I won't have my daughter dragged into all this. You stay away from her, do you understand? I don't want her anywhere near you.'

Anita took a step towards Laura. She looked smaller in her towel. Wisps of curled wet hair stuck to the side of her neck girlishly.

'Laura, listen to me. I haven't been playing any tricks. I'm sorry about what's happened tonight with Ava and Tilly, I really am. But as for anything else, I honestly don't know what you're talking about.'

Laura shook her head, and glanced at Tilly as if to say, *Are you hearing this?* She scrabbled around in her handbag and drew out a photograph, which she flapped in front of Anita.

'I found my mother's diary,' Laura said. 'At the back was this photo. That's when I realised the truth. All that time you spent with Eliza. Playing on her suggestibility, on her vulnerability. Frightening her, and my dad. It's sick. You made them feel unsafe in their own home. You made them believe that some kind of presence wanted them out of the house. I mean, for god's sake! You wanted them to think an old woman was coming for them in the night.'

Anita took a small step away. She was trembling.

'Laura, I swear on my kid's life. I never *did* any of that. Eliza and I chatted about history, politics, that kind of thing. But that was it. The house, that was her idea. I know nothing about . . .'

'How do you explain this photo then, huh?' Laura was shaking her head. 'Why was it with my mum's diary?'

'It's just a photo,' Anita cried. 'A keepsake. We took it last year. Me, your folks, and my mum.'

Behind them, from the street, a thick swathe of moonlight tunnelled between the figs. It lit up the dim hallway. Tilly raised a hand to her eyes, her vision for a moment shuttered by the glare, and when it returned she saw her. Tall, stooped, those tight grey curls gathered on top of her head. It was the woman from the delicatessen. She was even wearing the same floral-print dress with a pair of mismatched slippers, a cigarette wedged between her fingers. She smiled at Tilly.

'I thought I heard you there, Laura. Well, come on in. Let's have a cuppa and a chat. It's been ages since we had a proper catch up.'

Tilly blinked back at her, waiting for the apparition to disappear. But when it didn't—when the old woman instead travelled towards her as if buoyed on a fog of cigarette smoke—Tilly looked to the others, expecting some reaction, either fear or surprise, but neither came, and so she took a hurried step away, coming up hard against the flyscreen door.

'Please,' she murmured. 'Stop.'

'It's all right,' Laura said. 'We're not going to have an argument about all this now.'

'Not you,' Tilly spluttered. '*Her.*' She pointed.

Anita looked behind her, then back to Tilly.

'Who?'

'Mum?' Heat flooded across Tilly's cool cheeks. She pressed her hands together like she was praying. 'Let's just go, okay. Please get me away from here.'

Anita glanced between the girls. She swallowed thickly.

'Laura?' It was the old woman again. 'What is the matter?'

Anita glared at Tilly, then spun around. '*Mum,*' she snapped. 'This is Tilly. Laura's *daughter.*'

'Who?'

Anita closed her eyes, her chin dropping to her chest, and muttered, 'For fuck's sake.' Then, after a deep sigh, she walked over to her mother and placed an arm around her waist.

'It's Tilly, Mum. Laura's girl. You know. My friend from next door. She moved away. To England.' She glanced at Laura, then to the floor. 'I'm sorry, Mum has dementia. She doesn't know who anyone is anymore.'

The woman blinked amiably in Tilly's direction and smiled. 'Oh no, I don't think so. I've got to watch this one; she's always trying to pull the wool.' She took a contemplative drag on her cigarette. 'You must come over more often, Laura. Anita needs a friend like you to keep her out of trouble.'

Anita smiled sadly at her mother.

'Nothing wrong with a bit of trouble, Mum. Come on. Let's get you back to bed. You'll be tired in the morning.' She glanced at Laura. 'We can't find permanent care for her. Everything is so expensive. She's been in and out of respite since January. It's been really tough for all of us.'

Tilly's legs went wobbly. She bit on her lip, clamping down on the urge to let out a thankful scream. She watched Anita lead her mother down the hallway. Denise was real. She hadn't been imagining her. But when she shot a look at Ava standing by the hall table, Tilly saw the girl's eyes were bright with laughter, and she felt breathless.

'What the hell, Ava?' she hissed. 'You told me your gran had died. Why did you do that?'

Ava ran her tongue over her teeth.

'You seemed . . . receptive.' She gave a slight shrug. 'It was only a bit of fun. The séance and everything. Just a laugh, a distraction. Don't take it all so seriously, yeah?'

'Don't take it all so seriously? You made me think your grandmother was dead too!'

Ava rolled her eyes, pressing her head into the wall with the impudence of a small child. *It meant nothing to her*, Tilly realised. *I'm just a broken toy, a plaything, to her; a joke gone wrong.* She noticed Anita had stopped and turned, her face drawn. She let go of Denise's arm and strode towards Ava. She seemed about to say something, until she drew back her hand and slapped the girl hard across the face. 'Shame,' Anita spat. Ava's eyes went wide, and then her shoulders began to heave. Meanwhile Denise stood by the lamp, her cigarette burnt down to the nub.

Tilly looked at Laura. She didn't know what to do. Laura took Tilly's hand, urging her towards the front door. Her mother's eyes never left Anita. Her face was glowing. Her expression vindicated, triumphant.

'Come on, darling,' she said. 'Time to leave.'

The night air was full of moisture and the smell of damp moss. From a tree nearby, a nightjar let out a small cry. They trailed down the stairs, Laura guiding Tilly towards the concrete drive below. When Tilly glanced back towards the house, Ava appeared in the doorway, watching their route across the garden.

'That's right. Run along, Matilda,' she called. 'It's what Lize and Bruce told you to do, remember? Go home.'

15.

AFTER THE DEBRIS from the storm had been cleared from the yard, Andrew delayed further work on the house for several weeks, and the builders did not return to the site until the poinciana had been uprooted and sawn into pieces small enough for the mulcher in the driveway. It took Andrew a whole day to reduce the tree to a brown mound. When he was done, Laura and Tilly came outside and shovelled the mulch into the wheelbarrow, which they took turns steering to the native garden beneath the master bedroom and distributing among the flowers and shrubs.

Since that night next door, Tilly had avoided Ava at school and on the walk home from the bus. They managed to present their history assignment without meeting up again either; the teacher, Ms Petrovic, said it was a terrifying account of a family riven with ghosts. She awarded them an A.

Laura was more like her old self after she returned from Charleville. She was making good progress on the novel about her parents, with half of the first draft already complete, and when she wasn't in the study she spent time out in the garden, bedding in the new flowers, and helping Andrew brick up the water feature in the back corner by the fence. Tilly observed this with some wariness; it was hard to forget what had happened between them all. Tilly wished they could have moved out of the house, but her mother did seem happier, and healthier, and that counted for something. After a while, it seemed easier to not talk about it, and gradually the memory of those strange events began to fade.

In August, the builders came back full time, and they finished the remaining work on the house in eight weeks. The upper floor was fitted out and furnished, the en suite installed. The last of the landscaping around the pool was completed, the fences repainted. The men even filled in the gaping hole and planted new turf over the spot where the poinciana had been. The absence would have been inconspicuous to a stranger, but Tilly still found her mother standing by the back door, staring over the yard, something wistful in her eyes. By mid-October the 'For Sale' sign was mounted on the verge, and at the end of the month the house was sold.

None of them had a swim in the new pool.

They left Central Avenue on a humid morning in early December. Tilly had spent her final night on a foam camping mattress in her parents' bedroom. Everything else in the house had been sold or donated or taken to the tip in Ferny Grove. To celebrate their leaving, her father had walked down to Rosalie Village and brought back a bottle of Perrier-Jouet with three plastic glasses, while Tilly ordered fish and chips on her phone. They watched the old *Picnic at Hanging Rock* on her laptop, and for once the bats nested quietly in the Moreton Bay fig across the road.

'Hey, Mum?' Tilly had asked as Miranda waved to Mademoiselle through the foliage, the panpipes trilling. 'Do you think your agent will like your new book?'

Laura rested a warm hand on Tilly head. She began stroking her hair.

'I don't know,' she said. 'I guess we'll have to wait and see.' Her hand withdrew. Tilly waited for Laura to say more, but her mother only reached for her champagne. On the laptop screen, the girls had begun their fateful ascent of the rock.

Now their taxi was waiting in the driveway to take them to the airport. From the front step where she sat to tie up her sneakers, Tilly watched Laura load her suitcase into the boot before climbing into the front passenger seat. Through the tinted window, Tilly could make out her mother chatting to the driver.

'All right, Til?'

Her father was standing behind her, a rolling suitcase propped against his leg. He was wearing a straw hat. Sweat seeped through the front of his cotton shirt. Tilly peered over to the house next door, wondering if Anita or Ava would make an appearance. She hoped they wouldn't.

'Do you think we'll come back?' she asked.

'Oh, yeah, I'm sure we will.' Andrew brushed at his damp brow with the back of his hand. 'Why—don't you want to?'

It wasn't a question of wanting, Tilly thought to say to her father, though she doubted he would understand. She walked down the drive, passing the letterbox, and caught sight of something sticking out of the slat. It was a postcard from somewhere called Adavale—Outback Pub, General Store, Post Office—with a cartoon of a house on the front. Tilly flipped it over. It was addressed to Laura at Central Avenue. Printed in the black spidery scrawl of her grandfather were the words:

You should have never come back.

Tilly took a raw, sharp breath. Her chest contracted, her bones clicked. She looked up and found Laura again, there in the taxi, almost within reach. She had wound down the window, her golden arm resting lightly against the door, her face tilted towards the sky, a soft smile on her lips.

The fig across the street rustled. The sun blazed between two clouds. Tilly felt her attention drawn towards her parents' bedroom window. The blinds were drawn, but there was some movement behind them, a shifting shadow. Tilly felt the blood drain from her face. She paused, waiting for more, but the blinds had fallen still.

Laura turned her gaze to Tilly and gave her a wave—encouraging her towards or away from the house, it was impossible to tell.

Acknowledgements

THE VISITOR WAS largely produced in Meanjin (Brisbane), unceded sovereign country of the Turrbal and Jagera peoples. I acknowledge the traditional custodians of this land, and pay my respects to their Elders, past, present and future.

An earlier version of *The Visitor* was written as part of my PhD in Creative Writing at the University of Queensland. I will always be grateful for the support I received during my studies. Returning to university to research questions around haunting in Australian literature was a privilege and a delight. Particular thanks go to Venero Armanno and Natalie Collie for their generous supervision and guidance during my doctorate.

Thank you to the wonderful team at Allen & Unwin, who continue to nurture my writing career, especially Alex Craig and Angela Handley, as well as Deonie Fiford for her close and insightful copyedit. Thank you to Jane Palfreyman, who first took a punt on me in 2013, and who provided incredible encouragement as I developed my work from book to book.

Thanks to my amazing agent, Pippa Masson at Curtis Brown, who has had endless patience and enthusiasm for this project, which has been years in the making.

And lastly, I would like to express my deep love for and gratitude to my wife and our children. I would drive across all the deserts of the world for you.